To: Mrs. Lizz
12-18-09

from: Tristan Pennington

Map of Ecuador provided by: www.worldatlas.com

Scanning, uploading and/or distribution of this book via the Internet, print, audio recordings or any other means without the permission of the Publisher is illegal and will be prosecuted to the fullest extent of the law.

This book is a work of fiction. Names, events and characters are fictitious in every regard. Any similarities to actual events or persons, living or dead, are purely coincidental.

The Calling
Deborah A. Hodge

Copyright © 2009 Romance Divine LLC
ISBN 978-1-934446-64-5
Cover Design by Viper

All rights reserved. Except for review purposes, the reproduction of this book in whole or part, electronically or mechanically, constitutes a copyright violation.

Published by
Romance Divine
Find us on the
World Wide Web at
www.romancedivine.com

This book is dedicated to all of those who are patiently trusting God and waiting for Him to work all things together for good.

I would like to acknowledge several people who helped with this book: Libera Garrett, Halle Childress, Inez Hill, Edward Hamil, Victoria Overton and Dylan Hill for proof-reading the manuscript and for their kind suggestions and encouragement.

I am very grateful to Jay Johnson for proof-reading and correcting my Spanish.

The Calling

Deborah A. Hodge

One

Cate felt like pinching herself to see if she was dreaming, but she knew she wasn't. It was real; and it was wonderful. She breathed it all in and joyfully savored every sight and sound. They invigorated her, the flight attendant's announcements and demonstrations, the taxiing of the plane to the proper runway, the roar of the engines at take-off, the movement of the plane as it sped faster and lifted into the sky. As the plane soared into the air, Cate's spirit soared too. She was on her way to a new beginning, another chance, and a new adventure with God.

As the plane leveled off, the pilot greeted the passengers, and Cate tried to follow along, even as she thought about her new adventure, "Good afternoon ladies and gentlemen. This is your pilot, Captain Daniel Ortez…approximate flight time…excellent weather between Kansas City and Quito…sit back and relax…We hope you have an enjoyable flight."

After the pilot finished his welcome, the 'unbuckle seat belt' sign flashed on, and Cate surveyed the faces of those accompanying her on her journey. To her left, seated in the aisle seat, was David Barnes, his handsome, compassionate face and penetrating, brown eyes framed by his thick, black, neatly, combed hair. She wondered what he was thinking. Could he be reminiscing about past times in Ecuador with his late wife Jenny, or maybe he was thinking about what lay ahead as he returned? To her right, was four year old, Sarah, David's daughter. Her hair, eyes, and smile were her father's, but the rest of her features were those of her mother. Sarah was playing with the doll that Cate's parents had given her as a going away present. As she spoke to her dolly, she was fastidiously straightening its dress and fixing its hair. She had named the doll Carrie. Cate didn't have to wonder what Sarah was thinking, she could hear what she was saying to the doll.

"Carrie, you'll like Ecuador. It's a very beautiful country. Where we live, you can see the mountains and you'll like our house. My mommy likes our house. Maybe, we'll see mommy there."

'Maybe, we'll see mommy there.' Those words rang in Cate's ears. She knew Sarah probably believed it, or at least hoped it with childlike fervor, but Cate knew her mommy wasn't there. Her mother had died in a plane crash when Sarah was three. She also knew that Sarah was too young to understand the finality of that event.

David also heard what Sarah had said. His daughter's words caused him to shift in his seat.

Cate glanced at him knowingly and whispered, "It'll be okay. Just give her time. She's too young to deal with finite concepts like death."

"I know. It's just difficult for me to hear her say that maybe Jenny will be in Ecuador when we get there."

Cate looked sympathetically into his eyes, filled with love and concern for his daughter. She detected lingering grief as he said his dead wife's name. She wanted to say more, but didn't know what. Her attempt to think of the compassionate, comforting, appropriate thing to say was interrupted by the cry of a baby somewhere behind them. Cate turned to see where and when she looked back, David had closed his eyes. That led her to believe that he wanted a few minutes of personal privacy to be alone with the feelings his daughter's words evoked.

Cate focused her attention back to Sarah, who was still talking to Carrie. Suddenly, the flight attendant interrupted the conversation to ask about the evening meal. David and Cate allowed Sarah to choose first.

Sarah answered in a very grown-up manner, "I would like chicken please."

The flight attendant smiled as she reached for Sarah's choice.

"What would you like to drink?"

"Milk, please,"

"Milk, it is." The flight attendant passed Sarah her dinner and beverage with David's assistance, while Cate helped her pull her tray down.

After Sarah was situated, Cate and David chose and received their meals. The trio blessed and ate their food; fairly appetizing, considering it was airline food.

Afterwards, Sarah announced, "I need to go potty."

Once again, David had closed his eyes after dinner. Maybe he was praying, or maybe napping. Whatever he was doing, he didn't respond to Sarah's announcement.

"No problem, I'll take you. The restroom is right up there," Cate nodded up the aisle. Unfortunately, the bathroom visit meant that they had to disturb David. Cate gently touched his arm, and he opened his eyes,

"I'm sorry, but Sarah needs to go to the restroom."

"Oh—sorry, I was in another world." David stood to let them out.

Sarah smiled as she walked by, "Daddy, we'll be right back."

"Okay, sweetie," David sat down.

Once in the restroom, Sarah was fascinated by how different it was from those at home and asked many questions. Cate answered her numerous questions, after which they returned to their seats and Sarah soon settled down and fell asleep.

After a few minutes, David noticed that Sarah had gone to sleep, "Look at her, sleeping so peacefully."

"Yeah, it's great to have absolutely no problems." Cate smiled as she brushed Sarah's hair back from her face.

"Oh," David nodded, "she has problems."

"None that her daddy can't solve," Cate smiled as she glanced in David's direction.

"She has problems that *I* can't solve, but none that the Heavenly Father cannot solve."

Cate nodded, "You're right. I tend to forget that sometimes."

"So do I," David admitted.

"You, Mr. Preacher Man?"

"Me, Miss Preacher's Daughter."

"But, not like me." Cate turned to gaze out the small window. "I struggled for such a long time after Justin to believe that God could solve all of my problems, beginning with my need for His forgiveness for my rebellion and sin. But, by His grace, He did forgive me and teach me that He truly can solve my problems, when I seek Him and His will for my life."

"I'm grateful for what He has done in your life. You're a very different woman than when I first met you."

"I know, and I give God the glory for it. I'm just sorry that I wasted so much time and made such mess out of my life—and Justin's—before I allowed Him to change me." Cate breathed a sigh of regret.

David knew her thoughts, and gently touched her arm, "Cate, don't go there."

"I can't help it. If I had been totally submissive to God seven years ago, I would've never married Justin and had a failed marriage."

Cate, we've been over this. Whatever you might think, your failed marriage was not your fault. Justin chose infidelity. He chose divorce, not you."

"That may be true, but we both know that I should never have married him." Cate sighed as pain creased her face and tears filled her eyes.

"Cate, you know that beating yourself up over the past won't do any good. You can't go back and change it," David softly took her hand in an effort to comfort her.

"That may be true, but I can regret it until the day I die." Tears trickled from her eyes.

"You've allowed God to do so much in your life. You need to focus on that. You've allowed Him to forgive you, and help you grow into a vibrant, committed Christian. Focus on that—and forgive yourself." As he spoke, Cate wiped her tears with her right hand as he squeezed her left.

"But, I should have known better. I'm a *pastor's* daughter. I should have known the hurt, scars and consequences that came with rebellion." Her tears were now flowing freely; there were too many to wipe away.

"Cate, you know that God can heal hurts and scars, and can help you live with the consequences. He's promised that His grace is sufficient for whatever we face. You can count on that."

"I know, but sometimes I just get sucked into that vortex of regret, and forget about God and His sufficiency." Cate once again tried to wipe the tears flowing down her cheeks.

"Sometimes we all get pushed around by emotions, and the only way to fight back is to focus on God and His promises. Remember He is the God of Second Chances. You know that by experience. You're on your way to Ecuador to teach at a mission school because God has called you to that. He has a plan for you, and His promises and His grace will be sufficient to carry you through." David gently squeezed her hand again as he spoke.

"Thank you for the reminder, and thank you for your friendship. I really appreciate all that you've done for me." With her head still lowered and trying to regain her composure, Cate closed her eyes, took a deep breath, sniffed to clear her nose and tried wiping away the remainder of her tears.

"You're welcome, but there's no need to thank me," David turned toward her, gently raised her head so he could look into her eyes and wiped away the remaining tears.

Cate became uncomfortably aware that David was touching her face. She squirmed, shifted in her seat, took a deep breath and whispered, "Thank you."

"It's all right, I'm here for you," he said.

She composed herself and began again. "I do need to thank you. You recommended me to Matthew Kennedy. Without you, I'd never be on my way to Ecuador to teach in a mission school."

"Matthew made his own decision about you."

"That may be true, but your recommendation helped a lot."

"I think God had more to do with it than anyone else," David said.

"I'm sure that's right, but I'm also sure that He used you and Matthew Kennedy to get me where He wanted me, and I am extremely grateful."

"Glad to be of service, to God—and you," David squeezed her hand.

"Me too."

They both smiled; he was still holding her hand. David had held her hand throughout most of the conversation. It was the first time they'd held hands in seven years. Back then, they were an engaged couple, but Cate had broken their engagement to marry Justin.

Almost simultaneously, they both realized that they were no longer holding hands in an effort to comfort, but were actually *holding hands*. The realization that they were affectionately holding hands jarred both of them. They knew that was no good.

David spoke first while extricating his hand in an effort to stop the hand holding without admitting what had happened. "Well, I think, I'm going to try to get a little sleep before we get to Quito." He withdrew his hand and folded his arms across his chest to sleep.

"Good idea. Maybe, I'll try it too," Cate said, but she quickly realized that sleep wasn't possible. The hand holding incident had rekindled strong feelings and painful regrets of the past. As she looked at David on one side and Sarah on the other, she realized how much she had lost by rebelling against God and marrying Justin. She battled to push the memories from her mind and drift off to sleep, but they refused to go. As Cate finally began to drift off to sleep, Sarah stirred as if she was having a bad dream. Cate rose to comfort her, and as she tried to settle back in her seat and drift off to sleep again, the memories re-assaulted her. She was transported back in her thoughts to seven years earlier, to relive it all again. As she began her journey back in time, she gazed intently at the man on her left, now asleep in the chair beside her. Her lack of submission to God *issue* had first confronted her when she met him.

Two

Cate met David at the University of Kansas when they were both freshmen and taking some of the same classes. Shortly after they met, David became the youth minister at Bethsaida Baptist Church, where Cate's father was pastor.

From the very beginning, Cate liked David and he liked her. They had many things in common. He was a committed Christian, who reminded her of her father. After they began dating, many people thought David and Cate made a perfect couple, and everyone began to contemplate their marriage.

Cate and David knew that people had already paired them for life, and even though both suspected that they loved each other, they took things slowly. David wanted to be sure of God's will in the matter, and though she never told David, Cate didn't want to think about marriage at all. She liked being with David, and knew that she loved him, but she did *not* want to be a *pastor's wife*. If she married David, not only would she be a pastor's wife, but a missionary's wife. If God wanted her in missions, He had never made that known to her.

The showdown between Cate and her submission to God came when David began to talk about marriage. She remembered the conversation vividly. David was visiting her in her parents' home and she was painting her toenails as David began.

"Cate, we've dated for a while, and I think you know how much I love you."

The seriousness of his tone caused her to pause from her task and listen intently to what he was saying. As she looked up, he continued.

"Cate, will you marry me?" he blurted out.

She knew he expected a "yes", but she also knew that even though she loved him, she couldn't say yes, at least not yet. She did *not* want to be a preacher's wife. She had grown up in a pastor's home and she knew what that was like. If anyone had asked her about growing up in a pastor's home, she would have answered that for the most part it had been a wonderful experience. The clue that one would notice was 'for the most part'. That experience colored her thinking, and when God asked her to submit her life to Him, even if it meant becoming a pastor's wife, Cate rebelled.

When Cate thought about becoming a pastor's wife, she remembered those times when people had not treated her father and mother well. She also remembered those times when her family had done without things that others took for granted. Her father and mother were the best Christians she knew. Dr. Johnathon and Carol Jones had sought all of their Christian lives to be, and to do, exactly what God called them to do. They lived their lives submitted to God; Cate knew that. But she also knew that through his years of ministry quite a few of her father's parishioners had not treated him, or his wife, very Christ-like.

Those unchristian Christians had caused Cate to rebel against the idea of submitting even to the possibility of becoming a pastor's wife, but there were other reasons. She knew what it was like to live in a "fish bowl". The pastor, his wife and his children were always on display. Everyone expected them to be perfect. People expected the pastor's children always to be happy, well mannered, and well behaved. She didn't want to live the rest of her life in a fish bowl. She told herself that since she had submitted in every other way that surely God would understand her lack of submission in that area, but David did not.

"David, I know that you want me to say yes, but I just can't right now," Cate said.

"Why not marry me? I know that you love me."

"Yes, I do, but you're going in the ministry. If God's ever called me to be a minister's wife," she shrugged, "I don't know about it."

"But, Cate-," he tried to protest further, but she cut him off.

"Are you absolutely sure of your calling to the ministry?"

"Yes, I am. Won't you please think about marrying me?" he pleaded.

"Sure, I will. I love you very much, but I just don't know about being a minister's wife."

Because he knew of her commitment as a Christian and her willingness to follow God's will for her life, he thought she was simply nervous. "Cate, you'd make a great minister's wife, and I'm sure that you'd be a perfect wife for me," he assured her. "Please pray about it and let the Lord guide you in this."

Because he was such a good man and she loved him, Cate reluctantly agreed to pray about the marriage. David was thrilled; Cate was not, but she had agreed to pray about it so pray she would. Over the weeks that followed, she prayed and she agreed to try missions.

The trial mission assignment was David's idea. He encouraged her to give God the opportunity to use her and to speak to her in the process. She found a summer mission opportunity at a children's camp near Lake Tahoe.

When she arrived at Tahoe, she intended to complete the summer mission service while giving God the opportunity to guide her as to His will concerning missions and David. However, things changed drastically when she met Justin Timmons. Like Cate, Justin was there for the summer. He was in charge of the camp recreational activities, a handsome, funny, mischievous and charming counselor. Cate was immediately attracted to him and he was attracted to Cate. She remembered the first thing he said to her.

The second day at the camp, he singled her out and with a wink and a grin said,

"Hello there beautiful."

Cate blushed. *Wow! I can't believe he thinks I'm beautiful.* Intrigued, she smiled. "Hello yourself," *I can't believe I'm flirting.*

"How would you like to take a walk with me this afternoon?"

"I–I don't know."

"I can assure you. I'm a good guy."

"And modest too." *I can't believe it; I'm really flirting.*

"Uh, I'm just trying to put your mind at ease. I'm asking you for a walk, nothing more."

"I guess a walk can't hurt."

"Not at all. You might even discover that I *am* a nice guy."

After that first walk, she was hooked. Without even realizing it, Cate's priority became Justin, not finding God's will concerning David or missions. In fact, Cate's feelings took over. Instead of growing closer to God, without realizing it, she moved away. She went through the motions of Bible study and prayer, but her heart wasn't in it. Justin was drawing her heart to him.

She found herself spending most of her free time with Justin. They went on long walks where they talked.

"So, your dad's a pastor?"

"Yep"

"How is that?"

"It's not bad, most of the time."

He stopped, took her hand and looked her in the eye. "Sometimes it's not so hot huh?"

Her face took on a serious look, afraid that she had been disloyal to her father's calling. "It's like anything else. You take the bad with the good, and the good usually outweighs the bad."

He raised her hand to his lips and kissed it. "You don't sound very convincing."

Embarrassed, Cate bite her lip and looked at the ground. "I promise; being a pastor's daughter is okay. My dad and mom are wonderful."

"They must be to have a *daughter,* like you." He raised her chin and gently kissed her.

Cate backed away. *Wow! I can't believe I let that happen and–I can't believe I liked it so much.* She stood silent for a moment, furrowed brow, eyes darting back and forth, as she tried to say what needed to be said.

"Justin. I–I'm engaged."

He cocked his head and narrowed his eyes. "You're *engaged.*"

"Well, sort of."

His head straightened, his eyes widened and his mouth opened slightly. "You'll have to explain that."

"I've been dating a guy back home for about a year and he's asked me to marry him?"

"And, you said?"

"I didn't say *no*."

"Ah... But, you didn't say *yes*?"

Cate shook her head. "I told him that I'd pray about it."

Justin smiled. "So you weren't sure."

"No, I wasn't sure. I'm not sure I want to be a preacher's wife."

"So, marry me," Justin winked.

Cate's mouth flew open. "Justin, I like you, but—"

"Okay, if you won't marry me, just walk with me," Justin laughed.

Cate punched him. "That's not funny."

"Really, I thought it was," he joked. "You were being way too serious. Let's just have fun this summer. That's all I'm asking—a little fun."

"Fun?"

"Yeah, fun. Do you know what that is Miss Preacher's Daughter?"

Cate pursed her lips and folded her arms. "I know what that is."

"So, do we have a deal? Will you be my partner in fun?"

She cocked her head, and considered his request. "It's a deal." She offered her hand for a shake. He grabbed her hand, pulled her close, kissed her and she surrendered.

Cate told Justin about David, but not David about Justin. She did everything she could to make sure that he never found out. Because she was afraid that he might hear something in her voice, or ask her a question that she couldn't answer, she came up with a plan to avoid phone conversations. Rather than talk to him on the phone everyday as they had planned, she persuaded David that they should correspond by letters and email.

David was supposed to visit her at Tahoe. However, Cate volunteered to work the weekend he was supposed to come so she would be able to tell him that if he came she wouldn't be able to spend time with him. He was disappointed and even more disappointed when he was unable to arrange another time for his visit.

Cate's parents did visit her, and she introduced them to Justin. Dr. and Mrs. Jones seemed to like Justin very much. Because of that, Cate felt more comfortable continuing her relationship with him.

Justin and Cate's relationship progressed steadily over the summer. She was sure that she loved Justin, not David. The catch was if Justin had real feelings for her, he never said so.

As the summer ended, Cate was in turmoil. She was about to go home, where she knew that David would be anxiously awaiting her arrival, and knew he would be expecting to hear what she felt God's will was concerning them. Cate shared some details about camp, though nothing about Justin. She assured David she had been seeking God's will, and in her own way, she had. The key words were *in her own way*. The feelings she had for David in no way compared with the feelings she had for Justin, and she decided that marrying David could not be God's will-for her. She was sure that Justin had to be God's choice for her. However, if that was true, Justin didn't seem to realize it. He never even told her that he loved her.

The day before Cate left Tahoe to go back home to Kansas City, she met Justin at *their spot* to say goodbye. She hoped Justin would finally declare his love for her.

"Justin, this has been the best summer of my life, and you're the main reason for that."

"I could say the same thing to you." Justin took her hand and smiled as he looked into her eyes.

"Then, say it. Girls like to hear things like that."

"They do, do they?"

"This one does." Cate looked deeply into his eyes to see what feelings were there.

"I'd say it if you were my girl, but—you're not—are you." He was making a statement rather than asking a question.

Cate looked away. "No; I guess not."

"I will say it's been *fun*. David Barnes is a lucky guy."

"Yeah"

He pulled her close. "We probably won't see each other tomorrow. I hope you have a great flight home."

Cate was stunned. "Yeah, you too."

He kissed her, "Cate I'm sorry, but I've got one more activity to lead tonight. I'm sure we'll see each other again some time."

Cate was confused. "I hope so."

"Got to go"

"Justin!"

"I'm sorry. I'm late now. Got to go."

Cate watched him walk quickly away. *Oh, I am such a fool! How could I have been such a fool?"*

For the rest of the night and all the way home, Cate reproached herself for falling in love with a man who apparently did not share her feelings. She had no desire to continue unrequited love, but she also knew that she also had no desire to marry a pastor. Even though she would not be marrying Justin, she could not marry David.

She knew what she did *not* want, and what she *did* want, she couldn't have. She didn't know how to tell David. Though she loved Justin, she cared about David too. David was a good man and she knew he loved her unconditionally. She didn't want to hurt him, and so she decided not to tell him anything-for a while. She'd go home, pick up where they left off, and wait for an opportune time to tell him that she could not marry him.

When her plane landed at the airport at Kansas City, David and her parents were waiting for her arrival. Her mother and father greeted her with kisses and hugs first. Next, David hugged and kissed her.

"I'm so glad you're home. I've missed you so much." David looked deeply into her eyes.

Cate turned away as she answered. She was afraid that he would see the truth in her eyes. "I've missed you too," she said, attempting sincerity. The truth was she *had* missed him, but there was also another truth, that wouldn't be said, at least not yet. Cate felt guilty; she was sure he had suspected something. If he did suspect anything, he never said so. He was very happy to see her and quite ready for them to get on with their lives.

The week after she returned home, Justin called, and even though he said he was just calling to say hello to an old friend, his call gave Cate a glimmer of hope. Subsequent calls fueled those hopes.

With Justin's calls came questions, first from David, and then her parents.

"Cate, this guy that keeps calling you, who is he?" David's face clearly revealed his irritation.

"He's just a guy who worked at the camp in Tahoe."

"Why does he keep calling?"

"Because we're friends, can't I have male friends? Don't you trust me?" Cate decided that pretending to be hurt by his questions would be the best way to handle the situation.

"I'm sorry. Of course I trust you."

Justin's calls not only bothered David, but also her parents. They were concerned that there might be more going on than Cate was telling them. When her parents asked about Justin, she told them the same thing she'd told David. She rationalized it by telling herself that she and Justin were only friends. Regardless of what *she* wanted, Justin never hinted that he wanted to be anything more.

The situation took a more complicated turn, when Justin surprised Cate by coming to Kansas City; he'd decided to transfer to the University of Kansas. Cate was overjoyed to see him, and hoped that his transfer was evidence that he loved her and had chosen to pursue her. Indeed, he seemed eager to resume the relationship that began in Tahoe.

David was not happy to hear that Justin had become a student at the University of Kansas. With clenched jaw, tight mouth and rigid stance, he confronted her. "Cate what is *he* doing here?"

"He's here to go to school." Cate's answer was curt.

"Don't they have colleges where he's from?"

"He said he liked what the University of Kansas had to offer."

"And, what would that be?"

"I don't know. He didn't tell me." There was a touch of sarcasm in her answer.

"I think it's you."

Cate shook her head feigning exasperation. "I told you; *we're just friends*."

"I don't think *he* thinks that."

Her hands on her hips, Cate asked, "What are you saying?"

"You know what I'm saying."

"Don't you trust me!" *It worked before, maybe it'll work again.*

"It's *him* I don't trust."

"You don't know him."

"Nor, do I want too."

"David, I can't believe you said that. That's not at all like you."

"I'm sorry." He sighed heavily, closed his eyes and bowed his head as if praying. "You're right. I guess I've got a problem where this guy's concerned."

Cate looked at him intently as he reproached himself for his jealousy and his dislike for Justin. *You have more of a problem than you know, and I can't admit it to you because I'm a coward.*

Cate kept hoping that Justin would tell her that he loved her and wanted to marry her. At the same time, she feared that the time would eventually come when she would not only have to tell David that she couldn't marry him, but that she was going to marry someone else. As much as she hoped that Justin would ask her to marry him, she dreaded the time when she would hurt David.

Caught between her love for Justin and her reluctance to hurt David, Cate lived a secret life, or so she thought. It wasn't a secret to her parents, and they lovingly confronted her, first her mother and then, her father.

"Cate, what are you doing?"

"What do you mean?"

"I mean it's clear to me that you're involved with two men at the same time," her mother said. "And, I expected better of you."

"I know, but I care about both of them."

"Well, you need to make up your mind which one you care more about and cut the other one loose."

"I know which one I love more," Cate paused and bit her lip, "but I don't want to hurt the other one."

"Cate, what you are doing is not fair to either of them. You need to straighten this out."

Cate knew her mother was right, but couldn't find the courage to hurt David, so she continued to keep him in the dark. She was in her room waiting for David to arrive for New Years' Eve when her father gently tapped on her door.

"May I come in?"

"Sure," Cate said.

"Catie, I know that your mother has spoken with you about the situation with David and Justin. I also know that she encouraged you to straighten things out, but you haven't." Cate stopped what she was doing as he continued, "Cate, I've never been ashamed of you, but I am now."

Cate hung her head. She had always been daddy's girl, and his words hurt.

"Cate, what you are doing is not right and I think you know it."

Her head still down, avoiding his eyes, Cate murmured, "Yes sir, but I don't want to hurt anyone."

"But, you are. You're hurting David, Justin, yourself and your mother and me. We expect you to be straightforward and honest in all of your dealings with people. You need to make up your mind which man you want, and tell the other one that you can't see him anymore."

"I'll tell David tonight."

"David," her father said.

Cate heard the disappointment in his voice. She watched him as he took his glasses off, rubbed his face, ran his hand across his hair and let out a deep breath.

"Catie, do what you have to do, but straighten this thing out."

"Yes, sir"

She watched him leave her room with a look of disapproval on his face. Her mother had reacted the same way when she confessed that she thought that she was in love with Justin. Cate knew he was not their choice for her, *but he's my choice*.

Cate couldn't put off telling David any longer, and it wasn't just because of her parents' insistence. Justin had proposed to her the night before. She had met him at a restaurant on campus and he'd finally confessed his love and proposed. Cate immediately said "yes" to his proposal.

After her conversation with her mother, and still dreading to hurt David, Cate decided to do the cowardly thing and break things off in a note. She carried the note around in her purse for days, but her father's confrontation reminded her that David deserved to be told face-to-face.

However, her plan to tell him face-to-face never materialized.. Before she could tell him, he found the note that she had written. It had fallen out of her purse and when he picked it up, he realized that it was for him. Cate entered the room just as he was reading the note. She could tell he was upset and pleaded with him to give her the note; trying to explain that she hadn't meant for him to see the note.

"David, I never intended for you to read that note. I–I, wanted to tell you in person."

His shaking hands held the note and his voice quivered, "So tell me."

"You've got to believe me. I *never* meant for this to happen. I love you-"

"Love me," he held the note to her face, "how can you love me and let this happen?"

"I'm sorry," she stepped back. "I do love you, but I love Justin more, and he wants to marry me."

"So, do I."

"Yes, but *I* want to marry *him*," Cate confessed, a wellspring of tears filling her eyes. "David, I tried to tell you that I wasn't cut out to be a pastor's wife, but you wouldn't listen. I know you don't believe that I love you, but I do. That's why it's been so difficult for me to tell you about Justin. I didn't want to hurt you. I knew you'd react this way."

"How was I supposed to react, Cate?"

"I don't know," she clenched her fists and wiped at the tears on her cheek, "but please believe that I never meant for this to happen. It just did. I'm sorry. Please believe how sorry I am," Cate tried to take him by the arm, but he refused.

"Well, I guess, there's nothing else to say, but have a good life." He quickly walked from the room.

Cate shook her head, knowing that she'd hurt him deeply. She told herself it couldn't be helped. As she continued to think about what had happened, she found herself experiencing a sense of profound loss and sadness. She was confused as to why, and decided to deal with it by hurrying to see Justin. That seemed to work, at least for a while, but the whole episode left Cate very unsettled. The memory of the hurt look on David's face haunted her, and she continued to feel sad and guilty.

"Come unto me, all ye that labor and are heavy laden, and I will give you rest, take my yoke upon you, and learn of me; for I am meek and lowly in heart, and ye shall find rest for your souls. For my yoke is easy, and my burden is light."

Matthew 11:28-30.

Three

She was jarred back to the reality of the present by David moving in his seat as he slept. Cate watched him; after what had transpired that night seven years ago, she'd never imagined that she would one day be on the way to Ecuador-with him, that she would be serving as his daughter's caretaker when he was away on mission business, or that she would become a teacher at the mission school. She thanked God for His grace.

As she continued to watch him, her thoughts again drifted slowly to the past. First one, then the other came, vying for her attention. She felt as if she was careening through the kaleidoscope of her life after her rejection of David.

After she had been painfully honest with David, she refused to face the sadness and guilt that she felt. She chose, rather, to stuff those feelings deep inside. When she began to have reservations about her marriage to Justin, she ignored them.

She refused to acknowledge anything that would deter her from achieving her desire to marry the type of man whose goal would be to make her happy; Justin was that type of man. He confessed to her that he came to Kansas City not to go to school, but to win her. She liked that attitude; Justin putting her first, being the center of his attention.

Her parents had reservations about her marriage to Justin, but she assured them that everything would be fine. Her father interviewed both of them before he would give his blessing and agree to marry them. Justin gave all of the right answers, as did Cate. Her father and mother acquiesced and withdrew their reservations.

She and Justin were married in her home church; her father performing the ceremony. Everything that day *seemed* to foreshadow a happy marriage. It was on the honeymoon, when Cate began to be aware of things that she *should* have been aware of, and would have been, had she taken time to get to know Justin before she married him. Justin had hidden his attitude toward alcohol and Christianity.

Cate remembered the argument that she and Justin had as they sat down to enjoy their first honeymoon dinner.

"Bring us your best bottle of champagne," Justin told the waiter.

"Champagne?"

"Sure this is a celebration. We've got to have champagne," he replied.

"Justin, I don't drink. I never have."

"You don't drink?" Justin cocked his head, his brow furrowed. "Everybody drinks."

"Not everybody. I was brought up to believe in abstinence concerning alcohol."

He shrugged, "Your parents' idea. Cate, you're a married woman now; you can do what you want."

She straightened in her chair, "And I don't want to drink!"

"Cate, don't you love me?"

"Of course I do."

"Don't you want to celebrate our marriage?"

"Yes, but I don't want to celebrate with alcohol."

"How can you be so against drinking if you've never tried it?"

"I just am."

"Please, Cate, just celebrate with me tonight. Try the champagne; if you don't like it, don't drink it," he pleaded.

Because she loved him, and against her better judgment, she gave in to his request and agreed to try the champagne. The waiter brought the champagne and poured each of them a glass. Cate tried it, and didn't like it. Justin, however, seemed so happy at her willingness to please him that she continued to drink. Consequently, the celebration did not have a good outcome for Cate. She became very ill. Justin thought it was funny; Cate did not.

With Cate still ill the following day, Justin continued the honeymoon activities alone. Cate protested and pouted, and Justin apologized and returned to his charming self. Once again, he catered to Cate's every desire and things were fine—for a while.

After the honeymoon, Cate and Justin moved to Baton Rouge to finish college at Louisiana State University. Once Justin was back in Louisiana, with his friends, his drinking became an issue in the marriage, and Cate found out quickly that alcohol use was a big part of Justin's life. As far as he was concerned it wasn't just for celebrating, it was for all occasions. Anytime they socialized with friends, at their home or their friends' home, alcohol was served. Cate felt uncomfortable and out of place, and Justin was embarrassed and angry at his wife's attitude toward alcohol.

"Cate, how dare you treat my friends like this!"

Cate'e eyes widened, "Justin, I don't understand. What have I done?"

"Your self-righteous attitude!"

"You don't have to yell. I don't understand at all. I *am* nice to your friends when they come over."

"Yeah, but you don't participate. You sit there in your *self-righteous smugness*. You watch us and don't participate."

"Justin, you know how I feel about alcohol."

"And, you know how I feel. You don't have to be so judgmental."

Cate shook her head, her eyes narrowed in puzzlement. "How am I being judgmental?"

"You're nice and polite, but the guys know how you feel about alcohol."

"How—how do they know. *I've* never told them. Have you?"

"No one had to tell them. They can see."

"What?"

"Yeah, they can; so can I. You make them feel uncomfortable."

Cate was shocked. "I make *them* feel uncomfortable? They make *me* feel uncomfortable."

"And, it's written all over your face. That's what makes them feel uncomfortable."

"Oh, I see."

"Finally," Justin softened his tone and sat on the couch.

"Justin, I'm sorry, I didn't realize that my face was betraying my feelings."

He stared at Cate, his tone rigid, "Yeah, well you need to do something about that."

A sigh was forced from her mouth and her body tensed. "I–I don't know what."

"It would help if you'd join in."

Cate looked him in the eye, as her heart sank. "You know I can't do that."

"Ashley and the other girls do, and they're not that crazy about drinking."

"I–can't."

Justin took her by the hand. "Well, work on that face of yours then. Don't be so judgmental."

"I'll try."

"For my sake, you need to do more than try." Justin gently pulled her down to him.

Their agreeing to disagree about alcohol didn't make things better, and as the problems with Justin continued, Cate sought refuge in a local church and began to get her relationship with the Lord resolved. Justin went with her-at first-but decided that it wasn't for him. The men of the church tried to reach out to him, but he refused. When Cate confronted him about the need for a Christian to attend church, Justin revealed his ideas about church, God and salvation. Cate realized during that conversation that she, a Christian and a pastor's daughter, had married a man who was *not* a Christian.

"Justin, you told my father you were a committed Christian. Why did you do that if you weren't?"

"I was hedging my bets. I knew what he wanted to hear, so I told him. I would have done whatever it took to marry you."

Cate's eyes gazed at him as though seeing him for the first time, "You intentionally lied to my father."

"I wouldn't call it lying. Call it hedging my bets. After all I *am* a Christian; just not your father's kind of Christian."

"My father's kind of Christian?" Cate folded her arms.

"Yeah, I believe that God loves everybody, and that He's not as down on all this *sin stuff* as most people think, but I could tell that your father was a straight laced, Bible-believing Christian. I didn't think he'd agree to our marriage if he thought I was different. Back then, I thought that *you* were my kind of Christian."

"I'm sorry for giving you the wrong impression." Cate shifted on her feet, "I never meant to do that. I'm sorry if I'm a disappointment to you, but I promise I'll try to be a good wife to you."

"I know you'll try to be a good wife, Cate."

This revelation of Justin's true spiritual condition and his impression of her before they were married devastated Cate, but she had taken vows and she meant to live by those vows. The situation with Justin caused Cate to do much soul searching and repenting for her rebellion toward God that had led her to get involved with Justin. She prayed, "Oh God, please forgive me for the rebellion that got me here, and give me the strength to be true to my marriage vows. Please Father, help Justin realize how to truly know Christ as Savior and Lord."

After the first six months of their marriage, he wasn't antagonistic as much as unresponsive to her. He made excuses to stay away from home and came home only to sleep. His attitude devastated Cate. But she did receive a glimmer of hope.

Her parents were coming for Cate and Justin's graduation, and she was beside herself. She didn't want her parents to know what was going on. Justin realized the spot she was in and decided to do the compassionate thing.

"Cate, don't worry about your parents. I'll play the part of the loving husband, while they're in town for graduation."

Amazed by his offered, she asked, "Why would you?"

"Because I know how much they love you, and I know you haven't told them about us."

Cate narrowed her eyes, bit her lip and looked intently at him. "You're serious, aren't you?"

"Of course I am,"

She decided to take advantage of the occasion. "Justin, I'd like to get things straightened out between us."

He shook his head, "After your parents leave, not now." He turned and walked out the door.

Cate was hopeful for the first time in months. She prayed that the Lord would work in Justin's heart and help heal their marriage, and she was encouraged by his actions and attitudes toward her while her parents were there. He played the part of a loving husband so well that Cate thought God was answering her prayers. However, after saying goodbye to her parents Justin made it clear on the way home that God had not answered her prayers.

"Cate, I did what I said. I played the part of a loving husband, but your parents are gone now, and I want to get things settled between us."

"Okay, so can I ask you something?"

"Go ahead," Justin answered.

"Will you go to marriage counseling with me?" Cate prayed he'd say yes.

He shook his head, "Cate, I thought you understood."

"Understood what?"

"I thought that you understood that I don't want to be married to you anymore."

She tried to speak but nothing came out, it was as if the air had left her body. Cate squeezed her eyes shut, hoping her world would be different when she opened them. "B-but, Justin you said we were going to try to straighten things out. You... Didn't you see, see how things could be this week? We were nice to each other again, considerate, even loving, I…"

"It was an act Cate! Don't you get it? I was trying to be kind. I knew that what's happened with us put you in a spot with your parents. I knew you hadn't told them anything. So, I told you that I'd help you out, and I did."

Cate sat, quietly wringing her hands, as she tried to make sense of what he was saying. Justin tried again to make her understand.

"An act of compassion, that's all this week was. I thought I owed you that."

"You thought you owed me. What does that mean?"

"Cate, I know that you love me and I love you, but you're not the girl I married."

"Yes, I am. You have to believe me. I *am* and I've tried to be a good wife."

"I know you've tried to be a good wife, but you're not the kind of wife I want. I want a wife that puts me first, and wants what I want," Justin shrugged, not even bothering to turn and look at her, "and that's not you."

"Justin, I've spent the last eleven months trying to be the kind of wife that you want."

"That's not exactly true. I know you believe it is, but it's not. You're so caught up in this Christian stuff that you'll never be what I want."

"You think my Christianity is the source of our problems?" Cate's stomach twisted, *this can't be true, it can't.*

"Yes, I do. You put God first, not me, and I know that's not going to change, but neither am I. I want a wife that puts *me* first, not God." He paused, "I believe I have found a woman who will do that."

"You—You've what?"

"I've found someone else."

"No," she shook her head, "no, I can't believe it."

"Cate, I'm sorry. I never meant to hurt you. You've got to believe me. I love you, but not like I love her. I don't want to be married to you anymore. I want to marry Ashley."

"Ashley, Ashley" Cate stared at the car's floor mats, but didn't see them. "Ashley."

She barely heard Justin tell her that he had filed for divorce and that she would receive the papers in a couple of days. He realized that she wasn't listening.

"Cate! I've filed for a divorce. You'll receive the papers in a couple of days. Please don't contest the divorce. It won't do you any good. I'm moving in with Ashley tonight."

When they arrived home, she went for a walk as he packed to leave.

Justin's adultery and his desire for a divorce signaled her complete and utter failure as a woman and a Christian; she plunged into despair and depression. Not only had she failed God and Justin, but she had ruined her life and quite possibly her mother's and father's too. There had never been a divorce in Cate's family; she couldn't cope with the fact that hers would be the first one, that her divorce might hurt her father's ministry because some people might consider her failure his failure. How could she ever admit to her parents what had happened? Surely, they would be disappointed in her. After all, all that had happened was her fault; she'd been the one who strayed from God. Moreover, there was David, *I need to apologize to him.* In telling her that he did not love her

or want to be with her anymore, Justin had used some of the same words she had used with David. She felt firsthand what horrible wounds those words made. She understood now that she should have married David, *too late now*. The thoughts circled constantly, round and round in her mind, crushing her heart and spirit.

Four

God, in His grace, intervened through Mica Pierce, a friend from church. Seeing how deeply the depression had taken hold of Cate, she sought to help. "Cate, how about going with me to church tomorrow?"

"I'm sorry, but I can't."

"Come on, you haven't been to church since Justin left you. As a matter of fact, you haven't been anywhere except to work. Cate, it's not good for you to be by yourself so much. Go to church with me tomorrow, please."

"Mica, I can't. I'm," Cate bit her lip, "I'm too ashamed."

"Ashamed of what? You didn't do anything. Justin did."

"I must have done *something* wrong. He left me for another woman."

"You're saying *his* adultery is your fault? I don't think so!"

"Mica, he said I wasn't the wife he needed me to be."

"Even I know better than that. I know how cold Justin was toward you. Cate, he was just trying to justify his infidelity."

"If I had been the kind of Christian I ought to have been, he wouldn't have been so antagonistic to Christianity."

"Whoa! I won't believe that one either. Cate, I know how hard you tried. You tried a lot harder than I would have. I wouldn't have put up with all his stuff."

Cate scuffed the ground with her shoe and avoided looking in Mica's eyes, "It wasn't that bad."

"Really?" Mica narrowed her eyes, "I remember the drinking, the carousing and only coming home to eat and sleep."

"Mica, I'm so ashamed. There's never been a divorce in our family. The fact that my dad is a pastor makes it so much worse. This whole thing is such a terrible reflection on him and my mother."

"I'm sure they don't think that."

"They would if they knew," Cate rolled her eyes.

"You mean—they don't know? You haven't told them?"

"No, I can't bear the thought of disappointing them and hurting them."

"Cate, do you mean to tell me that you're trying to go through this whole thing alone? *Girl*, you need your family. You need their support. Call them. Tell them."

"Mica, I can't. I just can't."

"Cate please,"

"I can't." Cate wiped at the tears trailing down her cheeks as Mica sought to comfort her.

"Okay, okay, for now. But, I want you to know. You've got *me*. I'll be here for you, but you've got to let me. Cate, I'm worried about you."

"You don't have to worry about me Mica."

But, she did worry; she couldn't help it. Nothing Mica tried to do helped. Cate's depression grew worse, and Mica decided to exhibit tough love for Cate. She called Dr. and Mrs. Jones and told them about the divorce and Cate's depression.

"Hello–Dr. Jones–You don't know me–I'm a friend of Cate's from Baton Rouge–Dr. Jones, I think you ought to know what's going on with Cate–Justin left Cate for another woman–Yes, sir that's right, and he divorced her–About three months ago–But, I'm calling because Cate's not handling it well–No, sir, she's terribly depressed; she doesn't go anywhere, but to work. She doesn't eat or sleep like she should–Yes, sir; I'm extremely worried about her–Thank you, I was hoping you'd say that."

Shocked and concerned by what they heard, Cate's parents made plans to come to Baton Rouge immediately. Only God's grace, through Mica's intervention, and her parents' loving care enabled Cate to climb out of her terrible pit of deep depression.

Cate moved from Baton Rouge back to Kansas City and into her parents' home during her recovery. After several months of her father and mother's patient counsel and the Lord's word, Cate was ready once again to face life.

God offered her a second chance to surrender her life to him, and to follow obediently wherever he led, and Cate responded happily to God's forgiveness. She hoped that she would have a second chance with David, hoped that he still had feelings for her. She decided to try to win him back.

"David, I'm sorry that I hurt you. I'm sorry that I married Justin- and not you."

David stood silent.

"David, I made a mistake. Can you please forgive me?

David responded with expected Christian charity, "Cate, I forgave you long ago."

"David, I should have married you. I love you," Cate gushed.

"Cate, too much has happened. We can't go back."

"Please don't let my mistake ruin things for us," Cate's eyes pleaded with him.

"Don't you understand; it wasn't just a mistake; you married another man. You can't just take that back."

"Are you telling me that there is no second chance for us?" Cate's hope had turned to despair.

"I'm telling you that your marriage to Justin changed things between us. It had too, Cate."

"No, it doesn't have to."

"Yes it does. You need to know that I've been seeing someone, and I'm going to marry her."

"Y-you have? Who?"

"Jenny, it's Jenny."

"Jenny Howard?"

"Yes."

"I see," Cate felt the tightness in her stomach, her knees quivered. "She isn't with Steve anymore. She's with——you."

"She's with me. Steve's somewhere playing basketball. He chose basketball over God. Jenny chose God."

"She chose God, and now she has you. There's a little irony here, don't you think?"

David looked uneasily at his watch. "Cate, I'm sorry, but I have to go. I'm supposed to meet Jenny in a few minutes." As he turned to leave, he stopped, turned around, and hugged her, "Goodbye, Cate," he whispered in her ear.

"Goodbye." Cate whispered as she watched him walk away.

David crushed her hopes. She had heard him say there was no second chance with him. He told her about Jenny and his plans to marry her. She heard him clearly, but her heart argued something else. The hug he'd given her as he said goodbye and the strong emotions that he'd exhibited led her to believe that he still had very deep feelings for her. She vowed to continue her efforts to win him back.

Cate's parents realized her determined desire to win David back, and Dr. Jones lovingly confronted his daughter, "Catie, honey what are you doing? David is engaged to Jenny."

"But, Daddy he loves me. I know he does."

"That may be, but he loves Jenny too, and I know that to be true."

"But, Daddy…"

"No *buts* Catie, you broke your engagement to David and married Justin. Would you have David do that to Jenny?"

"Daddy," Cate crossed her arms over her chest, "you're not being fair."

"Are you sure that it's me who's not being fair? Catie if you were to succeed in winning David back, you would ruin his ministry plans. The International Mission Board, is about to appoint him and Jenny as missionaries to Ecuador, and the IMB would never appoint a couple if one of them were divorced."

"But, Daddy I *love* him."

"Baby Girl, I'm going to be straight with you. You messed up when you married Justin, and unfortunately, that mistake has consequences. I know that you really love David but, you need to love him enough to let him go."

Knowing her father was right and having no desire to mess up David's life, as she had messed up hers, she gave up her efforts to win David back, but not before Jenny confronted her.

"Cate, I'm sorry for what happened with Justin, but David is not available."

"Jenny, I know he's engaged to you."

"Yes, he is, and I'm not about to give him up. I know he loves me, but I know he also loves you. I've seen how torn he's been since you've come home. Cate, don't you realize that you could destroy him without meaning to?"

"I would *never* do that! Never."

"Then, leave him alone! Let him marry me. Let us serve God together in Ecuador."

Jenny's words stung, but Cate couldn't argue with them. The talk with her dad had already made her see the truth of what Jenny said. "Of course, I'm sorry; I never meant to cause so many problems. I guess, I was only thinking of myself. You don't have to worry anymore."

"Thank you, Cate."

Cate kept her promise. She made herself scarce from that night on. David married Jenny, and they went to Ecuador as missionaries.

Reconciled to having no second chance with David, Cate began a new life. By God's providence, she had chosen to get a degree in elementary education with a reading specialty. She found a job, an apartment, and moved out of her parents' house.

While she was teaching third grade at Glendale Elementary School and getting her life together, David and Jenny were having a baby daughter. Try as she might to get over David, every bit of news from David and Jenny in Ecuador only caused her to think about what might have been. She tried many times to surrender this to God, but her feelings for David never faded. Neither did her regrets about marrying Justin.

"And the Spirit and the bride say, Come, And let him that heareth say, Come, And let him that is athirst come. And whosoever will, let him come and take of the water of life freely."

Revelation 22:17

Five

After three years of teaching, she accepted a summer position at the camp where she had met Justin five years earlier. The job at the camp gave her the opportunity to get away and have time for God to speak to her in new surroundings. She knew that the camp at Tahoe would be conducive to her spending time alone outdoors where she could walk and talk with God. Maybe there, God would give her clear guidance as to His will for her.

She was right. God did speak to her at Tahoe, and He led her to consider teaching in a missionary school. It was also at Tahoe that she heard some very bad news. The day before she was to leave for home, her father called.

"Hello," Cate was cheered to hear her father's voice.

"Catie, I've got some bad news."

"Is it mom?"

"No, honey, it's Jenny Barnes. The plane that was taking her to an inoculation point crashed—Jenny was killed."

"What! How's David?"

"Devastated, I spoke with him briefly. He's bringing Jenny back to Kansas City for burial."

Life was changing. David was without a wife; Sarah was without a mother, and God had given Cate another chance to follow His leadership.

She began taking steps to be obedient to God's leadership by teaching in a mission school. She applied to a mission school in Mexico,

and was accepted. Shortly before she was to leave for Mexico, Cate received a letter withdrawing their offer due to lack of funding. Cate read the letter repeatedly in disbelief. Surely, the letter was a mistake; she'd been so sure of God's guidance.

Having had her parents' support and constant encouragement in her efforts to follow God's leadership, Cate appealed to them to help her make sense out of what had happened.

She held up the letter. "The mission agency has withdrawn its offer."

"What!" Her mother was wide-eyed at the announcement.

"Why Catie?" her dad asked, as he took the letter.

"Funding issues," Cate sank down on the couch in a lump. "I was so sure about God's leadership. I can't believe I got it wrong."

Her dad looked up from the letter. "Maybe you didn't get the leadership wrong, perhaps you got the location of where God wanted you wrong."

"Really?"

"I suggest you settle down and pray," her father counseled.

Since she had given up the lease on her apartment and her job, Cate spent the next few months looking for a job while temporarily living with her parents. Her father advised her to settle for a part-time job, to continue to live at home, and to consider becoming a seminary student while waiting for God to lead her further.

God's providence was definitely at work during this period of Cate's life. The first night of her seminary class on missions, she discovered David was the teacher. The seminary had offered him a temporary position while he was on furlough, and desiring to keep busy as a means of coping with Jenny's death, he readily accepted.

Then, there was Sarah. When Cate first met Sarah, she was amazed; the child mesmerized her. Sarah was three years old, was very smart, and fluent in Spanish and English. Sarah looked more like David than Jenny. Yet with all her charming qualities, Sarah was sad and grief stricken, and rarely smiled. She pulled at Cate's heartstrings.

Cate made Sarah her special project; she was intent on helping Sarah cope with Jenny's death. Even though Jenny had been her rival for

David, Cate had always liked Jenny, and envied her for not having any qualms about marrying David and going to Ecuador. Cate admired Jenny for that. Consequently, helping David and Sarah was the least she could do.

Cate spoke Spanish and did so quite often to Sarah. She brought her little gifts, but most of all she took time with Sarah. Within a few weeks, Sarah responded to Cate's efforts to draw her out of her shell of sadness and grief. Sarah was less sad, more outgoing and smiled at times.

David saw the changes, and expressed his appreciation to Cate, "I want to thank you for all that you have done for Sarah."

"You're welcome, but there's no need for thanks. Sarah's a great little girl."

"Thank you, I think so too," David agreed. "I appreciate you helping her deal with Jenny's death, and how you've helped turn a very sad little girl into a happy little girl again."

"The staff at the preschool deserves a lot of the credit too."

"That may be true, but *Miss Cate* is the one she talks about the most. I know how much you mean to her."

"She's a sweetheart. I'm glad I could help her." Cate gently touched David's arm, "If you don't mind me asking, how are you doing?"

"I'm making it, one day at a time."

"I know it's hard," Cate said.

"Yeah, it is hard, but God is good and His grace sustains me."

That night was the first time that they had a conversation in almost five years. Before that night, they had been cordial, but kept their distance from one another. After that night, they were friends again, and both seemed relieved.

Realizing Sarah's affection for Cate, and that she was no longer the same Cate who had dumped him for Justin, David included her in some of his and Sarah's activities.

Cate accepted this as a gesture of forgiveness and friendship, but nothing more. Though she had very strong feelings for David, she reconciled herself to the fact that she could never be his wife. He was still a missionary, and though he was on furlough, his year was almost up, and he would be returning to Ecuador.

Cate enjoyed their times together, as did Sarah and David. They had much in common, including a call to missions. He confessed to her that he had been quite shocked when he saw her in his class that first night and even more shocked when she wrote in one of her papers that she felt that God was leading her to teach at a mission school. Through the times they spent together talking and doing things with Sarah, David and Cate became good friends again.

David confided his concerns about leaving Sarah behind when he returned to Ecuador. He hated the thought of it, but with Jenny gone, there was no one in Ecuador to be her caregiver when he had to be gone on his trips as a church planter. His family in Kansas had offered to take care of her, and he knew that he could count on them for that. However, he hated the thought of leaving his little girl behind. She wasn't even five yet; how could she understand her daddy leaving her behind? He prayed and prayed about what to do and had not received God's clear guidance on the subject.

The answer to everyone's prayers came with a teacher's vacancy at the mission school in Ecuador. David sought out Cate one night before class, "Cate, God may have just answered both our prayers."

"How?"

"A friend of mine, Matthew Kennedy, needs a teacher at his mission school in Peguche, Ecuador. Would you consider teaching at the mission school?"

"What?"

"You heard right. The position is yours if you want it."

"Are you sure?" Cate was having difficulty wrapping her head around it all.

"I'm very sure."

"This may be God's answer to my prayer, but I still want to pray about it. I don't want to make a mistake."

"Of course, pray about it. This may be God's answer to both our prayers, but I want you to be sure about it, and if God leads you to Ecuador, I want to ask you to be Sarah's caregiver if you take the position."

"If God leads, I'd love to be Sarah's caregiver."

Cate sought her parents' advice. They agreed that this might be the Lord's answer to her prayers and David's, but that God would have to confirm it to her. They promised to help her pray for guidance.

Cate decided to spend time alone in prayer and fasting. Over the next few days, God led her to complete peace about His will concerning teaching in Ecuador and becoming Sarah's caregiver. Having received God's confirmation, Cate willingly accepted Matthew's offer of a position at his mission school outside of Otavalo, Ecuador.

Cate's reflection on the events of the past seven years made her realize how good and gracious God had been to her. He had been faithful to lead her into His new direction for her life. Her journey to the center of God's will had been a long winding road with a few rocky detours. She determined never to forget what it had taken her to get there. She was grateful for the memories of the last few years. Memories of God's forgiveness and God's grace which made the memories of the wrong choices and the irreversible consequences of those choices easier to bear. She was thankful that God was the God of the Second Chance and the God of Many Chances.

"And Jesus said to the woman at the well, "Whosoever drinketh of the water that I shall give him shall never thirst, but the water I shall give him shall be in him a well of water springing up into everlasting life."

John 4:14.

Six

The pilot's announcement that they were about to land in Quito, interrupted Cate's memories. David stirred and stretched as Cate turned her attention to Sarah, who was still sleeping, and she fastened Sarah's seat belt.

"We're here, huh?" David rubbed his eyes.

"That's what the pilot said."

"Sleeping beauty is still out I see."

"I thought I'd let her sleep until we actually touched down."

"Good idea," David agreed. "Are you ready for your new adventure to begin?"

"I've been ready," Cate nodded, "for a long time."

As the plane touched down smoothly on the tarmac, Cate awakened Sarah,

"Come on, Baby Girl. We're here."

David retrieved their carryon luggage from the overhead compartment and they took their place in line to leave the plane. With Sarah's hand in hers, Cate took a deep breath, not a sigh of anxiety or a breath of relief; rather it was a deep breath of excited anticipation. *This is it; this is my second chance at service and to submit to God in all things.* Even though it was the beginning of night in Quito, she knew it was the dawning of a new day in her life. She couldn't help but be excited at the possibilities that lay ahead. She was certain that she was in the very center of God's will for her life. That one fact alone caused her heart to overflow with joy; she could not stop smiling.

Even though she was tired and had not been able to nap on the flight, there was no trace of fatigue. There was a spring in her step; she was eager to begin experiencing Ecuador, and all that it held for her.

As she, David and Sarah walked to Customs to declare their reasons for coming to Ecuador she was overjoyed to tell the official that she was there to teach. Officials of the mission and the mission school as well as some of David's friends met them at the airport. All were anxious to welcome David and Sarah back, and to meet the new teacher for the mission school.

Cate remembered her impressions of each. Dr. Patterson, the director of mission work was a likeable, gray-haired, godly man. Cate could tell immediately that he loved the Lord, the mission work and was grateful to have David back. Matthew Kennedy, the young, handsome director/headmaster of the mission school, was there. Cate knew that he and David were very good friends and that was why he had trusted David's judgment in recommending her to teach at the mission school. Matthew greeted her warmly, and Cate marveled at how much he reminded her of David. She was sure that she would love working with him.

Matthew introduced Cate to Miss Janet. Janet Cook, a petite woman in her late forties, had taught at the mission school for twenty years, and was Matthew's trusted right hand.

Cate also met Kim Davis, a blonde-haired, brown-eyed, attractive teacher, who'd been teaching at the mission school for the past five years. She and Cate were approximately the same age, and Cate would share a house with Kim and Miss Janet.

Cate also meet Mr. and Mrs. Garcia, who were in their late forties. Mrs. Garcia had worked at the mission school as the janitor and cook, but retired. She knew David and had known Jenny well. She came to offer her services as a housekeeper and cook to David, who gratefully accepted her offer.

Once the greetings were finished and the baggage retrieved, everyone headed to the mission van, except Mr. and Mrs. Garcia, who brought along the luggage in their truck.

As she stepped from the airport building, Cate was amazed by the beauty of the Ecuadorian night. Though it was the last day of July, the temperature was chilly, and spring-like. She saw the silhouettes of mountaintops in the distance against the night sky. They reminded her of Tahoe, where she had worked in the summers. However, she would soon find out how really different Ecuador was.

The little caravan made its way to Otavalo, a small town about thirty-five miles north of Quito, stopping only to drop off Dr. Patterson at his home in Quito. Otavalo was nestled in a valley surrounded by mountains. Cate knew the population numbered fewer than 30,000 and their main industry was textiles. The Otavalenos, the most highly developed modern tribe, were master artisans, who sold their wares at a Saturday market, a famous tourist attraction and one of the main sources of income for the surrounding area. She looked forward to meeting some of these wonderfully skilled and talented people.

As the van proceeded to its destination, Cate reveled in the beauty that God had bestowed upon the magnificent landscape within this part of the Andes. Cate realized that this place was very different from her home, or anywhere else, she had ever been. *Cate, you're not in Kansas anymore.*

As they passed small villages along the way, she realized that the living standard was nothing she had ever experienced. Even though the American Way on which they were traveling was a well-paved highway, the streets of the villages they passed were unpaved. The houses and buildings were very simple; their builders constructing them from readily available, cheap materials. Simple as they were Cate found them beautiful. Everything she saw was beautiful; deep within her, she had the overwhelming feeling that everything was exactly as it should be, and in her heart she praised God for the opportunity that He had given her.

"For God so loved the world that He gave His only begotten Son that whosoever believeth in Him should not perish, but have everlasting life. For God sent not His Son into the world to condemn the world but that through Him the world might be saved."

John 3:16-17.

Seven

After a two-hour drive through the mountains they arrived at Otavala, which had more paved streets than the villages before. There was a large square for the market, buildings that were more complex and beautifully ornate, a train station and bus service. However, Otavala was not their final destination. The mission school, David's house and ministry, Cate's new home and school were located in Peguche, a small village on the outskirts of Otavalo. The little caravan traveled until it arrived at the small village about ten minutes further down the road.

    A crowd of local people waited at David's home to greet David and Sarah, welcoming them home with much joy and love. A representative for the group delivered a brief speech expressing the group's sympathy for the loss of Jenny and their tremendous love for, and memory of her. David and Sarah's departure from Peguche had saddened the people of the village and they were overjoyed at their return.

    The generosity of the village's people deeply moved David, and his friends. Finally, he choked out the words, "Thank you friends. May God richly bless you for your generosity and love."

    Because she was more attuned to his feelings than she wanted to admit, and knew how deeply the generosity of these people had moved David, Cate found herself fighting back tears. She breathed a quick prayer that God would help her not to cry. She didn't want to intrude with what was going on between David, his friends and the town's people.

    Sarah had fallen asleep in Cate's lap during the trip from Quito.

When the group arrived at David's house and the people were waiting to greet David, Matthew had taken her into his arms to allow Cate to get out of the van. Sarah, who was a deep sleeper, continued to sleep during the speech. When she awoke and realized where she was, she automatically cried out, "Mommy! Mommy! Where are you, Mommy?" Immediately, every eye was on David, who moved toward his daughter.

As he gently took her into his arms, Sarah, rubbed her eyes and continued, "Daddy, isn't mommy here?"

"No, Sarah, Mommy's not here."

"But, Mommy was here." Sarah had a look of remembering on her face.

"Yes, she was here, but she's in heaven now."

Understanding flooded Sarah's face, "That's right. Mommy's in heaven now."

Seeing the look of sadness on her daddy's face, Sarah apologized, "I'm sorry Daddy. I thought Mommy was here, but I know that Mommy's in heaven. I miss Mommy, Daddy."

"I know, Baby. I miss her too."

The joy that everyone had felt now turned to sadness. They could not help but feel that they were intruding upon a very personal moment between father and daughter. One by one they quietly said their goodbyes and excused themselves.

Matthew and his entourage continued on to the house Cate would occupy with Janet and Kim. Matthew and Mr. Garcia carried Cate's bags into her room. It was a simple house, but adequate for Cate's needs. Miss Janet and Kim had shared the responsibilities of cleaning, cooking and taking care of the house. They also shared the expenses involved in providing food and other necessities. Cate assured them that she was quite willing to share in all these things.

After a quick tour, Cate and Kim returned to the living room where Miss Janet had provided refreshments. Miss Janet and Matthew were talking about the upcoming school term and included them in the conversation.

"Miss Jones," Matthew began.

"Mr. Kennedy, please, call me Cate."

"I will, but only if you will call me Matthew. *Mr. Kennedy* is my father," he answered.

"Okay."

"Cate, I understand that you taught third grade for four years, but haven't taught for the past year," Matthew said.

"That's correct."

"May I ask why you didn't teach last year?" Matthew continued.

"You may," Cate nodded and smiled, "At the end of my fourth year at the elementary school I resigned in anticipation of teaching at a mission school in Mexico. When that didn't materialize, my job at the elementary school was no longer available, and neither was any other teaching job around Kansas City. After much prayer and advice from people I trusted, I took a part-time job at a preschool and began seminary."

"May I ask why you wanted a job at the mission school in Mexico?" Matthew asked.

"I wanted to teach in a mission school because I felt that was what God wanted me to do. I applied for the job in Mexico because I was being obedient to God's call. I was accepted, but the mission organization had financial problems, and had to withdraw their offer of employment."

Throughout Matthew's inquiries, Miss Janet and Kim sat quietly, listening with interest to each question and answer. Cate seemed to read an expression of approval upon their faces as she answered each question.

"What age groups did you work with at the pre-school?"

"I worked with three and four year olds mainly, but also some five year olds who had not yet entered school."

"Did you teach things like colors, shapes, alphabet, numbers and things like that?" Matthew continued.

"Yes, I did. I also taught some reading."

"Reading! You taught reading to three and four year olds?" Miss Janet exclaimed.

"Yes, I taught them very simple reading: vowel sounds, phonics, simple sight words and such."

"And, they learned that?" Kim inquired.

Cate nodded, proud of her accomplishment, "Most did well."

Miss Janet smiled in amazement and nodded to Matthew.

"Cate, how would you like to teach kindergarten at the mission school?" Matthew asked.

"Kindergarten, I thought I'd be teaching third grade."

"I thought so too, until I talked to David and the head of the

pre-school and found out what you had been able to accomplish with your pre-school students."

"Teach kindergarten?" *Maybe this is one of my callings?* "Yes, I would like that."

"Cate, I want to make sure that you understand that kindergarten here will not be like kindergarten in America. Some of your students will be older than five, and some younger," Matthew cautioned.

"Really?"

"As a mission school we try to provide not only a traditional education, but a service for the people of the area. We take students as early as possible to help the parents with childcare issues and we take students who are older, but have been unable to attend school for whatever reason. The government is unable to provide schools in all areas and even then, our school tends to be better than the government schools. We actually have people move to the area, or travel a long way so that their children can attend our school. These people greatly value education. They particularly value the ability to read. Many value Christian education. They want their children steeped in the teachings of Christianity as well as traditional education. We are very pleased that the Lord has put us here to be used in these people's lives," Matthew paused and smiled at Cate, "and we are glad that He sent you to us. We're hopeful that you will be a very valuable asset to help us to minister to the needs and expectations of these people."

"Wow, I don't know what to say, I feel so very humbled by the opportunity that God, and you, are giving me. I promise you that with God's help I'll do my very best."

"I know you will. You came very highly recommended," Matthew added.

"Yeah, David's opinion carries a lot of weight around here," Kim chimed in.

"How long have you known David?" Miss Janet inquired.

"About eight years."

"David was youth minister at your father's church. Wasn't he?" Matthew asked.

"Yes, he was."

"So, your father's a pastor," Miss Janet stated.

"Yes, he is."

"How long has he been a pastor?"

"He's been a pastor for about thirty-five years. He's been at his present church for twenty-seven years."

"So, your father has been a pastor all of your life," Kim reflected.

"That's right."

"Mine too," Kim added.

"Your dad's a pastor also?" Cate asked.

"Yep."

"Mine too," Matthew added.

Cate looked at Miss Janet expecting to hear her say, 'Mine too'. However, Miss Janet said, "My father was a farmer all of his life, until he died last year."

"I'm sorry about your father," Cate gently touched Janet's arm.

"Thank you."

"Well, Cate, I know you must be tired from your flight. It's getting late; I guess I should be going." Matthew rose, "But there's just one more thing. We're having a reception in your honor tomorrow night around six at the school. We thought it would give the other staff, parents, students, and interested parties an opportunity to meet our new teacher from Kansas."

"A reception in my honor, that's very nice." Cate blushed, "Thank you."

"You're most welcome. However, I can't take credit for the idea. Janet and Kim were the brains behind it, and now that I have met you, I believe that it's one of the best ideas that they've had in a while." Matthew paused, and before Cate could respond, he continued, "I don't believe that Job would mind if I paraphrase a little. 'I had heard of you with my ear, but now I see you for myself and I am amazed.' Yes, I'm certain that the reception in your honor is a wonderful idea."

"Thank you all very much." Cate was embarrassed by Matthew's obvious interest in her.

"I'll look forward to seeing you tomorrow night at the reception." Matthew exited after a reluctant goodbye.

Kim watched with a grin as Miss Janet showed him out, and giggled with glee once he was out the door. "Well, Miss Jones, it seems that in your short time here that you've made a conquest," Kim's face held a broad smile and a twinkle in her eye.

"Trust me." Cate held up her hand, "I am *not* interested in making any conquests. I'm here to teach."

"Evidently, you could teach me a thing or two." Kim looked to the door where Matthew left. "I've been here for five years and Matthew has *never* looked at me like he looked at you from the moment you got off the plane."

"Yeah," Cate rolled her eyes, "right,"

"She *is* right, my dear. Matthew does appear to be rather smitten with you," Janet agreed.

"Smitten with me?"

"Yes, indeed." Janet arched her eyebrows, "I suspect that we shall have a very interesting school year."

"The headmaster will most likely spend a lot of time in a *certain* kindergarten classroom," Kim chimed in.

"Look ladies, I'm only here because I'm interested in serving the Lord by being the best teacher I can be." Cate wanted everyone to clearly understand why she was there.

"I am quite sure that's true," Janet replied, "and I'm also quite sure that's *one* of the things that attracts Matthew to you."

"That's *one* of the things?" Cate leaned back, eyeing her two new friends.

"Yes, one of the things, you *are* quite beautiful you know," Janet continued. Janet noted Cate's beautiful auburn hair and lively green eyes.

Cate choked back a laugh, "Yeah, right."

"Yeah is right," Kim spoke up reluctantly, "Cate, aren't you aware of how beautiful you are?"

"Please, ladies, this is getting a little absurd. I do *not* go around preening in front of a mirror. I do not have a problem with vanity."

"Poor eyesight or low self esteem maybe, but certainly not vanity," Kim joked.

Miss Janet chimed in with a laugh, "There's nothing wrong with beauty of appearance or spirit, my dear, if you do not let it go to your head. It's very apparent you do not. In fact, it seems that you are not even aware of your beauty."

Cate felt embarrassed-and uncomfortable. Janet and Kim both apologized and asked her to forgive their bluntness and humor. They assured her that when she came to know them better that she would realize that they had not meant anything. Cate accepted their apology, assuring them that she took no real offense, but she was concerned about Matthew. If they were correct about Matthew, the situation might present complications for which she was not prepared. *I'm not ready for this.*

As she fell asleep that night, even though she was quite tired, thoughts prevented her from drifting into a deep, restful sleep. She was quite sure that she was exactly where God wanted her to be, but she found herself anxious about the complications that Miss Janet and Kim predicted. She did not want anything to interfere with carrying out her teaching assignment. Friendship was fine, but anything else would be an inconvenience. In addition-there was David. He would always occupy a special place deep in her heart. She knew he was the only man that she would ever love deeply and completely, and his presence would constantly remind her of that fact. However, she was also sure that her love for him could only be love from afar. He was a missionary through and through, and the International Mission Board would never sanction the service of any couple, one of which was divorced. She could never have any hope of a life with David as long as he was a missionary, *and he'll always be a missionary.*

She remembered how he looked when the man who gave the speech had mentioned Jenny. She saw how much of a grip grief still had on David, and knew he still deeply loved and missed his wife. Even if the IMB obstacle wasn't there, Cate knew that Jenny still filled David's heart, and that left no room for her.

To combat the possibility of falling into the grips of depression as she had in Baton Rouge, she concentrated on her relationship with God and her relationship with Sarah. Sarah needed her after Jenny's death, but she also realized that she needed Sarah. She had helped Sarah with the grief she felt because of the loss of her mother, and Sarah helped her deal with the depression that had reared its ugly head after she once again began a *relationship* with David. God and Sarah helped her keep balanced. God because of his strength, truth and grace, and Sarah because of her love and innocence, and she kept Cate busy. Whether at the preschool or after school, once David had given his blessing, Cate spent lots of time with Sarah. God used that to renew her friendship with David and to bring about the teaching assignment in Ecuador and the caretaker assignment concerning Sarah. She knew God had worked in and through every part of the last year of her life, but in ways she did not always expect-or understand.

To comfort herself that first night in Ecuador, she reminded herself that as Romans 8:28 says God indeed did work all things for good, for those who love Him. Though His ways were often mysterious, she was convinced they were the best and that God's faithfulness and trustworthiness were unending. Cate knew that whatever lay ahead God could handle it, and she could handle it with His strength.

Eight

She awoke the next morning refreshed and with a renewed sense of purpose. She committed the day, and the whole Ecuador experience, into His hands, confessing that because of Him, she could face whatever lay ahead in Ecuador.

After breakfast, Cate offered to help with the dishes, but Miss Janet and Kim refused to allow her to help. They told her that she had the rest of the week off to adjust, but after that, they would inaugurate her to her share of the household chores. Consequently, she turned her attention to unpacking and to picking out what she would wear to the reception that night.

Not wanting to commit a cultural miscue, Cate asked Miss Janet and Kim for advice as to what to wear. They helped her settle on a simple, but beautiful, peach dress, simple white sandals, would complete the outfit.

Once Cate finished unpacking and choosing her wardrobe for the reception, Kim offered to take her on a tour of the village. Cate readily accepted and off they went for her first real adventure.

The day was bright and sunny. Even though it was the first of August, it was a delicious spring-like day. Cate loved the spring, and delighted in the fact that in this area of Ecuador the temperatures were usually mild. Cate breathed deeply the fresh air and her senses soaked in the sights, sounds, and smells that she encountered as they walked. She was most interested in the people. Cate knew that they were descendants of the Incas and therefore, had an ancient and proud heritage. She loved

their beautifully distinctive clothing. The women wore embroidered blouses, beaded necklaces and skirts. The men wore their hair in long braids, ponchos, white trousers and sandals. They were friendly people; everyone they met seemed to know Kim, and Kim quickly introduced them to Cate. When they found out that she was the new teacher from America, they were anxious to meet and welcome her.

"Kim, do any of these people have children in the mission school?"

"Some do; they will be at the reception tonight. Others are just interested in meeting the new teacher from North America."

"Oh, I see." Cate smiled.

After about twenty minutes of walking, meeting, and greeting, Cate and Kim ran into David and Sarah at the local general store.

Sarah grinned broadly, as she spied Cate coming through the door.

"Cate," Sarah screamed, as she ran toward her.

"Hey, Baby Girl. How are you today?" Cate swept her up in her arms.

"I'm good," Sarah answered.

"I'm glad." Cate hugged her and kissed her cheek.

"Hello, you two," David greeted Kim and Cate, as he came toward them, hugging Kim briefly.

"Hello," they both echoed.

"How's the new girl doing?" he asked, as he embraced Cate warmly.

"The new girl's doing fine." Cate noticed Kim observing the whole event with the same expression on her face that she had the night before when she and Miss Janet had teased her about Matthew. She dreaded the prospect of being teased again, especially about David. Trying to run interference against the prospect of teasing and questions, Cate quickly withdrew from David's embrace. She withdrew so quickly and in such a manner that David noticed, but didn't comment.

"She's doing much better than *I* ever did," Kim remarked.

Cate knew she was not talking about adjusting to Ecuador.

David didn't help by commenting, "Cate's amazing."

"I think so too," Kim agreed, but not to David's meaning.

"You two need to stop." Cate protested. She was not being coy; she really did want them to stop.

"Cate, can you come to my house and play with me?" Sarah asked.

"Not today," David answered, "Cate needs to relax and get acquainted with her new home."

"But, isn't Cate going to live at our house?"

Everyone but Sarah laughed. For David, it was a laugh of amusement at what his little daughter had said. For Kim, it was a mischievous, nosey laugh. For Cate, it was a nervous laugh, a very nervous laugh.

David explained, "Cate lives at Miss Kim and Miss Janet's house."

"But, Daddy, you said that Cate would stay with me."

"Yes, honey, Cate will stay with you when Daddy has to go on trips," David brushed a lock of hair away from Sarah's face, "but, most of the time she will stay at Miss Kim and Miss Janet's house."

"Okay." That was enough explanation for Sarah.

Kim and Cate had been silently looking on as David was explaining to Sarah. Once he finished with Sarah, David said his goodbyes and promised that he and Sarah would see them at the reception that evening.

As David and Sarah left, Kim began her dreaded comments. "Well, well, this promises to be one of the most interesting school years we have ever had."

"Kim, I hope you aren't implying what I think you are," Cate responded.

"I wouldn't know. What do you think I'm implying?"

"Whatever it is, you're wrong!" Cate warned.

"Oh, I don't think so. David has never, *ever* hugged me like that."

"Like what?" Cate protested.

"Like he *meant* it, really meant it."

"We've been friends for years. That's all it was," Cate confessed.

"We've been friends for years too, but he's never hugged me like that."

Knowing there was nothing she could say to change Kim's mind, Cate shook her head and sighed deeply. "Is it okay if we go back to the house now? I'm a little tired."

Kim agreed, but commented as they left the store, "Yes sir, it's going to be a very interesting school year."

Cate tried to be congenial on the way home, but Kim wanted to continue her implications about Cate and David and her attempts to probe into their relationship.

"So you're Sarah's caregiver when David is away?"

"That's right," Cate said.

"If I may ask, why did he choose you?"

"Maybe, he chose me because I was coming to Ecuador to teach and because Sarah had been my student at the preschool."

"Forgive, me Cate, but there seems to be more to this whole thing than that," Kim continued to probe.

"David and I are friends." Cate stopped in the street and turned to face Kim. "We have been for a long time. I trust him and he trusts me. I helped with Sarah after Jenny died. When the teaching position became available he knew I felt God was leading me into teaching in a mission school and he recommended me to Matthew. I prayed about it and felt that God was leading me here. David had been praying about what to do about Sarah and when God confirmed that he wanted me in Ecuador. He felt that was God's confirmation that he wanted me to be Sarah's caregiver." Cate paused, "Is that what you wanted to hear?"

"That's part of what I wanted to hear, and that's probably all that you're going to tell me, but I can't help but feel there's more."

Nine

Lunch and conversation were pleasant, and Kim made no mention of David. Miss Janet was busy telling Cate what to expect at the reception. She pointed out that Cate, as guest of honor and the particular point of interest to the parents and students, did not need to be nervous or overly concerned about first impressions. Miss Janet assured her that the parents and the students were very anxious to make her feel welcomed to their town and their school. Matthew had been excited about the things that David had told him that he had been broadcasting her praises long before he met her face to face.

"Miss Janet, that makes me even more nervous, how in the world can I live up to their expectations?" Cate admitted.

"Just be yourself, my dear. From what I've seen since you've been here, that will be quite enough."

I don't know about that," Cate protested.

"I do, Cate. Trust me; you'll make a great first impression. Everyone will love you," Kim reassured.

"I hope you're right."

"Why don't you rest after lunch?" Miss Janet suggested. "I'm sure you have a little jet lag. You have plenty of time to take a nap, before getting ready for the reception."

"Please, let me help you clear the table and clean up first."

"Nonsense, I told you that you are a guest for the first week. Trust me; your turn for chores will come. Rest now; you'll want to be at your very best this evening."

Cate reluctantly, but appreciatively, agreed and excused herself to go to her room and rest. As she entered her room and gazed out the window, she was grateful for the view, the mountains in the distance. Their beauty overwhelmed her and provoked her memory of Psalm 121: 1-2. "I will lift up my eyes unto the hills. From whence cometh my help? My help cometh from the Lord, who made the heavens and the earth." She gave thanks to the Lord, for she knew that He had given her a visible reminder of that truth. She didn't know that this visible reminder of God's presence and strength would become vitally important to her.

As she tried to rest, she couldn't help but evaluate her first few hours in Ecuador. She felt joy at the prospect of coming, and that joy had continued as she arrived. She was sure that she was being obedient to what God had called her to do. However, she failed to understand why almost immediately, the *David issue* had confronted her again. Had she not given all of that to the Lord? Why would He allow it to pop back up? She prayed that He would take control of the situation and resolve it in accordance with His will and purpose. She also prayed that He would give her grace, strength and wisdom to deal with the issue, and all that lay ahead; that night, and in the future. She drifted off to sleep with the assurance that God's grace would be sufficient.

She awoke to a gentle tap on her door and Kim's voice telling her that she needed to get up and begin to get ready for the reception. She stretched and looked at the clock. She couldn't believe that she'd slept for almost two hours. *Evidently, I'm suffering from jet lag more than I realized.* As she began to get dressed, she realized that she felt much better; she found herself humming and singing.

Matthew picked Cate, Miss Janet and Kim up and drove them to the reception. He confessed that he wanted to walk into the reception with Cate on his arm. "After all," he reminded his passengers, "she was my find."

"Nonsense," Kim retorted, "she was David's find."

"I'm the one who hired her. David simply recommended her. Therefore, I deserve the credit, and I aim to have it."

"Yes, boss; anything you say, boss," Kim joked.

"I am the boss, and don't you forget it." Matthew smiled as he winked at Kim.

"Never, Sir, never," Kim replied. Everyone laughed, even though Cate's laugh was forced.

There was the whole David issue again and she was certain that a Matthew issue was looming in her future. She said a quick prayer under her breath. "Dear Father, you know that all I want to do is obey you and be a good missionary teacher. Please, please, help me."

Once they arrived at the school, Matthew did indeed make a grand entrance with Cate on his arm. Cate was embarrassed, but smiled broadly, as everyone began his or her introductions and hellos. They were extremely gracious and nice to Cate, yet try as she might she knew she'd never remember all of their names. She met her fellow faculty members, not only of the elementary grades, but also, of the secondary grades. Those in the community who helped the school financially, those who volunteered, and those who served on the local advisory board were also there to greet her. She met many of the parents whose children attended the school, and met the parents of the children who would be her students. As much as Cate enjoyed meeting everyone, it was the children, many of whom would be her students, that she enjoyed the most.

Some of the children were children of missionaries, or of Americans living in Ecuador. Those children boarded in quarters owned and operated by the mission school. Others were children of locals, who were well-to-do, and others who were not so well off. Cate was pleased to see how well mannered the children seemed to be and all were anxious to meet the new teacher. Each one, flanked by his or her parents, introduced himself or herself to Miss Cate. The parents seemed proud of their children, and extremely anxious for them to learn. The parents' excitement about the possibilities and expectations for their children was contagious. Cate was looking forward to getting into the classroom to work.

Once the introductions were over; the children sang a song of welcome for Miss Cate. She enjoyed the sincere emotions exhibited by the children and their parents. The time for refreshments came, and again Cate became the center of attention. More than once, she heard the word

"*bonita*" connected with her name. She could not help but be embarrassed. It always embarrassed her when someone called her beautiful because she did not see herself that way. She was more concerned about being beautiful on the inside, and constantly prayed that God would make her beautiful from the inside out.

Finally, the time for the reception to end neared, and people began to say their goodbyes and leave. Cate saw David and Matthew standing to the right of the room. David was holding Sarah, who had fallen asleep. As she looked in their direction, she realized that they seemed to be talking about her. When she walked over, she confirmed her suspicions, *they are talking about me.*

"There she is, the belle of the ball. The beautiful new teacher, who has won everyone's heart," Matthew said.

"Belle of the ball, maybe. Beautiful… I'm not so sure. Having won everyone's heart… I doubt it." Cate was embarrassed.

"Belle of the ball, for sure. Beautiful…I can prove it. Isn't she beautiful, David, my friend?" Matthew responded.

"Yes, she is beautiful. She's very beautiful." David smiled as his eyes sought Cate's.

Cate, disarmed by the tone in which he had answered, turned her gaze slowly toward David. Hearing him say that she was beautiful caused her to look into his dark brown eyes to seek to discover any indication as to why he'd answered as he had. As she caught a glimpse of David's face, she wasn't sure what she saw. She only knew that she had to try to understand what she had heard. As her eyes met David's, the spell of the moment was broken as Matthew continued, "See, Cate, it's unanimous. You *are* beautiful. You might as well admit it."

"I dare say that a lady admitting she is beautiful would make her less so." Cate hoped that she had covered up her reaction to David's words.

"She's got you there, Matt," David said. They all laughed.

"Cate, I'd be glad to show you your classroom and give you a tour of the school, or if you'd rather, we could wait until tomorrow," Matthew said.

"Well, I'd hate to make Miss Janet and Kim wait while we did that."

Cate looked at David as he replied, "Go ahead if you'd like. I'll be glad to escort the ladies home. Matt's dying to show you around."

She looked at Matthew, "Okay I'll have the ten cent tour please. David, I guess I'll see Sarah and you tomorrow at church."

"Yes, you will. You two have fun," David replied.

Matthew offered Cate his arm; she smiled and said another goodbye to David. As Matthew ushered her through the door, Cate turned her head to catch one last glimpse of David as he walked toward Miss Janet and Kim.

Matthew's tour of the school was very informative. He talked about the school and its mission as a proud parent would talk about his child. Cate realized how much he loved what he did. She also found out that his father had established the mission agency and school thirty years earlier and had served as its director/headmaster. He retired from the position because of illness, and he and his wife returned to the U.S. for his medical treatment. Since the time of his father's retirement, Matthew had been the director/headmaster.

Cate asked about his upbringing and found out that he spent most of his life in Ecuador. He had earned his bachelor's degree at the University of North Carolina and his Masters at Dallas Theological Seminary. After seminary, he returned to Ecuador to help his father at the mission school.

"Enough about me," Matthew said, "I want to hear about you."

"There's not much to tell."

"*That*, I do not believe," Matthew answered.

"Well, there's not much that you don't already know."

"Tell me about your family," Matthew probed.

"My family lives in Kansas. I have two older brothers, who are both married and have two children each. My father is a pastor. He's been the pastor of Bethsaida Baptist Church in Kansas City, Kansas for the past twenty-seven years."

"So you've basically lived in Kansas all of your life," Matthew added.

"Yeah, basically,"

"May I ask a very personal question?" Matthew asked.

Cate narrowed her eyes, "Sure, I guess."

"How come such a beautiful girl like you isn't married?"

"I was married. You know that," Cate answered, honestly.

"I know you were married. David told me that before I hired you. He also told me how your marriage ended."

"David told you about that?" Cate felt a lump in her throat.

"Yes, he did. David and I have been friends for years and I specifically asked."

"Of course, you did," Cate replied, "you'd want to know what kind of person you were hiring."

"That's right and I found out."

"You found out that you were hiring one with a lot of baggage," Cate looked away, unable to meet his eyes.

"We *all* have baggage, Cate."

"I guess, so, but not baggage that disqualifies."

"Disqualifies you from what?" Matthew asked.

"Oh, nothing; I was just thinking out loud."

"You're not the only person ever to get divorced. You're not even the only pastor's daughter ever to be divorced," Matthew pointed out.

"All of that's true, but what I did, I did when I was rebelling against God, and I didn't even know it. Before I married Justin, there were questions I should have asked and things I should have recognized, but I was blind to my motives for marrying him and blind to myself. Consequently, I married a man that I should never have married. I hurt a lot of people, people I love, that should never have been hurt."

"But, you weren't the one who left the marriage," Matthew reminded her.

"No, I wasn't, but that doesn't matter. Lots of people got hurt."

"It *does* matter, if you were faithful and your husband wasn't. You were the offended one. You had biblical grounds for divorce."

"That may be true, but I think my husband felt like he had been sold a bill of goods," Cate's shoulders fell.

"What do you mean?"

"I mean that I wasn't living as a Christian ought to live at that time, and later I found out that Justin wasn't a Christian at all. When I began to try to live as a Christian should, that caused big problems in my marriage. Therefore, I have to bear some responsibility for what happened."

"But, your husband was the one who left the marriage wasn't he?"

"David told you a lot, huh?" Cate asked.

"Yes, but only because I asked. I hope you don't mind. I promise I wasn' trying to pry. I just wanted to know about you."

"No, I don't mind. It's not like I'm trying to hide anything," Cate replied. "I'm just amazed that you hired a divorcee to teach in your mission school. Some boards would have never considered a divorced person."

"I hired you for two major reasons. You had impeccable recommendations from your previous employers and David vouched for you. David's recommendation goes a very long way with me and our board. He thinks a lot of you, you know." As Matthew explained, he saw Cate blush.

"Yeah, David's a great guy."

"Yeah, he is a great guy, and I hope when you get to know me better that you will think that I'm a great guy too."

"I already think you're pretty great. After all, you've given me a chance to follow God's calling and teach in a mission school," Cate confessed, with a big smile.

"Just wait. Give me a chance and you'll have many more reasons to think I'm a great guy." Matthew tried to sound as if he was joking, but decided to be serious, "Cate, I think you're special, and based on everything I know about you now, I really would like for us to get to know each other better. I think you and I might be good for each other."

"Matthew, I really just want to focus on getting use to things here and doing a good job. Really, for now…"

"I understand and trust me, I'm all for that, but that doesn't necessarily exclude us getting to know each other. Does it?"

"No, I guess not," Cate answered, reluctantly agreeing. "But, I want you to know up front that I'm not looking for romance. Friendship is fine. Romance is not."

"Friendship is good, but why not allow for the possibility of romance?"

"Too many complications," Cate answered, shaking her head 'no'.

"Complications can be dealt with."

"Some can, some can't, and I don't even want to think about it all," Cate answered. "Please, for now…"

Matthew took her hand, and looked into her eyes. "Okay, friendship," and then kissing her hand, he added, "for now."

Cate breathed a big sigh and shook her head again.

"When you get to know me better, you'll find that I am an eternal optimist," he responded with a broad grin. Looking at his watch, he continued, "I suspect that if I don't want Miss Janet to fuss at me for keeping you out so late, I had better get you home."

As they drove home, they continued to make small talk. Matthew was very easy to talk to about anything. Cate found herself wondering why God had brought Matthew into her life. He was very nice and *very handsome*: blonde hair, blue eyes, and a tanned face with rugged features that greatly enhanced his winning smile. He was tall and well built. His was the kind of handsome man that women find very attractive, and more importantly, he was a godly, plainspoken man. He was open, honest, sincere, and up-beat. She could tell that he really *was* an eternal optimist. She also could tell they were going to be good friends.

The possibility of romance on the mission field was not something that she had consciously considered. Most mission agencies frowned on dating while on the mission field. That was fine with her. She knew there would be no romance for David and her, but she'd never considered the possibility that God would allow someone else to cross her path. Friendship with Matthew would be fine, but she did *not* want anything more.

Ten

Finally it was the day for Cate to assume her duties at the mission school. She greeted her students; they came with bright, shiny faces, eager for the adventure of learning. One thing she liked about kindergarteners and the early grades was that learning mesmerized the students. Their minds were sponges eager to soak up knowledge, and they were anxious to please their parents and teacher.

Her life finally seemed to make sense. The students were a constant source of joy and surprise, and teaching them was what God had created her to do. Teaching had always been a source of delight, but now it was a source of meaning and fulfillment. God was blessing her abundantly.

Over the several weeks since her coming to Ecuador, she and Matthew had become good friends and, as he had hoped, they were more. Cate had not wanted, nor had she expected to feel anything other than friendship for Matthew. However, proximity conspired against her.

She loved talking with Matthew. He challenged her both professionally and spiritually, encouraging her in everything she did. He was her biggest cheerleader and she found herself responding to his sincere feelings. However, along with closeness to Matthew came a distance between David and her. They were still very good friends, but she realized that David was intentionally withdrawing from her. She knew that he and Matthew talked often, and was sure that Matthew had confided to David how he felt about her. Knowing David, Cate understood why he was

withdrawing. She was still Sarah's caregiver and regularly stayed at David's home with Sarah while he was away on mission business. David was always cordial when he came home, and was genuinely glad to see her, but there was an intentional distance. She and David never talked about personal matters anymore, not important ones anyway. That part of him David had withdrawn, and Cate reciprocated.

That particular part of her life, she didn't like, but she understood that kind of closeness was reserved for people who had a future together. She was sure that she and David had no future together. After she began seeing Matthew, Kim made a play for David and he responded. Consequently, two months after her arrival, David and Kim were 'a couple' and Matthew and Cate were 'a couple'. In fact, Cate helped the David and Kim relationship along.

Kim had approached Cate. "Do you think enough time has passed since Jenny's death for David to be interested in someone else?"

"I guess," Cate's answer was cautious.

"I know that the IMB policies prohibit dating on the mission field, but that's not what I'm interested in. I'm interested in getting to know David better, first as friends and then, well, maybe more. Do you think I would have a chance with him?"

"As good a chance as anyone else,"

"Do you really think so?"

"Kim, you're a great girl. David would have to be crazy not to see that."

"I don't know. He was crazy to have passed you up."

"David and I... We're just friends."

"I didn't believe that until you and Matthew began to see each other, and when I saw how happy you seem to be, I decided to try for a little of that happiness myself."

"You deserve to be happy. Go for it. David is a great guy."

"Thanks," Kim considered the possibilities.

Once they were a couple, Kim seemed to be happy, and so did David. Actually, David seemed to be happier than he had been for a long time, causing a deep sadness to creep into Cate's heart. She prayed that the Lord would take it away and thought it was gone until she'd see David and Kim together. She was sure at times the sadness and jealousy surfaced enough to be seen on her face or in her eyes. But, if Matthew ever noticed, he never mentioned it. Still, she was constantly afraid that he, or someone else, would notice.

Many nights she looked out her window to the mountains in the distance and prayed, "Lord, please help me with this. I don't want to be sad or jealous. David deserves to be happy, even if it's not with me. Maybe, it's Your will that Matthew and I have a future together, and David and Kim. Oh, Father please, help me to yield to you. I want to honor you." Afterwards, she would try to sleep. Sometimes the sleep came quickly; often it didn't.

During this time, Matthew became even more attentive. Cate was bewildered and frightened and wondered if this was the answer to her prayers. She knew she still loved David, but she might have feelings for Matthew too, and realized that it was possible to love two men at the same time. Cate knew that the most important thing she could do was seek God's will. She tried to concentrate on really *being with* Matthew when she was with him. She refused to think about David. She gave Matthew her constant, undivided attention, and her solution seemed to work.

Things seemed to be progressing at lightning speed with David and Kim. Kim hinted that wedding bells might be ringing, and she had asked David to allow her to occasionally stay with Sarah while he was away. When David approached Cate with the idea she reluctantly agreed.

Cate had difficulty being edged out with both Sarah and David. She struggled with losing David and Sarah, *but that's crazy because they're not mine to lose.* Once again, she found herself trying to submit the whole thing to God.

One day while Cate was staying with Sarah, Sarah began to ask questions.

"Cate, is Miss Kim going to be my new mother?"

Her question stabbed at Cate's heart, and she struggled to come up with the right answer, in the right tone. "I don't know, Baby Girl. That's a question you need to ask your daddy."

"I did," Sarah said.

Cate was surprised, "You did?"

"Uh-huh,"

"And what did he say?" Cate was more eager to hear the answer than she should have been.

"He said he didn't know."

Cate was pleased with what she heard. She smiled, "Well, there you go."

"Cate, I want *you* to be my new mother." Sarah spoke with the innocent candor and determination of a child.

Cate found herself searching for just the right thing to say, *I wish I could be her mother.* "Sarah, it's up to your daddy to choose your new mother, and he'll make the right choice."

"But, I love *you*, I want you,"

"I love you too." Cate quickly gathered Sarah in her arms and hugged her.

Sarah's five-year-old mind came up with the answer to their dilemma. "Tell daddy that I love you and you love me and that if he'll choose you, you'll be my new mother."

"I can't do that, Sarah. Your daddy has to make his own choice." Cate tenderly corrected her suggestion.

"Well, I'm gonna tell daddy to choose you."

Cate laughed and hugged her again, remembering the verse, "Out of the mouth of babes". Even though she was still confused about God's will concerning Matthew and her, she admitted to herself that she wished David would choose her.

When she awoke the next morning, Cate checked on Sarah, who was sleeping soundly. She decided to make coffee and have her quiet time. She had settled into her Bible reading and prayer, when she heard the door open, and David entered. He and his bags were wet from the rain that was falling.

"Hi. We didn't expect you home today," Cate said, cheerfully.

"I didn't expect to be home today." David set down his bags and reached for a towel to wipe his face and his hair.

"I've made some coffee. Would you like some?"

"Yes, but I'll get it. Looks like I've interrupted your quiet time."

"You're tired from your drive. Please, sit, I'll get your coffee."

"Thank you, that's very thoughtful. I am a little tired."

David sat in his favorite chair and Cate poured him a cup of coffee. "How long has it been raining?"

"For about four hours," David held the cup in both hands, welcoming the warmth, "it's rained on me all the way home."

"So, it's probably an all day thing."

"Probably," David sipped his coffee, "how's Sarah?"

"She's fine. I can't believe that she's still sleeping, but we did stay up a little later than usual last night. We were reading."

"She does enjoy reading. Thanks for reading to her."

"I am glad she enjoys it so much. I hope it continues."

"I do too."

The entrance of the young reader interrupted their conversation.

"Daddy!" Sarah yelled, as she rubbed sleep from her eyes. He sat down his cup of coffee as she ran and jumped into his lap.

"Hey, Lady Bug," David hugged her.

"Are you home to stay?"

"Yes, for now. Daddy won't have to leave again for another week or two."

"Yea!" Sarah said, as she looked at Cate. "I'm hungry. Can we have breakfast now?"

"Sure, we can." Cate rose to make breakfast.

"How 'bout," David tickled Sarah, "I fix your breakfast while Cate finishes her quiet time."

"Nonsense," Cate said. "I was through with my quiet time. You're tired from your trip. You just rest and I'll fix breakfast."

"Okay, it's a deal." David said, as he yawned and stretched.

Realizing how very tired he was, Cate suggested, "Sarah, why don't you help me?

"We'll make a special breakfast to celebrate Daddy coming home," Sarah agreed and they departed to the kitchen.

David fell asleep while breakfast was being prepared. Cate put a plate back for him for later, and she and Sarah ate quietly.

Once they finished breakfast, she and Sarah retired to Sarah's room to read her favorite story.

Finally, David awoke; he'd slept for almost three hours. He heard Cate and Sarah as they were reading and went to investigate. "Why didn't you wake me when you finished cooking breakfast?"

"I knew you were tired and figured the rest would do you good."

"Thanks. I do feel better."

"We've been having a good time daddy."

"You have," David said, as he swept her up in his arms.

"Uh-huh, we've been reading *Cinderella*."

"Your favorite book."

"It's my very, very favorite book. Will you read it to me again?"

"May I have some breakfast first?"

"Yes," Sarah said. "We left you some breakfast in the kitchen."

"Did you now? I'll bet you're ready for lunch."

"I *am* hungry," Sarah giggled.

"Come on," Cate said. "Daddy can have breakfast while I make lunch."

As David was eating breakfast and Cate was making lunch, Sarah decided to strike up a conversation. "Daddy, can I ask you something?"

"Sure, Lady Bug,"

"Daddy, can Cate be my new mother? She said it was your choice."

David stopped chewing, swallowed hard and searched for an answer.

Cate paused in the middle of stirring macaroni, held her breath, and remained turned away from David. When Cate heard him take a big breath and release a sigh, Cate turned toward him.

"Sarah, Cate and Daddy are friends, good friends."

"I know Daddy, but I love Cate, and Cate loves me. Maybe, she would love you too."

"I know you love Cate, and Cate loves you, and Cate loves Daddy as a friend. She also loves Mr. Matthew, so Daddy cannot ask her to be your new mother." With the last words he looked directly at Cate.

Cate wasn't sure what she saw in his eyes, and decided to add some words of her own.

"And, your daddy loves Miss Kim." As she said those words, David's expression changed, and he looked away. Cate wasn't sure what she had seen in his expression.

"Do you, Daddy? Do you love Miss Kim?"

Without raising his head, David answered. "I don't know, Lady Bug, maybe so." David excused himself and left the table, walking to the living room and then through the side door.

"Where's Daddy going?"

"I don't know," Cate patted Sarah's shoulder.

Cate wondered what to do and what to say when David returned. His words didn't confuse her, but his actions had. He had purposefully not looked at her when he spoke about Matthew and her, or about Kim.

Sarah was confused by her daddy leaving and continued to question Cate about where he was. Cate suggested that he had forgotten some business that he needed to take care of and would return soon. An hour later, Sarah fell asleep, as Cate sang softly while rocking her. Cate rose from the rocking chair and carried Sarah to her bed.

Cate waited for David. She found herself praying that God would give her wisdom in what to say when he returned. She had no idea as to why he had reacted as he had and she had no idea what to say. She tried hard to give her feelings for David to the Lord and submitted herself repeatedly to His will in the matter. Regardless, she knew she still loved David in a way that she would never love another man. She wondered if it was fair to continue her relationship with Matthew. She knew that his feelings for her were sincere, deep, and real. Matthew's loving her like that was an honor. She also knew that she had sincere and real feelings for him, but they were nothing like the love she had for David.

"Oh, Lord, why don't you take my feelings for David away? That would make my life so much simpler," she prayed fervently. "Trust Me," were the Lord's words, she heard deep in her heart. She turned in her Bible to Psalm 37:7 and read, "Rest in the Lord and wait patiently for him." Those words had become words that sustained her when things were difficult and perplexing-an often occurrence in her life. She devoured those words and the truth they contained; they were food for a hungry, hurting, fearful soul, and a satisfying ointment for this moment. Words of gratitude welled up deep within her, "Thank you, Lord."

The opening of the side door as David entered interrupted her thanksgiving. He noticed the Bible in her hands.

"Where's Sarah?"

"She's down for her nap."

"Good, I'd like to talk to you without her hearing." He shifted on his feet, "I'm sorry she put you on the spot this morning."

"She's five years old. Five year olds do that."

"I know, but it was embarrassing nonetheless."

"I wasn't embarrassed," Cate admitted, "but I noticed you were, or at least uncomfortable."

"Yes, I guess, I was. Sarah's been asking a lot of questions about Kim and me, and I gathered from what she asked this morning that she had been talking to you about the same thing."

"Yes, she has," Cate said. "She asked me if Kim was going to be her new mother. I told her that was up to you."

"She asked you to be her mother, didn't she?" David's tone and expression made Cate uneasy.

"She did, and I'm sorry about the spot that puts you in."

"She asked me that before. I explained to her about your relationship with Matthew and my relationship with Kim."

"I tried to also," Cate said.

"What did you tell her?" David seemed very interested to hear her answer.

"I told her that you were seeing Miss Kim and I was seeing Mr. Matthew and that you and I were just very good friends."

"That's what I've told her both times, but I guess she just wants what she wants."

"That's just being five years old," Cate said.

"Yes, it is, but I know she loves you very much and is deeply attached to you. I'm not sure any other woman could fit into her life the way you have."

"Sure, someone else could." *But I want it to be me.* "She's five years old. She's got lots of room in her heart."

"Yes, she does have lots of room in her heart, but I see in her a love for you like she had for Jenny. Sometimes I'm afraid she's transferred her love for Jenny to you."

"David, I don't think that's true. Sarah and I talk about Jenny all the time. She remembers her and loves her still."

"We talk about her too, and I show her Jenny's picture often, but Cate, she talks a lot about you too. In Sarah's heart, you've taken that special *mother* place and I don't know what to do about it."

"You talk like Sarah's love for me is a problem." Cate's tone revealed hurt.

"One I failed to foresee when I asked you to be her caregiver."

"I don't understand exactly what the problem is," Cate's voice betrayed her hurt. Suddenly she understood, "David, are you concerned about Sarah's attachment to me, because you're going to ask Kim to marry you?"

"No, that's not it."

"Well, what is it then?"

"I'm sorry, but I can't explain."

"You've got to explain. I'm totally lost here. Do you want me to stop being Sarah's caregiver altogether?"

"No, not really," David mumbled.

"Not really? That means that on some level you do. You have to help me here. I just don't understand what's going on." Cate ran her hands through her hair, "If you're not going to ask Kim to marry you, why should my relationship with Sarah change?"

"Because Matthew's going to ask you to marry him," David answered reluctantly.

"What!" Cate locked eyes on David, "How do you know that?"

"He told me before I left on my trip."

"Well, he hasn't mentioned it to me."

"He's trying to get up the nerve. Plus he's waiting for just the right time."

"Wow! I can't believe it; Matthew and I've only known each other for a couple of months."

"He knows a good thing when he sees it."

David's tone surprised Cate. Searching for what it meant, she looked directly into his eyes. "Thank you."

As her eyes met his, David swallowed hard, cleared his throat and looked away. "Yep."

"I knew you two talked about things, and I even figured he confided in you about us, but I never had any idea that he would ask *you* about marrying *me*."

"He knows that we've been friends for a long time. He figured talking with me about you would be one way to get to know you better."

"Does he know—everything?"

"Everything."

"Does he know that we were engaged?"

"No, he doesn't know that," David answered.

"But, you told him all about Justin."

"Yes, I told him about that before he hired you, but I didn't tell him about you and me. I didn't see why he needed to know about that," David said.

"How did you explain our friendship?"

"I told him that we met in college, that I was youth minister at your father's church and that we reconnected after your divorce and Jenny's death."

"He never asked you if we'd been romantically involved."

"Not–uh–directly," David answered.

"Indirectly?"

David shrugged, "Yes, indirectly."

"How?"

"He asked me how I couldn't be interested in a girl like you."

"What did you say?" *I'm not sure I really want to know.*

David breathed a sigh before he answered. "I told him that my appointment as a missionary and your divorce were mutually exclusive."

Cate was shocked and hurt to hear him say those words. She lowered her head so he didn't see the tears welling up in her eyes.

"Cate, I'm sorry. I didn't mean to hurt you," he rose from his chair, sat down beside her on the couch and put his arm around her. His actions only made his words hurt worse. As her tears began to drop on the pages of her Bible, he continued, "Cate, you're a wonderful, Christian woman, and I told Matthew so. He was thrilled to know the way was clear for him to pursue a relationship with you. When he told me the other day that he was going to ask you to marry him, I told him that he'd be a lucky man if you agreed to marry him-and I meant it."

Cate struggled to stop crying and to summon the courage to speak. David's arm of compassion around her didn't make it easy. Finally, she gained her composure and found the strength to say, "Thank you."

"Cate, you know I would never intentionally do anything to hurt you. I didn't mean to…"

"It's okay. I know my divorce disqualifies me as far as the IMB goes, but," she sighed and bit her lip as she continued, "but, I had never heard you say it. I'm sorry I'm so touchy about it. You don't have any reason to apologize; after all it's the truth."

"Cate, don't."

"Don't what?" Her hands gripped her legs so hard her knuckles turned white, "Don't say what we both know? My divorce disqualifies me in many important ways."

"Cate, the divorce wasn't your fault."

"Wasn't it?" Cate asked, sobs choking her throat.

"He left you for another woman."

"That's true, but we both know that I never should've married him."

"You thought you loved him and that he loved you." David sought to reassure her.

"Yes, I did, but I never bothered to really get to know him." Cate decided to be more honest with him than she ever had been. "David, I married Justin because I was running away from God, and you."

"What!" David shrank back.

"I'm sorry." Cate said, in response to the shock on his face. "Remember, I told you that I didn't want to be a preacher's wife; that's why I married Justin. I talked myself into believing that it was God's will, but later I found out that Justin wasn't even a Christian. I tried to make a go of the marriage. I had made a commitment to Justin before God, my family, and my friends. But, when I got things straightened out with God, Justin didn't want any part of my Christianity or me. So, you see the failure of the marriage was my fault, as much as Justin's.

"Cate."

The way David said her name made her stop, and look directly at him. She saw compassion in his eyes. It was more than she could take; once again, the tears came, and no matter how hard she tried, she could not hold them back. She choked out words through her sobs.

"Don't you see the irony in what's happened?"

"Irony?"

"Sure, I married Justin because I was rebelling against the idea of marrying a preacher-and now, I never can."

"Cate," David uttered, again with compassion in his voice while taking her in his arms and holding her. Little did he know he only increased the irony and the sobs, because she had been talking about being unable to marry *this* preacher.

Hearing Cate's sobs, Sarah called from her room, "Daddy, Cate, what's wrong?"

Brought back to reality by Sarah's question, David stopped hugging Cate, and she tried to stop crying.

"Everything's all right," David reassured her, as he straightened in his seat and Cate dried her eyes.

"Why is Cate crying?" Sarah's eyes were wide, her voice concerned.

"I'm all right. I'm not crying now," Cate wiped her cheeks and brushed a lock of hair from her face.

"But, why were you crying?"

"Cate was just a little sad," David answered.

"Why were you sad Cate?"

"I, I was thinking about some sad things."

"Sometimes people cry when they do that," David explained.

"Like you do sometimes when you remember mommy," Sarah said.

Now Cate looked at David with compassion, and he looked away, feeling embarrassed at what his daughter had said.

"Yes, like Daddy does sometimes when he remembers your mommy," Cate answered for him.

"Oh," Sarah said, "Cate, I'm sorry you were sad."

"It's okay, Baby Girl." She swept Sarah up in her arms and hugged her, "Did you have a good nap?"

"Uh huh, but I'm thirsty. May I have some juice?"

"Sure, you can. I'll get it," David went to the kitchen to get Sarah's juice.

Sarah, still concerned about Cate, offered, "I'll get *Cinderella* and we can read it together. That always makes me happy. Maybe it'll make you happy too."

"That's a great idea."

Sarah climbed down from Cate's lap and ran to get the book. She came back with a broad smile and the book as David returned with Sarah's juice.

"Daddy, Cate and I are going to read. That'll cheer her up."

"That's a fine idea. You two read, and I'll cook dinner."

"I'd be glad to make dinner," Cate said.

"Nope, you just relax, and I'll fix us a gourmet meal of beans and franks."

"Beans and franks," Cate laughed.

"Beans and franks," David wagged his finger, "are a delectable delight."

"Beans and franks are what you fix when you don't know how to fix anything else."

"Oh, I know how to fix something else."

"Really, what else?" Cate demanded.

"Macaroni and cheese, but I'm afraid you had that for lunch."

"Wow, you have an amazing culinary repertoire," Cate grinned.

"Yeah, I know. That's why Mrs. Garcia cooks for us, when you aren't here."

"Smart man," Cate laughed again.

"I try."

"Well, may I offer an alternative to beans and franks? Why don't Sarah and I go to the kitchen, and while she reads, I'll cook something?"

"Sounds like a plan, but only if you let me help," David said.

Cate narrowed her eyes, "I don't think so."

"I can help, if someone tells me what to do."

"We'll see," Cate and Sarah rose and headed toward the kitchen, followed by David.

Once in the kitchen, Cate gathered the ingredients for dinner, while Sarah began to read *Cinderella* aloud. David took inventory of the proposed menu and gathered the necessary cooking utensils. Cate told him what to do and he did it, as she supervised Sarah's reading, and took care of her part of the preparation. She stopped for a moment to watch David with the pots and pans and Sarah reading, *this feels right, this is what I want.*

Finally, the dinner was finished, and they sat down to enjoy the fruits of their labor. David said grace, and they began to eat; as they began, there was a knock at the front door. When David answered the door, Cate heard Matthew's voice, but couldn't understand what he was saying. She did hear David's answer.

"Yes, she's still here. We're having dinner. Would you like to join us?"

Cate started into the living room and met David and Matthew coming into the kitchen. Matthew reached out to greet her with a hug and a kiss and David continued to the kitchen where he took another table setting from the cabinet and placed it on the table.

"Mr. Matthew!" Sarah said, with genuine affection.

"Hello, Sarah; how are you?"

"I'm very well," Sarah answered, as David, Cate and Matthew smiled at her grown up answer.

"Are you now?"

"Uh-huh,"

"Uh-huh, What are you suppose to say?" David corrected her, along with his parental stare.

"Yes, sir," Sarah said.

"Well, it sure looks like you're eating well." Matthew smiled as he noticed what Cate had cooked.

"Yes, sir," Sarah looked toward her father for his acknowledgement of her manners this time, and continued, "Cate is a very good cook."

Matthew smiled at Cate, "I agree with you wholeheartedly."

"I second that," David chimed in.

Cate blushed as she accepted their generous compliments.

"But, Mr. Matthew, you haven't eaten anything," Sarah said.

"Right you are," Matthew agreed, "but we can remedy that if your daddy will pass the mash potatoes and gravy."

"My oversight, here you go. Have some meatloaf too."

"My favorite," Matthew said, with a grin.

"Mine too," David said, as he looked toward Cate, "And, it's very good."

"Thank you," Cate said, as she smiled. "Glad you like it."

"I like it too," Sarah joined in.

"Me too," Matthew said, as he swallowed his first big bite.

Cate shook her head, "It doesn't take much to please you all."

Everyone smiled and continued to eat their 'sumptuous' meal. Conversation was minimal as both men ate as if they had not had a good home-cooked meal in a while. However, Cate knew that was not true. Cate cooked for Matthew regularly on weekends and Mrs. Garcia cooked for David every day.

After dinner, they cleared the table, and Cate suggested the men retire to the living room, while she and Sarah took care of the dishes. Even though she was quite small, Sarah was a good helper and it was a time of sharing and joy for both of them. After they put away the final dish, she and Sarah went to the living room, where they found the men discussing David's mission work. Cate was fascinated to hear the details of what David had been doing on his latest trip. She was impressed at how much Matthew understood and how knowledgeable he was about David's work.

She had always known that David and Matthew were alike, but until now, she hadn't realized how much. Before her sat two men, two godly, Christian men, who loved God and had a heart for sharing the gospel. Both men were committed to missions, one as a church planter, and one as the headmaster of a mission school. Both men loved people-*and I love both men.* She admitted it. She loved them both. Though she loved one more deeply than she would ever love the other one, the one less loved was about to ask her to marry him. *The one I deeply love-he'll never ask me.*

As Mr. Matthew and her daddy talked, Sarah sat in Cate's lap, holding her dolly and playing with Cate's long hair. She had once told Cate how much she loved playing with her hair. "Cate, you have hair like my mommy's, except mommy's was light and yours is dark." Cate didn't mind Sarah's twirling her hair through her fingers; she knew it was a source of comfort and security for the little girl.

Finally, David and Matthew were finished with their conversation about missions and included them in their new topic of conversation.

"How would you ladies like to watch a movie?"

"A movie?" Sarah echoed.

"A movie," David repeated.

"What movie Daddy?"

"We'll let Cate decide."

"No, you two guys decide."

"Lady's choice, right, Matt?"

"Right, as long as she chooses a guy movie," Matthew agreed.

"A guy movie, huh," Cate said. "Sarah, what guy movie should I chose?"

"*Chicken Little*," Sarah answered. Cate, Matthew and David laughed. Sarah added, "*Chicken Little* is a guy, so it's a guy movie."

"That's exactly right, Baby Girl," Cate said. Outvoted, Matthew and David watched *Chicken Little*.

Toward the end of the movie, Sarah yawned and rubbed her eyes as she struggled to make it to the end of the movie without falling asleep. David asked if she was ready for bed and she said "no". When the movie ended, he asked again. This time she answered "yes" to the question about bed, but "no" to David's offer to tuck her in.

"I want Cate to tuck me in Daddy." Sarah looked at Cate, pleadingly with her big brown eyes.

"Sure, I'll tuck you in," Cate swept her up with a hug and carried her to her bedroom.

As Cate tucked her in, Sarah hugged her tightly and said, "I love you Cate."

"I love you too, Baby Girl. Sweet dreams, I'll see you tomorrow." Cate walked to the door, blew Sarah a kiss and turned out the light. As Cate walked back into the living room, David and Matthew, who had been talking in hushed tones, became very quiet. Cate wondered if she had interrupted a private conversation—*about me?* She wondered if Matthew was asking David if he should ask her to marry him that particular night. *What will I say?*

"Well, Sarah's all tucked in."

"Thanks," David said.

"Anytime,"

"Are you about ready to go?" Matthew asked, as he looked at the clock on the wall.

"Go where?" Cate responded, unaware of the time.

"Go home." Matthew pointed to the clock.

"Oh, it *is* kind of late." Cate said.

"Well, I guess, I'll see you two in church tomorrow," David rose as Cate and Matthew prepared to leave.

"Yep," they answered.

"Cate, thanks for taking such good care of Sarah," David said, as he walked them to the door.

"You're welcome," Cate replied, as Matthew put his arm around her and they left.

They walked out into a clear, tropical night. The rain had stopped a couple of hours earlier and though the dampness lingered, it was a beautiful night. The moon and the stars had a brightness that they could only have in that part of the world. In the distance were the mountains that Cate had come to count on as a symbol of God's strength and help. They stepped into the street, and Matthew took her hand as they walked down the narrow street toward her home.

"I love the nights here," Cate said.

"Me too, especially since you've been here," Matthew stopped, still holding her hand.

"That's sweet," Cate looked into his eyes. "You're sweet."

"So are you," he leaned over and kissed her. "Cate, I love you."

"I love you too," and for the first time, she really believed what she was saying.

"You do?" Matthew asked, with a grin.

"I do," Cate smiled.

"Cate, I've been thinking."

"*That* could be dangerous."

"I'm serious."

"Okay; what about?

"I'd like to ask you something," Matthew's tone was solemn. Before he could say anything, a voice in the night called out.

"Cate!"

Cate recognized Kim's voice, and the excited tone with which she had called her name.

"Kim, what's wrong?"

"Your Dad called. He needs to speak to you right away."

"Is there something wrong?" *Late night overseas phone calls- can't be good.*

"I don't know. He didn't say. He said that he needed to speak to you as soon as he could. I called David's, but he said that you had left. I was afraid that you two might not come directly home so I decided to try to find you."

"Thanks," Cate hurried toward the house.

"These things I have spoken unto you that you might have peace. In the world you shall have tribulation: but be of good cheer; I have overcome the world."

John 16:33.

Eleven

She was nervous as she dialed the number. The phone rang twice before her dad answered.

"Dad, what's wrong?"

"Catie, it's your mom." Cate heard the concern in his voice.

Before he could finish, Cate blurted, "What's wrong with mom?"

"She has breast cancer, honey."

"Breast cancer," Cate echoed, in shock.

"Catie, she's having surgery on Monday at eight a.m. I'm sorry for calling so late, but we decided that you should know."

"Sure, I should know. What will they do in the surgery?"

"They will probably have to remove her right breast and some lymph nodes."

"Oh, Daddy, what can I do?"

"You can pray."

Cate closed her eyes and saw her mother and father, "I know, but what else can I do?"

"There's really nothing else to do, but trust God with the situation."

"How's mom?"

"She's a little shaken, but she'll be fine. Your mother has strong faith."

"Yes, she does. I envy her faith."

"Catie, you have strong faith too. You got that from your mother."

"I thought I got my faith from you."

"Maybe, you got it from both of us. Anyway, you have faith and I know you'll rely on it."

"Dad, can I speak to Mom?"

"Sure, honey, she's right here, waiting to talk to you."

Her father passed the phone and Cate choked up when she heard her mother's voice, "Cate.".

Cate searched for words, but found only sobs.

"Cate, honey, don't cry. Everything will be all right."

Even with her mother's pleading, Cate couldn't stop crying.

"Honey, please don't cry."

Finally, Cate found words, "Mom, I am so sorry… so very sorry."

"I'll be fine, honey. God is in control."

"But, Mom, why you? Of all the people in the world, why you?"

"Why not me? What makes me different from anyone else? I have no exemption from cancer."

"But, Mom, you're one of the best people I know."

"Cate, I'm not so sure about that, but I'm sure that good people get cancer. I trust that God knows best in what He allows and that He will take care of me no matter what. Honey, I need you to trust Him too."

"Mom, what can I do to help you?"

"I just told you. You can entrust me into God's Hands and trust that He will do the right thing no matter what that is."

"But, Mom…"

"Cate, we've got to trust Him. There *is* no other way."

"But, Mom, I love you so much."

"I know you do, honey, and so does He. We have to trust that Love."

"Mom, I'm coming home."

"No, Cate, don't. It costs too much and they need you there. I just wanted you to know, and I wanted to hear your voice; I wanted to tell you that I love you."

"Oh, Mommy," Cate uttered, sobbing again, "I love you so much."

"Darling, I know that, and I know that we'll get through this. I promise you that."

"Mom, can I speak to Dad again?"

When her dad took the phone again, Cate renewed her argument, "Dad, I want to come home."

"Honey, your mom is right. It's too expensive, and you have a job to do there. We'll keep you in the loop. I'll call you Monday as soon as the surgery is over."

"Daddy, will you hold the phone so you and mother can both hear?"

"Sure," her dad answered. "Okay, we are both here."

"I love and appreciate you both. You have always been there for me. Even in my darkest times, I knew that I could count on you. I want both of you to know you can count on me. I wish I could be there to give both of you a great big hug and tell you in person how much you mean to me. I don't know what I would do without either one of you. I promise I'll be praying and I'll be trusting."

"Thanks honey. We knew we could count on you."

"You'll call me on Monday, right after the surgery?"

"Sure, I will," her dad assured her.

"Call me at the school, okay? You've got the number, right?"

"I've got the number, honey."

"Daddy, I hate to hang up."

"I know, but I promise I'll call you on Monday. By the way, we are praying for you too."

"I know. Thank you. I'll talk to you on Monday," she reluctantly hung up.

Cate sat silently on the couch for several minutes. Tears were streaming from her eyes and a prayer was rising from deep within her. "Oh, Lord, please I pray that my mother will be all right. Please help the doctors get all of the cancer. Please Lord, I'm not ready to give up my mother. Please Lord; let my mother be all right."

Finally, Kim ventured into the room. "Cate, is everything all right?"

Cate shook her head.

"What's wrong?"

"My mother has breast cancer."

"Cate, I'm so sorry."

"Thanks."

"Is there anything I can do?"

"Just pray for her."

"You know I will. Matthew is quite worried. Is it okay to tell him and Janet?"

Cate shook her head that it was all right. She was still battling tears and praying silently.

Kim disappeared into the kitchen and minutes later Matthew came through the kitchen door into the living room. Matthew walked directly to Cate, put his arms around her and drew her in close. As he held her, he whispered, "I'm so sorry."

Cate cried as Matthew held her. He didn't say anything, he simply held her and let her cry. Finally, she stopped and took comfort from Matthew's embrace. After several minutes, Cate spoke, "Thanks for being here Matthew, and for letting me cry."

"I'm glad I could be here."

"I know it's really late. You need to go home and get some rest."

"I'm here for as long as you need me."

"I'll be fine now. I think I'm cried out," Cate assured him.

"You think you can sleep now?"

"I think so."

"I'd like to pray for your mother, your family and you before I go."

"That would be great," Cate said, as she accepted his offer.

They bowed their heads and clasped each other's hands as Matthew prayed a beautiful prayer of intercession and compassion. When he had finished, he looked Cate in the eyes and assured her, "Everything's going to be all right; you know."

"I know; thanks again," Cate answered, as he drew her close again.

"I love you, Cate," he kissed her softly.

"I love you too," Cate said, still in his arms.

"I'll see you tomorrow." He gently released her and headed for the front door.

Cate silently nodded as she followed him to the door. As he opened the door and started out, he kissed her softly one more time.

Cate went to the kitchen; the light was on, but no one was there. Kim and Miss Janet had already gone to bed, so Cate followed their example. She fell asleep while looking out of her bedroom window at the silhouetted mountains in the distance. Those moonlit silhouetted mountains comforted her; they had become a constant symbol to her of the Lord's help and strength.

Twelve

She began the next day conscious of God's gracious watch-care. She was sure this was because of God's gracious watch-care. When she realized that she had slept late, she dressed for church and went in for a quick breakfast.

Miss Janet and Kim were already dressed and sitting in the living room, reading newspapers from home.

Cate greeted them, "Good morning."

Miss Janet looked up from her newspaper, "How are you this morning?"

"I'm fine. I see you're both ready for church. Thank you for allowing me to sleep a little longer than usual today."

"We weren't quite sure when you finally got to sleep," Kim said.

"I'm not quite sure either, but I'm sure the extra rest did me good," Cate forced a smile.

"I'm sure it did," Miss Janet said, "You look refreshed."

"I am, and I'm hopeful."

"About your mother's situation?" Kim asked.

"Uh-huh."

"That's wonderful," Miss Janet said.

"Is your mother going to have surgery and treatments?" Kim asked, with genuine concern.

"She's having the surgery tomorrow morning, but I don't know about treatments. My parents didn't say, and I forgot to ask."

"They probably don't know about the treatments yet," Miss Janet said. "That determination will probably be made once the surgery has been completed."

"I guess. I don't know much about breast cancer."

"I know about it," Miss Janet continued. "My sister had breast cancer."

"What happened with her?"

"She had to have a double mastectomy and months of both chemotherapy and radiation."

"But, everything turned out okay?" Kim asked.

Cate held her breath as Miss Janet hesitated to answer.

When Miss Janet saw the look of panic on Cate's face, she answered, "Yes, she's alive and well in Sacramento. She's a teacher too, and has been cancer-free for fifteen years."

"How old was your sister when she was diagnosed?" Cate inquired.

"She was only twenty-eight."

"Twenty-eight," Kim echoed.

"Twenty-eight," Miss Janet nodded.

"Wow," Cate said.

"She was the same age as Cate and me," Kim said.

"That's right. Cate, how old is your mother?"

"She's almost fifty-two."

"There have been tremendous breakthroughs in treating cancer since my sister's recovery. Your mother has an excellent chance at full recovery."

"Yeah, I'm sure that's right," Cate said. *I hope so.*

Miss Janet pointed at the clock on the wall, "Well, girls, we had better start walking so we won't be late."

As they walked the two blocks to the church, Cate's heart felt lighter. Miss Janet's words about her sister had encouraged her.

When they arrived at the church, the other parishioners greeted them. Matthew motioned for them to sit with him, and Cate, Kim, and Janet took their seats. Mrs. Garcia brought Sarah to sit with them and when Cate inquired as to where David was, much to their surprise, Mrs. Garcia pointed to the front. As they looked up, David entered from the pastor's study and took his seat on the platform. Because the pastor was suffering from laryngitis, David would preach the sermon that Sunday.

Cate whispered to Matthew, "The last time I heard David preach was seven years ago when he was on staff at my dad's church."

"I don't know how he was back then, but I've heard him many times and he's a good preacher."

Kim leaned over to add her comment. "He's one of the best I've ever heard."

"She might be a little prejudiced," Matthew winked.

"I'd say she's a *lot* prejudiced," Miss Janet said, with a smile.

Kim shook her head, and defended her opinion, "Cate, I promise you'll be inspired by his preaching."

Cate's eyes held promise, "I'm looking forward to it."

Every song, every scripture, and David's sermon about Lazarus' sickness and death, spoke to her. He spoke of Jesus weeping at the tomb of Lazarus and his words to Martha as he reminded her that she would see the glory of God if she believed. Cate knew this had application for her life and her situation with her mother. She knew God was speaking to her heart about trusting Him with her mother, in the midst of perplexity and uncertainty.

When the service was over, Cate hugged David tightly, "Thanks for the sermon. I needed it."

"You're welcome," David said awkwardly, embarrassed by her depth of gratitude and method of expression, especially since Matthew, Kim, and Janet were standing there. In Matthew, Kim, and Janet's faces, he saw empathy for Cate.

"David, I liked your sermon too. Its applications were very practical," Matthew said, as he nodded toward Cate.

David realized there was something wrong, "Cate, are you okay?"

"Sure, I-I'm okay."

Confused, David looked at the others, "Is there something going on?"

Matthew, Kim and Janet nodded their heads 'yes', and Cate saw them point toward her. Haltingly, she began, "I found out last night that my mom has cancer."

This time David hugged *her*, "I'm sorry, Cate."

"I know," she wiped her eyes.

Matthew was holding Sarah, who was confused about what was happening.

"Mr. Matthew, why is Cate crying?"

Cate answered, "Sarah, I'm all right… I'm just a little sad." She took Sarah in her arms and Sarah helped Cate brush away her tears. Cate smiled at the love and thoughtfulness of such a little girl.

Matthew put his arm around Cate. "Hey," he said, "why don't we all go to *Mama's Hacienda* for lunch?"

"Sure, let's do it," David agreed.

Madre's Hacienda wasn't fancy, and wouldn't be the choice of most tourists, but it was clean and had authentic local entrees. The children of the restaurant owner attended the mission school. They were proud that the headmaster and his teachers came to their establishment.

The restaurant had begun to fill up, but when they arrived Mama Rosa saw them and ran to greet them.

"*Buenos Días,* if you will follow me, I have special table for you."

She led them to a table that would accommodate the party of six, and ordered the servers to make the dining festive and special.

"May I suggest our special entrée?"

"Is it your special chicken, Mama Rosa?"

"*Si, Señor* Matthew."

With a smile and a wink at Mama Rosa, Matthew said, "Well, that settles it for me."

Everyone concurred.

"Six specials it is," Mama said, as she motioned for the two servers, "If I may, I would like to have the servers bring you some of the punch that you like. It is my gift to you."

Everyone smiled and said, "Thank you Mama."

The servers had arrived at the table and began to serve the punch.

"I will go to the kitchen now and prepare your plates myself," Mama said, with a smile.

"*Muchas gracias,*" came the chorus from the table.

Everyone took a sip and finished with an "ummm." Mama's punch hit the spot.

Kim dreamily closed her eyes, "Fruit never tasted so good."

"You can say that again," David agreed.

"This punch is the best," Sarah added her seal of approval.

"I've never had better," Miss Janet said.

Cate had remained silent during the conversation. She was drinking her punch, but was in another place. Everyone noticed, but said nothing. Mama and the servers brought their plates; and once again everyone raved over the food, except Cate. She picked at her food with her fork, but didn't eat much and everyone left her to her thoughts.

When lunch was almost finished, David decided a little intervention was necessary.

"Matthew, Kim, can I see you outside for a minute?"

Matthew and Kim looked confused until David nodded toward Cate.

"If you ladies will excuse us for a moment, it seems we are needed outside," Matthew helped Kim with her chair.

"Of course," Miss Janet replied.

Realizing that he was leaving, Sarah asked, "Daddy, where are you going?"

"Be back in a minute. Finish your chicken and rice."

"Okay."

Miss Janet motioned for the server to bring Sarah some more punch. Mama Rosa saw her and came instead.

"*Si, mi bambina*, you need some punch."

"*Si, Mama Rosa.*"

Mama smiled and filled her glass.

"*Señorita* Cate, do you need more punch?" Mama Rosa asked.

Cate's eyes stared at the wall across the room.

Sarah said loudly, "Cate, Mama Rosa is speaking to you."

Cate came back from where she had been. "What, Baby Girl?"

"Mama Rosa wants to know if you would like more punch."

Cate saw Mama standing with the pitcher, "No, thank you; I'm fine."

"Are you well *Señorita* Cate?"

"Yes, yes, I'm well."

"She has a lot on her mind," Miss Janet said.

"I see," Mama returned to the kitchen.

David, Matthew and Kim returned, and sat down.

David brushed Sarah's hair away from her face, "Sarah, if you're finished, Kim and Miss Janet are going home. They would like you to go with them."

"But, Daddy I want to stay with you."

"Sarah," Kim said, "how about we take you to see Mr. Ramon's ducks?"

"I'd like that," Sarah clapped her hands.

"Well, let's go see the ducks," Miss Janet rose and offered Sarah her hand.

Sarah wiped her hands and mouth. She kissed her daddy and Cate goodbye, and left singing one of her favorite songs.

Cate folded her napkin, placed it on the table and leaned back in her chair, "Okay, what's going on?"

"We sent them home because we didn't want to talk in front of Sarah," David answered.

"I understand," Cate refolded the napkin, "I'm guessing that you want to talk about my mother."

"Yes, if you don't mind," David replied.

"If you do mind, we'll understand," Matthew said.

"I don't mind. What would you like to know?"

"Kim told us she would be having surgery tomorrow morning," David answered. "But, how are she and your dad doing?"

"You know my dad. He's a rock. He's trusting God, but I could tell by his voice that he's very concerned."

"I'm sure he is," Matthew added.

David nodded; he knew Cate's dad. "And your mom, how's she holding up?"

"She's trusting God, and surrendering the whole thing to Him, just like Dad."

"And," David paused, "how are you?"

"I'm trying to do the same thing. That's why your sermon meant so much to me. But, I can't help but worry about Mom and Dad. They've always been very close. They count on each other. I know this is hurting Dad deeply."

"I'm sure you're right. I've always envied your parent's relationship," David said.

"You have?" Cate's eyes showed surprise.

"They've always made marriage look good."

"Yeah, they have."

"Your parents sound great," Matthew said.

"They re great," David said.

Cate watched Mama Rosa work her magic with the other diners, "But, they'd tell you that marriage is tough and challenging."

"Yeah, they would," David said. "I talked with your dad about it when I was on his church staff."

"Cate, we were wondering if you wanted to go home to be with your parents during this time," Matthew probed.

"I thought about it, but my parents don't want me to. They say it would cost too much and that I'm needed here."

"Yes, but do you *want* to go?" David asked again.

Wondering what they were up to, Cate asked, "Why?"

"If you do, we'll make it possible," Matthew chimed in.

"What do you mean, you'll make it possible?"

"We'll both chip in and help pay for your trip home," David said.

"Thanks guys, I appreciate it and I'm really tempted, but I'll stick to the plan I made with my parents. I'll prayerfully wait on my dad to call tomorrow. Anyway, they may need me to come home later. Besides, neither one of you have money to spare."

"Cate, money is not any issue for either one of us."

She knew different. "Thanks again, but no thanks."

"Don't you know that I'd do anything for you?" Matthew realized he had left David out. He pointed to David and himself and stated his words differently. "Don't you know we'd do anything for you?"

"You're both sweet, but no."

"Cate," Matthew pleaded.

"No, Matthew," Cate said gratefully, but firmly.

David spoke to end the argument, "You heard her Matt. She said no."

Cate put finality to the conversation, "We'd better go. David needs some rest before he preaches again."

"You're right; he does," Matthew said.

They walked the four blocks to Cate's house. David was going to retrieve Sarah, but Cate suggested that he leave her so he could get some rest. As Cate and Matthew were about to enter the house, David called out, "Hey Cate, I love your mom and dad, you know."

"Yeah, I know," Cate smiled.

Cate and Matthew entered the house and found everyone napping.

Matthew suggested that he go so Cate could nap. He kissed her goodbye and she went to her room for a short nap.

She had been asleep for about an hour when she felt her bed move, and opened her eyes to find Sarah lying beside her.

"What are you up to, Baby Girl?" Cate grabbed her and tickled her. Sarah giggled with joy and tried to tickle Cate. The sound of their laugher brought Kim to the door.

"What's going on in here?"

"She's tickling me," Sarah yelled, through intermittent giggles.

"It's not me who's tickling, it's her," Cate said.

"It sounds like you're having fun."

"Yep," Sarah said, still giggling and tickling.

"Well, it's almost time to start for church."

"Okay," Cate said.

"Okay," Sarah echoed.

Cate sat up on the bed, "Guess we had better get up and get ready to go."

They washed their faces, fixed their hair and announced that they were both ready to go. Sarah slipped her hand in Cate's as they headed out the door and began the walk to the church.

Matthew was there as before, saving seats. As before, David's sermon touched Cate's heart. This time it was on Psalm 46 and reminded her that "…the Lord is a very present help in the time of trouble," no matter what the trouble is.

After she left the service, she thanked David for his sermon.

"Once again, I needed to hear what you said."

"Glad God could use me. I'll be praying for your mom, dad and you. I'll check with you tomorrow for news from your mother."

"Thanks again,"

Matthew took Cate's arm as he nodded to David, "Good sermon, pal."

"Thanks."

She and Matthew said a quick goodbye and took a walk beneath the beautiful night sky.

As they walked, she drank in the night-and Matthew's rugged good looks. She couldn't believe how attentive he was. She knew he was concerned about her, and how she was dealing with the news about her mother. He was very sweet, slipping his large hand around hers and allowing her to walk for twenty minutes without having to say a word.

Suddenly, he stopped. "Cate, could we talk a moment?"

"Sure,"

He held her hands and looked deeply into her blue eyes. "Cate, I want you to know that I'm here for you. I know that you know, but I want you to understand- how much I love you."

Cate bite her bottom lip, fearful he was about to propose, and thought about what she would answer.

He released her left hand and tenderly touched her faced. "I know that you're stressed about your mother, and I respect that, but once she's okay, I want to ask you something important."

"Matthew-"

"I'm sorry, I didn't mean to add to your stress."

"No, it's okay."

"Please forget I said anything. We'll talk when your mom's better."

As they began to walk again, Cate caught a glimpse of David and Sarah in the distance; they were walking toward their house. She could tell that they were carrying on a conversation. She said a silent prayer of thanksgiving for David, Sarah and Matthew's presence in her life at this particular time of trouble.

When they arrived at her house, Matthew kissed her good night, once again told her that he loved her and she reciprocated. As she readied for bed she stood looking at the mountains in the distance, and prayed for her mother, dad, the doctors, and the surgery the next day. She crawled into bed and fell asleep while looking at the mountains.

"*Call unto me, and I will answer thee, and show thee great and might things, which thou knowest not.*"

Jeremiah 33:3

Thirteen

The morning came quickly, sunshine streaming through the windows of her bedroom and the brightness of the day awakening Cate. She glanced at the clock, realized that it was not yet time for her to get up and get ready for school, but decided to spend time with the Lord in Bible study and prayer.

Her time in the word was sweet that day. The Lord's presence seemed to fill the room as she prayed a prayer for her mom, dad and the surgery. As she prayed, she felt the Lord immediately answering her prayer.

She left for school with joy in her heart. She wasn't sure what was happening at home, but was confident everything would be all right. Everyone at school was especially nice; all knew that this day was a critical day in her life. She felt a sense of belonging and security for which she was grateful on this particular day.

The hours crept by. Every time she heard steps outside her classroom door, she was sure that Matthew was coming to tell her that her father was on the phone, and each time she was disappointed. With each passing hour, Cate became more and more anxious, and wondered why her father had not called.

The children noticed Miss Cate's nervousness and anxiety, and they listened for footsteps too. Finally, they heard steps getting closer and closer. Matthew entered and told her that her father was on phone.

Cate hurried from the classroom to the office and the phone. "Hello, Dad. How's Mom?"

"Catie, she's okay. She's groggy and is going to be very sore, but she's okay."

"Did they get all of the cancer?"

"They got all that was in the breast. They removed the right breast and three lymph nodes, but we won't know about the lymph nodes for two or three days."

"Will Mom have to have chemo or radiation?"

"Both, but we won't know how much until we hear from the lymph node biopsies."

"Daddy, can I talk to Mom?"

"Sure, honey, but she might not remember talking to you."

"That doesn't matter. I'll know that I talked to *her*. I want to hear her voice, dad."

"Okay, honey. I'll hold the phone so she can hear. Okay, Catie go ahead."

"Mom, this is Cate. How are you?"

"Cate?" her mother answered, the voice weak.

"Yes, Mom, I love you."

"I love you too."

Her dad took the phone back. "See, honey. She's fine. She's just really sleepy."

"Daddy, will you call me when you hear from the lymph nodes and about the treatments?"

"Of course, honey. We told you we would keep you in the loop."

"Daddy, how are you?"

"I'm fine, Catie."

"Daddy, I love you."

"I love you too."

"I wish I was there."

"I know, but you're where you're supposed to be. Your mother and I have loved reading your letters. We've enjoying learning about everyone and everything. We've been glad to hear that you feel you are exactly where God wants you. That's worth more to us than you know. We are thankful for you, and proud of you."

"Thanks, Dad."

"I'll call you in a few days. Your mother will be able to talk to you then."

"Okay, I'll say goodbye for now."

"Bye, Catie,"

Cate hung up, and realized that several people were outside Matthew's office. As she walked out, they all inquired about her mother. She was happy to give them the news about the surgery. Everyone rejoiced and encouraged her to keep trusting the Lord.

By the time, she returned to her classroom, school was dismissing, but the children, as well as Matthew, stayed.

"We want to know about your mother," Matthew said, as spokesperson for the group.

"My mother made it through the surgery fine."

"Miss Cate, we are so pleased to hear this," Tomas responded, as representative for the class. All of the children nodded.

"Thank you, children," Cate said, and she began to hug each one. "I'll see you in the morning."

"Goodbye, Miss Cate. God bless you. We love you," said the little voices, as they received their hugs and left the classroom.

"We love you, Miss Cate," Matthew echoed, as he hugged her. "Cate, I'm glad your mother is doing well."

"Yeah, I am too. We won't hear from the lymph nodes for about three days. We won't know her prognosis until then."

Matthew continued to hold her, "We'll keep praying."

Kim and Miss Janet entered while he was hugging Cate. Kim thought a little levity was in order. "In all the time, I've been teaching here, he never hugged me like that. Did he you, Miss Janet?"

"You're just jealous," Matthew said.

"Jealous? Not me, I've got my own man," Kim said. "As a matter of fact, I expected him to be here to hug me by now."

"Well, you young folks make me feel left out," Miss Janet chimed in.

"Miss Janet, don't you know you'll always be my best girl," Matthew said, as he tried to hug her.

Miss Janet pushed him back, "Enough of this nonsense, Cate, we wanted to tell you how glad we were to hear how well your mother is doing."

"Thank you. We'll hear about the lymph nodes in a few days and we'll know the prognosis."

David and Sarah walked in as she finished. Sarah ran to Cate and hugged her. David asked about her mom. Once again, Cate explained.

"I'm glad things went well. How's your dad doing?"

"Dad's fine. I could hear the relief in his voice."

"Daddy, can we go home now?"

"What's your hurry?" Cate asked, as she tickled Sarah.

Sarah tried to get away from the tickling, "I want to go home and play."

"I guess it's time for all of us to go home," Matthew said.

"Cate, I'm sorry for such short notice, but could you possibly stay with Sarah tonight? I received a call about an hour ago requesting that I attend a meeting tonight in Quito. I also have a meeting tomorrow, so I'll be staying overnight with the Pattersons."

"Sure, how soon do you need me there?"

"Mrs. Garcia will be there until six, anytime before that will be fine."

"Yay!" Sarah jumped and clapped her hands. "Cate's coming to our house."

"So, you're taking my girl tonight," Matthew joked with Sarah.

"She was my girl first," Sarah replied triumphantly. Everyone laughed.

"I sure was, Baby Girl. I guess she put you in your place, Mr. Matthew."

Matthew smiled and everyone laughed again. Matthew moved close to Sarah, made a face, while giving her the 'evil eye', "But, I'm going to walk her home. Sarah, you'll get her later."

Sarah tried to make the same face, "Okay, Mr. Matthew."

Matthew did walk Cate home, while David, Sarah, Kim and Miss Janet walked behind. When they arrived David and Sarah said goodbye to Kim and Miss Janet, but Matthew did not get the 'alone' time he wanted with Cate. She was anxious to pack for her stay at David's house. He had to be content with a little small talk, a hug, a quick peck on the cheek, a goodbye plus a hurried, "I love you."

Cate arrived at David's home around five. David had already left for Quito, and Mrs. Garcia was giving Sarah her dinner.

"Miss Cate, I kept your dinner warm. It is in the oven."

"Thanks, that's very nice of you."

THE CALLING

Even though Mrs. Garcia was about the same age as Cate's mother, she and Cate had developed a warm relationship. Mrs. Garcia's smile and sparkling dark eyes evidenced an inner joy. During Cate's times of taking care of Sarah, they'd had opportunities to sit and talk, and both had grown to appreciate the other as a sister in Christ.

After dinner, Cate and Sarah spent two hours reading and doing homework before Sarah went to bed. After she was in bed, Cate made a cup of tea and relaxed. She liked David's home; Jenny had done a great job making it nice and homey, and she was sure that David had not changed anything since Jenny's death.

The living room was simply furnished, nothing fancy, but comfortable and inviting. A tufted, well-stuffed couch, mingled beige, brown and blue in color, accompanied by a matching chair and ottoman occupied the west and south side of the room. At each end of the couch were end tables with matching lamps. On the north side of the room was David's favorite chair, a blue rocker recliner he'd had ever since Cate had known him. Behind and to the right of David's chair and against the wall that led to the kitchen were bookshelves, filled with classics, children's, and favorite books. Along the wall opposite the couch, there was an entertainment center with a television, a VCR/DVD player, a CD player and numerous movies and videos. A number of beautiful plants adorned the room. Jenny had loved plants and had a green thumb; Mrs. Garcia continued to take care of the plants after Jenny's death.

It was not a large house. Besides, the living room and kitchen, there were three bedrooms, a bathroom and a small room that David used as an office/study. There was a patio and a little garden out back.

It was odd that Cate could feel so at home in a house that Jenny had decorated and shared with David. Strange as it might be, she did feel at home. She was grateful that was true, because David was away often, so she stayed with Sarah.

She thought about Matthew, that he was going to ask her a question after the crisis with her mother passed. That probably meant he was going to propose. Things with her mother seemed to be going well, so she needed to be considering what her answer would be.

She was sure she loved Matthew, *but do I love him enough to marry him?* When she married Justin, had she loved him or did she only think she did? She wondered what about the marriage had been real. She thought he loved her and she loved him. *Was any of it real?* Moreover, she had loved David, but when Justin came along, she thought she didn't love him anymore. Now, she thought she was sure she loved David-and Matthew. *Maybe I'm crazy, and shouldn't marry anybody.* She was more confused than ever. Finally, she did what she should have done in the first place-she prayed. "God, help me, please. I believe Matthew is going to ask me to marry him. I don't want to hurt him and I do want to do your will. Lord, I don't know right now who I love, or if I know *how* to love. I've made such a mess of my life in this department and I want to stop. I want to love the man you want me to, and how you want me to. God, help me please. I don't know what to do here. I submit to you. I'll do whatever you want me to."

Just as she finished praying and was about to finish her tea, she heard Sarah call out. She hurried to check on her and found that she was talking in her sleep. Cate sat on her bed for a few minutes and patted her back as she settled down to a deep, peaceful sleep. She kissed her softly on the forehead, went to the living room, turned out the light and went to bed.

Cate could see 'her mountains' in the distance from her bedroom at David's house too. She always thanked God for these mountains and their special symbolism to her. She repeated the verse again, "I will lift up my eyes unto the hills. From whence cometh my help? My help cometh from the Lord who made the heavens and the earth." She fell asleep looking at the mountains.

Morning came. She and Sarah awoke, dressed, ate breakfast, said hello to Mrs. Garcia and left for school. Cate deposited Sarah in her classroom and hurried to her classroom to greet her own students. One by one they came, each one greeting her with smiles and hugs. Cate loved each one.

"Miss Cate, me and my family prayed for you and your *madre*," Stefan said.

"*Muchas gracias*, Stefan."

"*De nada*, teacher."

"I prayed too teacher," Maria said and then, the others.

"I am grateful to you all. How about, we say our morning prayers as we begin? Who would like to pray?"

They all raised their hands to volunteer.

"Juanita, will you lead us in prayer today?"

"*Si*, teacher." She prayed a beautiful child's prayer.

One thing Cate particularly liked about mission school was the freedom to talk about Jesus, read the Bible, and pray. It was a delight not only to teach these children the regular kindergarten things, but also about God.

This day was wonderful, and so were the next two. People were nice, concerned and encouraging. Cate was aware of God's sustaining grace, and she prayed constantly for her parents and about the prospect of marriage to Matthew.

"For I know the thoughts that I think toward you, said the Lord, thoughts of peace, and not for evil, to give you an expected end. Then shall ye call upon me, and ye shall go, and pray unto me, and I shall hearken unto you. And ye shall seek me, and find me, when ye shall seek me with all of your heart."

Jeremiah 29:11-13.

Fourteen

Midday on Friday, Matthew came to her room and told her that her father was on the phone. Leaving her students under Matthew's supervision, she hurried to the phone.

"Dad," Cate answered.

"Hi, Catie,"

"What did they find out?"

"There was cancer in one lymph node."

"What does that mean?"

"It means that after your mom has recovered from the surgery, she will need some chemotherapy and radiation."

"Oh, Daddy."

"Cate, the doctors believe your mother will be fine. As far as they can tell, they got all of the cancer. According to the CT scans, there isn't any cancer anywhere else. The chemo and radiation are precautionary."

"But, Dad, I know it usually makes people really sick."

"That's true, but not everyone." He heard her concern over the phone line, and imagined the anguish on his precious daughter's face. "We'll have to pray your mother is one of those."

"Can I speak to Mom?"

"Sure, here's Mom."

"Cate," her mom said.

"Mom, how are you?"

"I'm fine, honey. I'm ready to go home."

"Do you have any idea when you might get to go home?"

"Maybe tomorrow,"

"Tomorrow, are you sure that's not too soon?"

"Well, the doctors don't think so. Besides, I can do the same things at home that they have me doing here."

"What do they have you doing?"

"I have to walk at least four times a day. Your father can help me do that."

"Mom, I'm sure you're terribly sore."

"Yes, honey I am, but I've got to get up and walk to prevent blood clots or pneumonia."

"I see. When do you begin chemo?

"In about four weeks," her mom answered.

"Mom, I love you and I'm praying for you."

"I love you too Cate."

"Can I talk to Dad one more time?"

"Sure, honey,"

Her mother handed off the phone.

"Daddy, will you call me in about a week and let me know how Mom is, and again after Mom has her first chemo?"

"Yes, honey, I'll call you."

"Thanks, Dad. I love you."

"I love you too, Catie."

"Daddy, email me every day or two."

"I will," her dad promised.

"Well, I guess we'd better say goodbye now."

"That's probably a good idea."

"Goodbye, then,"

"Bye, Catie," her dad hung up the phone.

When Cate returned to her room, her class had already gone to lunch. She sat down at her desk and said a quick prayer. Afterwards, she made her way to the cafeteria. Matthew and her fellow teachers met her to inquire about her mother. She told them what her parents had said and her colleagues assured her that they would continue to pray for her mother's recovery.

Though she was trying hard to cover up, Matthew knew that Cate was upset. He finally got her alone long enough to ask. "Cate, I know you're upset. Is there anything I can do?"

"No, Matthew. I'll be fine. I just need a little time to adjust. I was hoping that Mom wouldn't have to have chemo. I am so afraid of what it'll do to her."

Matthew took her hand and looked into her eyes, "Cate, I know you have a very special relationship with your parents, and that your mother's illness has been particularly hard for you to handle. Why don't you take the rest of the day off?"

"I can't do that. Who'd cover my class?"

"I will."

"You have responsibilities of your own."

"And one of those is to take care of my faculty. Please take the rest of the afternoon off."

Cate hugged him and whispered, "Thank you."

"You're welcome. Now go home, or for a walk, or do whatever would be most helpful."

Cate shook her head 'okay' and left to follow his instructions.

She chose a walk. She had spent a lot of her life walking and talking to the Lord. It always helped. It helped this day. She had been walking and praying for about two hours when she ran into David. He had been looking for her.

As he caught up with her, he asked, "Cate, are you all right?"

Still entangled in her thoughts about her mother and the chemo, Cate answered, "Yea, uh-huh."

"Matthew told me about your mom and the treatments, and that he had given you the rest of the day off. He was worried about you so he called me."

Somewhat bewildered, Cate responded," He called you?"

"He knows that I have a special connection to your parents. He figured maybe I could commiserate with you and pray with you. It's taken me an hour and a half to find you."

"I'm sorry. I wasn't heading in any particular direction. I was just walking and talking to the Lord."

"I'm not scolding you, Cate. I'm just glad I finally found you. Is it okay if I walk with you? We don't have to talk. I'd just like to walk with you."

"Where's Sarah?"

"She's with Mrs. Garcia. She's fine. We can walk as long as you want."

Still amazed, Cate said, "I can't believe Matthew sent you to look for me."

"He was worried about you."

Cate smiled, "He's such a great guy."

David looked away as he spoke, "Yeah, he is, and he loves you very much."

"I know," Cate said with a sigh.

Still looking away, David awkwardly said, "I love you too." He paused slightly and continued, "I love your parents too."

"I know you do."

"I'm sorry your mom is going through all of this."

Cate nodded in agreement and they walked several minutes in silence.

"David, my mom was always such a beautiful woman, so attractive, inside and out. Now, she has to deal with having part of her body removed. On the heels of that, she's going to have to go through chemo and radiation that may make her tremendously sick. She'll probably lose her appetite and her beautiful dark brown hair."

She felt safe in sharing what she was thinking. David nodded and allowed her to keep talking without interrupting.

"And, Dad has to watch, as his precious wife goes through it all. I know that he would give anything if he could take her place. That's the way I feel."

David stopped and took her by the hand. This time he looked her in the eye as he said, "Cate, I know your mom well enough to know she'd rather be the one going through it all. You three are just alike. You love each other so much that you try to spare each other all the pain you can. The problem is, you can't. I'm sure your mother has committed her trials to the Lord, and trusts His grace and strength to carry her through. And, I'm sure your dad is doing the same."

"You're right." Cate squeezed his hand. "You're exactly right. That's what they told me."

"Then, the question is, what have you decided to do? How have you decided to handle it?"

"The same way, but I have all of these feelings, these anxieties..."

"I know you do. Trusting God doesn't mean you don't have feelings contrary to that trust. It means that you choose to keep trusting God in spite of those feelings."

"Sometimes it's hard not to be overwhelmed by the feelings and the fears," Cate said.

David decided to be just as honest with her as she had been with him. "I know; I've been there. I was there after Jenny died-and I was there when you married Justin."

"David, I'm sorry. I didn't mean to bring all that up."

"You didn't; I did. And, I probably wouldn't have admitted it to anyone else but you. Guys aren't too good at talking about their feelings, you know, but, I wanted you to know that I understand what you're going through."

"Thanks, I appreciate the openness."

"Also, I've found that it helps if you have someone to talk to, especially someone who'll listen and not judge. I promise I'll do that for you."

"If you don't mind my asking, who'd you talk to when Jenny died?"

"Dr. Patterson when I was here, my dad and your dad, when I got home," David answered, as they started walking again.

"My dad?" Cate said, with surprise.

"Actually, I talked to your dad more than anyone else."

"I didn't know that."

"It's always been easy for me to talk to your dad. He always listens, non-judgmentally, and I respect his counsel."

"Yeah, he *is* like that."

"I've tried to follow his example."

"I'm glad," Cate said. "May I ask who you talked to when I left you for Justin?"

"Even before that, I talked to your dad. I trusted his advice. When the whole Justin thing began, I sought your dad's counsel. When you decided to marry Justin, I didn't talk to him as much. He was willing, but I felt funny talking to him about my feelings for you, and the whole Justin thing. I talked to my dad."

"I never realized. I–I never knew. I..." Cate felt something inside, but didn't know what she was feeling.

"I don't doubt it. Your dad always considered confidentiality a sacred trust. That was one of the reasons people felt free to talk to him about their problems."

"That's true. Heaven knows I don't know what I would have done if I hadn't been able to talk to him and get his advice about things in my life."

"Cate, since your dad's not here, I'd like to be here for you, if you'll let me."

"As busy as you are? I'd be a burden."

"Cate, you're never a burden. Besides, I count on you for so very much concerning Sarah. What kind of person would I be if you couldn't count on me now?

"David, I appreciate the offer, but I wouldn't want to impose and besides, I have Matthew."

"I know you have Matt, but I want you to know that you have me too, if you need me."

"Thanks, I may take you up on that. You know my parents."

"Yep, that's why he sent me today."

"It seems I've heard this before," Cate gave a little laugh.

"Yep, but I think Matthew made a wise choice."

"Me too,"

"Yep, you feel better about your mom and dad and I think we both understand each other a little better."

"Thanks for finding me and talking with me."

"You're welcome," David hugged her.

Cate felt very close to him at that moment and hugged him back. Neither seemed too embarrassed by the genuine affection they shared. As they continued to walk toward Cate's house, small talk and laughter replaced the seriousness that had dominated the last hour. David left her much happier than he had found her. She went to sleep that night with a heart full of hope. She was confident she could face whatever the future held.

Fifteen

Throughout the next two weeks, Cate and her father emailed back and forth. Her mother seemed to be healing well from her surgery; she'd visited the oncologist's office and made all of the necessary preparations for her chemo which would begin on the following Monday. Her dad had cleared his schedule so he could be with his wife through the duration of the first session. Cate was aware of how much her parents loved each other and how devoted her dad was to her mom. She was grateful for parents like that.

True to his word, her dad called as soon as the treatment was over and he reported that her mother had suffered no side effects. Cate's mother took the phone and spoke with her. Cate was reassured when she realized how strong her voice was and how cheerful she seemed.

Over the next few weeks of emails, Cate learned that her mother would take eight chemo treatments in all, followed by radiation. Her chemo would be every two weeks. Everything seemed to be fine for the first month, but during the second month, the nausea, chills, fever, and lack of appetite began, and her mother began to lose her beautiful dark brown hair.

Each email from her father was both a comfort and a curse to Cate. The news from home comforted her, but each email telling of her mother's suffering was also like an arrow piercing Cate's heart. What she had feared was happening.

Cate suffered with her mother; she couldn't help it. She struggled in prayer, with her fears and feeling. She repeatedly had to choose to have faith, to trust, and to lean upon the Lord. She prayed for her mother's health and freedom from nausea, chills, fever, pain and that she would be able to eat.

During this time of struggle and identification with her mother, Cate wasn't eating much, and it became very noticeable. Kim and Miss Janet wondered if she slept much. She didn't go to bed until long after they had, and was up before they were. To their way of thinking, she couldn't be sleeping much.

As far as school went, she was the same hard-working, caring teacher she had always been, but the children noticed that though she had always been slim, she was now skinny. Everyone, including Sarah, became concerned about her.

Matthew tried to be a comfort to Cate by listening and by sharing how he'd coped with his dad's cancer. Matthew knew that Cate was trying to trust God day by day. He knew that she was praying constantly and relying on His strength, but he also knew there was something going on that he couldn't identify. He decided to seek David's advice.

"Dave, you've known Cate and her family a long time, and I know that you've been friends with Cate for quite some time. I need your advice; I don't know how to help her. I listen, I try to comfort and encourage her, but, regardless of what I do, I can tell that she's not eating or sleeping much," Matthew's voice held genuine concern.

"I know exactly what you're saying. I try to do the same thing when she and I talk."

"So what do we do? She looks so tired and thin," Matthew said. "Kim and Janet think that she's depressed."

"I don't think that's it."

"I don't either. I think she's so concerned about and sensitive to what her mother is going through that she's going through it too."

"I think you're right, and I think she's battling fears and feelings and choosing to have faith in God's plan and purpose. But, the fears and feelings don't go away simply because we choose faith. Sometimes they get stronger, and we have to continue to choose to have faith in God. I think that's what's going on with Cate," David said.

Matthew nodded, "So, we have to choose faith too, faith that Cate's going to be all right."

"My friend, I think you've got something there."

"But, it's hard to watch her suffering the way she is," Matthew said.

"Yeah, it is, but Cate and her mother have a very close, special relationship. I think that's why she is identifying with her mother's suffering so much, and not being able to be where she is, is hurting too."

"I wish we could do something to make things easier for her."

"Yeah, me too, even Sarah has said the same thing."

"She did?"

"She sure did. She asked me what we could do to make Cate happy again. I told her we needed to pray for Cate and be nice to her. She told me that she was worried about Cate because she doesn't smile as much as she used to."

"I guess you're right. We need to continue to pray for her and be nice to her. Maybe, the Lord will provide a solution," Matthew said.

After Matthew left, David wished he had the answer to make things better for Cate, but there didn't seem to be a simple answer. He had tried to quiet Matthew and Sarah's concerns by assuring them that Cate would be all right. That's what he'd said, and that's what he hoped and prayed, but he wasn't completely convinced. The ordeal had convinced him of one thing, *I still have feelings for Cate.*

He had ignored those feelings when he married Jenny. Jenny had always known about his feelings for Cate, but she also knew that he loved her and had chosen her. Their marriage had been a real marriage, a great marriage. But Jenny died, and Cate had come back in his life. He had not sought her out, nor had she sought him, but it had happened. He remembered the day she walked into his seminary class, *There she is, my first real love, the girl who callously broke my heart. I can't believe she's sitting in my class.* He had forgiven her long before this, but the memories were still there.

She also worked at his daughter's preschool. It seemed that everywhere he turned, Cate was there. The more he was around Cate, the more he found himself pushing his feelings down. Even though he had become successful in his efforts, the feelings were still there, undeniably there, but the only one he'd admit it to was God, and he found himself reluctant to do that.

Because of her divorce, he didn't see any future for them. The

IMB would never continue the appointment of a missionary married to a divorced woman, and God had given him no indication that he was to serve Him in any way other than missions. Therefore, admitting his love for Cate to God, himself, or anyone else served no purpose. But it was there, deep in his heart, and it had been there for years; steady, unending, and strong. Seeing her in such pain and grief over her mother brought it to the forefront of his heart and mind. But, he had to ignore it, because now, there was Matthew-and Kim.

David knew that he had practically handed Cate to Matthew. When Matthew came to David for advice about a relationship with Cate, he had given his full blessing and encouragement. He had done this in the hopes that he could do as he had done before, turn his back on his feelings for Cate, and at the same time help a friend, and provide a godly partner for each of them.

Beginning a relationship with Kim was also part of the effort to turn his back on his feelings for Cate. Unfortunately nothing he had done had worked. Seeing Cate with Matthew hurt, and hurt badly. Being Matthew's confidant concerning Cate was almost unbearable. David continued to pray fervently that God would take away his feelings for Cate.

Throughout the continuing weeks of her mother's chemo, Cate continued confiding in both David and Matthew. Even though he was struggling, David continued to try to be there for Cate. Regardless of what he or Matthew did or said, Cate grew thinner and more tired.

It was so difficult for her to be so far away from her parents during the time of her mother's illness. She admitted to Matthew and David that though the emails and phone calls were good, they were not as good as being there, and being able to see her mother, hug her mother, and talk to her parents.

Matthew and David finally came up with a solution. They called Edward Randall, a friend of theirs who lived in Quito. Edward worked for an American corporation that did export business in Ecuador. Edward had access to corporate jets and corporate seats on regular airlines, and he had on occasion offered Matthew and David free trips to the U.S. or else where. Neither one had ever taken him up on his offer, but both were willing to approach him about helping Cate go home for a visit. This would be the best early Christmas present they could give Cate, and maybe the best medicine for what was ailing her.

Edward was glad to help. With transportation for the trip home taken care of, Matthew and David began to take care of the other things so Cate could go home. Once they had taken care of all the arrangements, the only thing left to do was to tell Cate. They decided to wait until the end of school that day.

As school was letting out, Matthew and David were standing in the door. Cate was hugging her students and telling them goodbye, when she looked up and saw them. Her first thought was something was wrong and that they had come to give her bad news.

"Is there something wrong with my mother?" she asked, holding her breath.

Realizing they had alarmed her by their presence, Matthew and David, both spoke, "Everything is all right. We have a surprise for you, an early Christmas present."

"An early Christmas present…" Cate's eyes narrowed as she looked at the two of them.

"Yes, we've made arrangements for you to go home for a visit," Matthew said.

Astonished at what she had heard, Cate asked, "Home?"

"Home," David said, "and you can stay until after the New Year."

"What? How?"

"Yep, it's all arranged," Matthew said happily.

"But, the cost," Cate objected.

"No cost, it's free," Matthew said.

Trying to grasp it all, Cate repeated, "Free."

"Free," David said.

"But, how?"

"Don't worry about how," Matthew answered.

"But, what about my classes?"

"All arranged," Matthew said.

"What about someone to stay with Sarah when you're away?" Cate asked, as she looked at David.

"Everything has been taken care of. All you have to worry about is packing," David assured her.

"When do I leave?" Cate asked, as it finally sank in.

"Tomorrow."

"Tomorrow, what time?"

"Around ten o'clock in the morning."

"I don't know who exactly is responsible for this or how it was accomplished, but I'm very grateful. I couldn't get a better present," Cate said, with a happiness in her voice that hadn't been there for a while.

"We, Dr. Patterson, and a mutual friend helped and we were all glad to do it," Matthew said.

"Well, I'll hug you two now, and Dr. Patterson and your friend later." Cate said, as she hugged them. "I guess I had better let my parents know that I'm coming home and then pack."

"They already know," David said. "I talked to your dad this morning."

Cate shrugged, "Well, I guess I need to pack."

Matthew took her arm, "I'll walk you home."

"And, I'll see you tomorrow," David said.

"Huh,"

"Matthew and I are taking you to the airport."

Sixteen

A trip home was just what Cate needed, to see her mother and know she was all right. Her dad met her at the airport, and she ran to his waiting arms.

"Catie, welcome home," he wrapped his arms around her and kissed her head.

Cate gladly accepted his hug and kisses, "Thanks, it's great to be home."

"Let me look at you sweetheart," he said as he held her at arm's length. "Don't they feed you down there?"

"Yes, Daddy they feed me. I just haven't been able to eat."

"Catie you look tired."

"Well, you look good to me. Daddy, it's good to see you," Cate hugged him and gave him a big kiss on the cheek. She had needed to see him too; he was a tower of strength for her and the perfect example of a godly man and father. She knew she was a lucky daughter and blessed to be home.

"Well, I guess, we had better go get your luggage and get home. Your mom is waiting."

They made their way to the baggage area, retrieved her luggage and started home. Now that she and her dad were face to face, she had nagging questions about her mother's illness and prognosis.

"Daddy, is mom going to be all right?"

"The doctors think so, and so do I."

"Really?"

"Sure, I told you that in my emails."

"I know dad, but when you're far away... It's sometimes difficult to really believe it."

"Believe it honey. Your mom is going to be all right." Her dad tried to prepare her for what she would see, "Catie, she's lost a lot of weight, and doesn't have much hair, she'll probably be wearing a scarf around her head."

"I'll be okay, Dad."

"I just wanted you to be aware that you'll probably be shocked when you see her."

"I know, Dad. It'll be okay." She reached over and placed her hand on her father's, "I just can't wait to be able to hug her and tell her that I love her." Cate was determined to master her emotions and be a source of strong support for her mother.

When she entered the house and walked toward the living room where her mom was waiting, she said a quick prayer. She was shocked when she saw her mom, but she prayed the Lord would help her handle it. She walked quickly toward her mother.

"Oh, Mom, you don't know how glad I am to see you."

"Oh, Cate, me too."

Cate and her mother hugged and held each other for a long time, exchanging "I love you and I'm so glad to see you" several times. They all talked until it was time to go to bed. Cate and her parents went to bed that night offering the Lord thanksgiving that she was home.

Being home was good medicine for Cate's mom. Even though she had given her only daughter to God, she missed her tremendously. She hadn't realized how much until Cate walked through the door. Having Cate home for the holidays made the holidays more special.

Cate had arrived home in time to help her father decorate for Christmas and finish shopping for Christmas presents. They enjoyed the decorating, and even though her dad had never liked shopping, this year, he seemed to. Cate liked shopping, but she loved spending time with her dad more.

She was glad to step in for her mom, even for the Christmas entertaining. Each year, her dad held a Christmas party at his home for the church staff and their families. He had wondered how he was going to do it this year.

"Dad, have you had the staff party yet?"

"No, honey I haven't."

"Can I help you prepare for it?"

"You want to help with the party?" her mother asked.

"Sure I do, it will be fun."

Her mother looked at her dad with a surprised but pleased expression.

"Well, if you're sure," her dad said.

"Great, when were you thinking about having it?"

"How about a week from today?"

"Sure, mom can help me decide on the menu, and you and I will shop for the food."

Her dad laughed, "You want *me* to be your shopping buddy?"

"Yep, unless mom feels up to it."

"I'm afraid not, at least not now," her mom said. "And, I have something else for you and your shopping buddy."

"What?"

"Christmas presents. We need Christmas presents for your brothers and their families."

"Okay shopping buddy," Cate said, "looks like we've got our work cut out for us."

"Yeah," her dad muttered.

"Jonathan, it'll be fun," Cate's mother chided.

"Carolyn, you must be delirious."

They all laughed. Cate loved it; she was home.

She and her father did have fun shopping, and her mother laughed as they talked about their escapades. They all wrapped presents together and reminisced about Christmases past.

Preparation for the staff party was something else they did together. Cate and her dad cleaned, cooked and her mother supervised. When the night came for the party everything was ready and looked beautiful, even Cate's mother. Carolyn Jones had always been a beautiful woman. And while the treatments had taken her dark brown hair, the sparkle from her blue eyes, and had caused her to have a sickly pallor and lose weight, this night no one noticed. Cate and her father bought her a pretty dress and turban for the occasion. Cate helped her with her make-up and everyone was amazed as she entered the room.

The Christmas staff party was a wonderful success. Everyone enjoyed the good fellowship, food and fun. Cate answered many questions about Ecuador and her work there.

"Cate, it's wonderful to see you," Mrs. Overton said.

"Is Ecuador as beautiful as they say?" Mr. Hill asked.

"How is the teaching going?" Clay Mitchell inquired with interest.

"How's Jenny's little girl?" Raven Taylor wanted to know.

"How's David?" Benton Powell asked.

Cate was glad to see everyone and told them what they wanted to know. It was fun to laugh and see her mother be the wonderful and warm hostess she had always been. When it was over Cate hated to see the night end.

In preparation for the rest of the family coming home for Christmas, Cate and her mom made sugar cookies and candies. Her brothers and their families would be home on Christmas Eve and Cate's sisters-in-law would help with the preparation of Christmas breakfast and Christmas lunch, Christmas dinner would be leftovers.

Her brothers and their families arrived right on schedule and Cate happily greeted them.

"Hey, you guys,"

"Hey, sis," her brothers yelled, as they walked toward the trunk of their cars.

"Hey, Cate," her sisters-in-law waved as they joined their husbands.

"Aunt Cate!" the nephews and nieces squealed as they swarmed her with hugs and kisses.

Cate stood back to eye the children, "Wow, I can't believe how much you all have grown."

Her brothers and their wives were taking the suitcases and boxes of goodies from their cars. Cate went to assist, "Can I help?"

"Sure," Thomas, her oldest brother, loaded her down.

"She's not a pack mule," Keaton, his wife, pointed out.

"My mistake. She looked a little horsey to me."

"Very funny," Cate said.

"She looks a little skinny to me," Paul, her other brother, said.

"So, she's a little philly," Thomas joked.

"And, she shouldn't be trying to carry that load you gave her," Keaton repeated.

"I'm okay," Cate replied.

"No, you're not," Hope, Paul's wife said.

"Okay, all ready. Sis, give me some of that," Thomas reached for the packages.

"Nope, I've got it, I told you."

"You're right Keaton. She's not a horse. She's a mule, a stubborn mule," Thomas said, as Cate started toward the house with her load.

Soon the cars were unloaded and everyone was settled in their rooms. The nieces and nephews occupied themselves with board games, card games and television, while the adults reminisced about past Christmases.

Observing family tradition, soup, sandwiches, chips, dip, Christmas cookies, and candies were consumed for Christmas Eve dinner, and afterwards, Cate's dad read the Christmas story from Luke 2. After he finished, he led the family in a prayer of thanksgiving for God's great gift of His Son, and prayed for his wife and his family. It was a wonderful time of family worship.

Cate watched her mother throughout the celebration and traditions of Christmas Eve and Christmas Day. Her mom was happy, and Cate was grateful she was there to witness it.

Cate had seen her mother gaining strength throughout her time at home. From the first day she arrived, she could tell the difference. Her mother had had a treatment on the Monday after Cate had arrived and still she seemed stronger than she had been the day Cate had arrived. She was smiling more and eating more. Cate and her dad thanked God for the improvement.

"Having you and the rest of the family home has been good medicine," her dad told her.

Her mom looked much different to her. She was still skinny, but she didn't look as sickly. Her family was a source of joy for her, and their presence this Christmas was particularly enjoyable.

As she talked with her brothers and their wives, Cate discovered they had also noticed the difference.

"Mom, sure looks better," Keaton observed.

Thomas smiled and added, "When I saw her two weeks ago, it hurt me to see how thin and sickly she looked."

"Cate must be good medicine," Hope said.

"I think having us all here is good medicine."

"I think you're right sis," Paul said.

"She does love her family," Keaton pointed out.

"I want to thank all of you for helping out while mom's been sick. I'm sorry I haven't helped more," Cate said.

"Hey," Thomas put his arm around Cate, "that's what family is for."

"Yeah, but I can't take turns staying to help take care of mom, cook and clean like you guys do, and I feel guilty," Cate's eyes moistened with tears.

"Cate, you're in Ecuador where God wants you to be. We're here where we are supposed to be and we're doing what we need to do. We're doing it for you too, so let us little sis," Thomas said.

"Cate, we're proud of you." Paul lovingly touched her shoulder, "You're an inspiration to us and your nephews and nieces."

"All of our kids pray for you every day," Keaton told her.

"They tell all of their little friends about you," Hope said.

"Wow, thank you. I love you guys."

"We love you too, sis," Thomas said, for all of them.

"Cate, how'd you get so skinny?" Paul squeezed her shoulder, "Don't you like the food in Ecuador?"

"Yes, I like the food in Ecuador. I've just been a little preoccupied with mom's condition."

"Well, you've got to stop," Keaton demanded, gently.

"I'll be fine now, Now that I see how well mom is doing."

"You'd better be fine. You'd hate for me and Paul to come to Ecuador to kick your tail," Thomas said, in big brother fashion.

"Nice," Cate shook her head.

"It could happen you know," Thomas assured her.

Cate smiled because she knew it was his way of telling her how much he cared about her.

"Anyway, mom's only got three more chemo treatments to go," Paul said.

"And, then comes the radiation," Hope replied.

"Yep, and after that, we're looking forward to hearing that there's no cancer," Keaton added.

"That's what we're praying for and the doctors are very positive." Thomas pointed out.

Cate loved talking to her brothers and their wives. Her brothers, Thomas and Paul were tall, dark haired versions of her dad, right down to their athletic build. They weren't preachers, but they were both leaders in their local churches.

They asked her about Ecuador, her work, and her friends. Cate had written them letters, but they had questions about things which she had not written.

"How's your work going in Ecuador?" Keaton asked.

"It's great; I love teaching there. I love the kids."

"How are David and Sarah?" Thomas asked.

"They're doing well."

"What about the caretaking thing? How's that going?" Hope asked.

"It's great. Sarah's a doll."

"What about your boss, Matthew Kennedy? Didn't he and David help make your trip home possible?" Keaton inquired.

"Yes, they did. Matthew's wonderful."

"Wonderful, huh?" Thomas arched his eyebrows, "Maybe you had better tell us more."

"Matthew is a really good, godly guy. We've been spending time together."

"You have," Keaton said.

"We have."

"And, how does David feel about that?" Paul asked, as Hope tried to shush him.

Blushing a little, Cate answered, "Paul, David and Matthew are very good friends."

Realizing how uncomfortable the question made Cate, Hope poked her husband, "Paul, don't tease your sister like that."

"I'm sorry, Cate. I was kidding."

"It's okay, Paul."

"Well, folks it's getting late and Christmas comes early tomorrow. I think I'll hit the bed," Thomas rose, trying to give his sister a break. He knew how she felt about David. They all did.

After everyone went to bed, Cate found herself thinking about Ecuador. Talking about it had made her homesick for Ecuador, but that didn't make sense, *I 'am' home.*

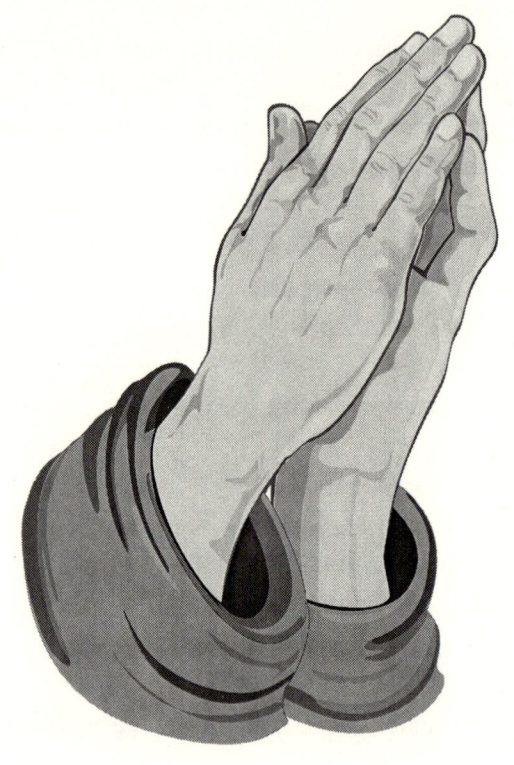

"...the Lord, the fountain of living waters. Heal me, O LORD, and I shall be healed, save me, and I shall be saved for thou art my praise."

Isaiah 17:13-14.

Seventeen

The day after Christmas, her brothers and their families left for home. Cate and her parents hated to see them go.

During her last week at home, Cate spent the time with her parents. She accompanied them to her mother's treatment. Her mother seemed to do better this time, with fewer side effects. Cate learned that her parents knew more about her last few months in Ecuador than she'd realized. "I've enjoyed my time here more than I can say."

"We're glad that you could share the holidays with us," her dad said, as he put his arm around her shoulder and drew her close.

"I'm glad you've put on a few pounds. We knew you were skinny, but we didn't know how skinny," her mom said.

"You knew I was skinny. How?"

Realizing that she had slipped, Cate's mom looked at her dad, who confessed.

"I've been talking to David."

Cate studied her mother and father, "Why… Have you been calling David?"

"I haven't been calling him, he's been calling me."

"Okay," Cate nodded slowly, "he's been calling you. He didn't tell me."

"He was worried about you honey," her mother said. "He called your dad to ask his advice."

"And, if I may ask, what advice did you give him?"

"I told him" her father said in his fatherly tone, "to pray for you and be supportive."

"And, he was."

"I know he was, and Matthew was."

Cate rolled her eyes, "He told you about Matthew?"

"Uh-huh."

"Matthew and David have been great," Cate admitted.

"They both are very fine men," her mother said.

"Yes," Cate agreed, "they are."

"David called us when they had figured out a way to send you home for the holidays. He and Matthew hoped this would be just what you needed. He told us how skinny you were, but we were shocked when we saw you."

"And, what else did he tell you Dad?"

"He told us that you hadn't been sleeping and they were very worried about you. And, we were worried too."

"I'm so sorry. I didn't mean to worry anyone. Mom's illness and other things were so important that prayer became more of a priority than eating and sleeping. But, I'm doing better," Cate patted her stomach. "Seeing mom face-to-face has helped me understand how much God has taken care of her."

"Honey, your mom and I are very glad about the prayer, and what God has been doing in your life. But everyone was worried about you not eating or sleeping."

"My eating and sleeping are fine now." She defiantly reached over and picked up a sugar cookie.

"Yes, we've noticed," her mom said, "and we're glad."

"Mom, I'm amazed at how well you've handled your tribulations. You are truly an example of courage to me."

"And, *you* are truly an example of love and empathy to me and your father."

Her dad nodded, as he hugged her again with arm around her shoulder.

"Honey, we want you to care and pray, but we don't want you to sacrifice your health in the process."

Cate took a bite of her cookie, "I promise," and wiped the crumbs away from her mouth.

"Catie, I appreciate how you stepped in for me and helped your dad prepare for and host the staff party, and all the rest you did to help us prepare for the holidays."

"I enjoyed it. It was fun."

"Quite a difference from how you use to respond to those types of things," her dad said.

"Yeah, but I've grown up."

"We know, we've noticed a confidence and a maturity that wasn't there before Ecuador," her mom said.

"You have a more confident trust in God, and deeper spirituality than when you left," her dad patted her shoulder, "I can see your faith in your eyes."

"I'm glad, but for the last several months I haven't felt very confident in my trust and certainly not very spiritual. Actually, I've felt weak in faith and spent lots of time in Bible study and prayer."

"Catie, it's during those times when the Lord is usually most at work in the lives of his people," her dad said.

Finally, the conversation turned to Cate's love life. Her parents knew that she had been seeing Matthew, but she hadn't really talked about it since she'd been home. There had been too many other things to discuss. Besides, there was the *proposal thing* that she had been praying about, and she was still confused. But, her parents were curious.

"What about Matthew?"

"He's great," she answered. "He's a godly man, understanding, compassionate. You both would like him a lot."

"From all that you've written about him, I'm sure that we would," her dad said.

Cate paused and bit her lip, "I think he's going to ask me to marry him."

"He is?" her mother glanced at Cate's father. "What do you think your answer will be?"

"I don't know. I wish I did."

"Do you love him?" her mom asked.

"I think so, but…," Cate began to answer, but stopped.

"But David," her mother finished her answer and saw Cate nod yes.

"Honey, how are things between David and you?"

"About like they have been for the last six years."

"I'm sorry, honey," her mother said.

"It's okay, mom. I just wish I could get over him. My life would be so much better."

"Are you sure about that?" her dad asked.

"Daddy, there's no hope for us."

"Cate, how can you be so certain?" her mother asked.

"David told me so."

"He did?"

"Yes, he did. Matthew had asked him why he wasn't interested in me and he told him it was because he was an IMB missionary-and I was divorced."

"I see," her mother folded her hands in her lap. "Honey, I'm sorry. I know that hurts."

"Yeah, it does; so you see, I just need to get over him, but I don't know how. And, I don't know what I'm going to do if Matthew asks me to marry him."

"I'm sure you've been praying about it," her dad said.

Cate's shoulders sagged, "Continually."

"We'll pray about it too," her dad said, as her mom nodded affirmatively.

"Thanks; I just wish the Lord would give me some clear guidance in this, and I wish He'd take my feelings for David away," Cate replied.

Her parents knew the situation was painful for Cate. They prayed with her about it. She appreciated their concern, prayers and support.

During her final days at home, Cate cooked meals to help out after she was gone. She made casseroles and things that could be frozen and reheated. She wanted to help all that she could. She also cleaned the house from top to bottom, did laundry and ironed. She wanted to leave them with a clean house and an empty laundry basket.

Eighteen

Her last two days at home were New Years Eve and New Years Day. Her parents insisted that she not spend those days cooking, cleaning, or doing laundry. On New Years Eve, she attend a party at the church and slept in on New Years Day. They ordered take-out instead of cooking and spent the day talking and watching television together. Late in the afternoon, Cate called her brothers and said a tearful goodbye to them and their families. That night she packed for her trip back to Ecuador. She'd leave at eleven o'clock the next morning.

The next morning came too quickly. Very reluctantly, she said a tearful goodbye to her mom, as they exchanged numerous hugs and kisses while her dad put her bags into the car.

"Mom, it's been so wonderful to be with you. I love you so much."
"Same here, darling. Take care of yourself."
"I will. You too,"
"I will."
Cate took a deep breath. "Bye mom."
"Bye, Cate."

Her dad pointed at his watch and reminded her that they had to go. As they drove away, she watched through the rear window as her mom became smaller, smaller, and finally she was out of sight.

Her dad spoke words of wisdom, encouragement and love all the way to the airport. Cate needed to hear everything he had to say.

"Catie, are you still sure Ecuador is where God wants you to be?"

"Yes, Daddy I am," Cate answered, with firm conviction.

"Then, you continue to trust and obey God, and He'll take care of things."

"Yes, Daddy,"

"Catie, you'll be all right now, right?"

"Yes, Daddy, I'll be fine."

"Please say thanks for your mother and me to the people who made the visit home possible."

"I will, Daddy."

"And, Cate," her dad paused as if he was trying find the right words to say.

"Yes, Daddy."

"Catie, remember that there are times we can't figure out what God is doing in certain areas of our lives, but He always knows. He always has a plan. He's always working toward a purpose. Trust him to guide you concerning Matthew, David and everything else," her dad continued, as they arrived at the airport.

"Thanks, Dad, I'll remember and I'll trust Him. I promise."

Her father helped her carry her bags to the terminal and waited for her to check in. After her check in, she proceeded to the metal detectors, but wanted to say one more goodbye to her dad. She turned to see him still standing where she had left him. He was having a conversation with a man who was waiting. His sincere interest in people always amazed Cate. She stood for a moment, simply looking at him, appreciating him. Finally, she caught his eye. He said goodbye to the man and made his way toward Cate for a final farewell.

As they embraced each other, Cate whispered, "Daddy, I don't know what I'd do without you. I appreciate everything you said to me in the car. I needed to hear it all. You always know the right thing to say."

"Thanks, Catie, but I don't always. Sometimes with the Lord's help, I just get lucky."

"Yea?" Cate responded, as she shook her head. "It's not a matter of getting lucky."

"It's not," her dad said, with a grin.

"No, sir, it's not. It's a matter of having the kind of relationship with the Lord that allows Him to use you."

"You just might be right," her dad smiled.

"I am right, and I want to be like that too."

"You are like that, my dear daughter."

"I hope so, Daddy," Cate hugged him one more time.

"Bye Catie."

"Bye Daddy, I'll email you when I get to Ecuador," she walked through the metal detector.

"We'll be waiting to hear from you," her dad yelled, as she began walking down the corridor toward her gate.

Cate found she was excited as the plane touched down. She knew Matthew, David, or both would be waiting to drive her to Peguche. As the plane taxied to the terminal and the departure ramp was connected, Cate retrieved her carry-on from the overhead compartment and waited to deplane. Walking down the corridor toward the international arrival gate, Cate felt happy to be back. As she presented her passport and customs declaration slip, she breathed a deep breath of satisfaction. *I'm home.*

When she walked through the arrival gate, Matthew and David were both standing there with broad smiles. Cate smiled too. As she hugged them both at once, she said, "Thank you, thank you both. You have no idea what the trip meant to me and my family. They made me promise to thank you."

"Well, we don't need to ask if you had a good time, do we?" Matthew responded, as he looked at David and then, Cate.

"It's written all over her face," David said, with a sense of satisfaction.

Cate smiled even more, and said, "It's because of you two and Mr. Randall. I wish I could thank him."

"Well, as a matter of fact, you can. He's standing right behind us," Matthew told her, as he stepped aside so she could see her other benefactor.

As he stepped toward her, Matthew introduced him, "Cate Jones, this is Edward Randall. Edward Randall this is Cate Jones."

"Mr. Randall, I'm so glad to meet you, and I'm grateful for you making my trip home possible. It meant so much to my family and me. They all asked me to thank you," Cate said, with tremendous gratitude.

"You're welcome. I was glad to be able to do it. I hope you found your mother doing much better."

"She is much better. Thank you for asking."

"And, I take it you enjoyed your trip home very much."

"I did indeed, Mr. Randall. I enjoyed it more than I can say."

"I'm glad, Miss Jones. My company and I were glad to help."

"I hate to interrupt," David said, as he pointed to his watch, "but we need to be going. We still have to claim luggage and people are waiting for us at home."

"I'll say goodbye then," Edward replied. "Once again, Miss Jones, it's been nice to meet you and I'm glad things are better at home."

"Thank you again, Mr. Randall."

"My pleasure," he said.

They picked up Cate's luggage, and drove home.

When they arrived in Peguche, Kim and Miss Janet had put together a small welcome home party. Sarah, a few of the teachers from the school, and the Garcias were all waiting to greet Cate.

Nineteen

Christmas break was not over until January sixth, and Cate had a couple of days to adjust to being back in Ecuador and to get prepared to go back to school. She slept until about eight o'clock, had a leisurely breakfast and, checked her e-mail to see if her dad had e-mailed her back from the night before. He had. She smiled as she read his e-mail and the p.s. that her mother had written. All was well. Even though her mother was still sick, things were great with her parents, and things were great with her. Bright sunshine, sapphire blue skies, with a few billowy white clouds beautifully adorned the day. She decided to go for a walk.

Cate loved the fact that a person could walk in the little village of Peguche without concerns for safety. Peguche enjoyed the reputation as one of the safest villages around Otavalo.

She loved the genuine friendliness of the people, and enjoyed chatting with the villagers as she walked. Before her visit to Kansas, she often walked down a secluded path that led to a waterfall, where she felt free to pour her heart out to God.

Today was different. Surely, prayer was just as important, but today she did not have a heavy heart. Therefore, she reached out to those she met on her way with a smile and a warm hello.

Everyone in the small village knew Miss Cate. They still considered her the new teacher. She would have to be there a couple of years to lose the title of *new teacher*, and teaching at the mission school for years and years would be wonderful.

Mrs. Ramos, whose grandson was a student in Cate's class, stopped to ask about her mother's health.

"Miss Cate, your madre is *mucho* better, *si?*"

"*Si, Señora* Ramos. Mi madre seems much better. M*uchas gracias*. How is Juan?"

"*Muy bien*, Miss Cate. Would you like some tea?"

"*Claro que si.*"

They drank tea and talked, about family, school and the village. After twenty minutes, Cate said goodbye and continued her walk.

Once again, Cate breathed in the beauty of her surroundings. Even though she would not have traded anything for the opportunity to be with family during the holidays, she enjoyed being back where she believed God wanted her. In the midst of thoughts, she heard Matthew's voice.

"I figured I'd find you out walking."

"Yep, you know me so well," Cate said, with a little laugh.

"I know you're fond of walking," he increased his pace, "and that you're hard to keep up with."

"Am I now?" Cate playfully bumped him.

A serious expression took over Matthew's face, "Yes, you are, and I'm glad that I found you."

Afraid that something had happened to her mother, Cate stopped, "Is there something wrong?"

He realized he'd scared her with his attempt to be playful, "Nothing's wrong. In fact, everything's right. You're back in Ecuador. That makes everything exactly right."

Cate's worried expression turned to an expression of appreciation for his tender affection.

"That's sweet, Matt."

He pulled her close and hugged her, whispering in her ear, "I'm glad you're home. I've missed you."

Cate responded to his affection and whispered back, "I missed you too."

As he let go of the hug, his eyes found hers, "I wish we were walking in a more secluded spot. I'd like to kiss you."

Cate blushed, embarrassed by what he said. He hugged her tightly again, but this time she did not respond as she had before. Realizing he made her uncomfortable, Matthew released her.

"I'm sorry—I made you uncomfortable."

"It's just," Cate nodded toward a nearby house, where several people were watching them.

"Oh," Matthew grinned, "Is it okay if I hold your hand while we walk?"

"I guess."

He slipped his hand around hers and they began walking again.

They soon ran into David and Sarah. Sarah was skipping while David was holding her hand. When Cate saw them, she called out, "Hello, there. What are you two up to?"

"We're going to *Mama Rosa's* for lunch," David answered.

"Daddy, can Cate and Mr. Matthew come?"

"Sure, if they'd like."

Cate looked at Matthew, and Matthew nodded.

"Yea!" Sarah responded.

Sarah slipped her free hand into Cate's hand while Matthew held Cate's left hand. David held Sarah's right. They laughed and paraded their way to the restaurant.

Like always, Mama Rosa greeted them and escorted them to their favorite table.

"Your table is available. Right this way por favor."

"*Muchas gracias* Mama Rosa, Kim will be joining us, so we will wait to order."

"*Muy bien* Señor David."

Fifteen minutes later, Kim entered the restaurant. "Hey, guys I'd like to introduce you to someone. Could you come outside a minute?"

"Sure," David said, as he got up to go with her. "You heard the woman Matt. Let's go."

Matthew nodded to Cate, "We'll be back shortly."

"Okay," Cate replied.

As they walked toward the door, Matthew turned to Kim, "Now, Kim what's this about?"

"The man standing just outside the door stopped me on my way to the restaurant and asked me about Jesus. I shared the gospel with him and he accepted Christ."

"Kim, that's great."

"Yeah, but there's more," she said, smiling. "He asked me to come to his village and tell his neighbors about Christ. I told him I couldn't, but I knew someone who could."

"You bet you do," David said.

While they were outside meeting with the man, Cate and Sarah entertained themselves.

"What have you been doing today, Baby Girl?"

"Oh nothing, just reading,"

"Just reading?" Cate said.

"Yep, and then, me and Daddy decided to come here for lunch. Daddy invited Miss Kim and when we saw you and Mr. Matthew hugging, I decided to invite you."

"You saw me and Mr. Matthew hugging."

"Uh-huh, Daddy said that we shouldn't watch, but *he* did."

"He did?"

"Yeah, I saw him. Daddy had a sad look on his face."

"A sad look…" Cate turned and looked to the door.

"The kind of sad look he has when he looks at mommy's picture."

Before any further conversation, David, Kim and Matthew returned to the table and began discussing what had happened outside.

"Wow, I really can't believe it," Matthew said.

"Believe what?" Cate asked.

"I can't believe that someone would approach a stranger," Matthew answered.

"Who did that?"

"A *Jivaro* man approached me on the way to the restaurant, and I led him to the Lord," Kim answered.

"That's great," Cate shared Kim's excitement.

"But there's more. He wanted someone to come to his village and share Christ with his neighbors," Kim said.

"I've never seen anyone as happy as he was when David told him that he would be glad to come to his village and tell his people about Jesus," Matthew said.

Mama Rosa interrupted the conversation as she came to the table to take their orders. Mama Rosa told them she'd bring them a surprise or two with their meals.

"Punch, Mama?" Matthew asked.

"Could be, *Señor* Matthew. Maybe, a special dessert also."

"You," Matthew teased, "are a woman after my heart."

Mama Rosa glanced at Cate and a slight smile curled the edge of her lips, "No, *Señor* that is not me."

Kim laughed while Cate flashed an embarrassed grin. Matthew put his arm around Cate and pulled her close as David looked down at the table.

"I will send your food out quickly," Mama Rosa said, as she left for the kitchen.

Once she left, the conversation returned to the *Jivaro* man.

"It's amazing what God can do," Kim said. "I'm humbled that God allowed me to be a part of it."

"Kim, you explained the gospel so clearly that he understood exactly. When I asked him what he would tell his neighbors when they asked about how to become a Christian, I knew he had it exactly right." David applauded her witnessing.

"David, you're going to his village?" Cate said.

"Yes, I am, and Matthew's going too."

Cate looked at Matthew, her hand instinctively touching his arm, "You're going? Along with David?"

"I guess, I am."

"I think Dr. Patterson might want to go too," David said.

Kim sighed, "I wish *I* could go, but I have to stay and teach."

Cate removed her hand from Matthew, and folded it in her lap, "When do you think you'll go?"

"As soon as we can get ready. The man is going to show us the way to his village. It's somewhere on the eastern slopes of the Andes," David's voice clearly indicated his excitement for the upcoming field trip.

"I can't believe he's *Jivaro*," Kim said.

"What does that mean?" Cate asked.

"It means that he is a member of a tribe called *Jivaro*, or the Shear," Matthew answered, "who go back to the days of the Incas."

"They were known," David paused, "for shrinking heads."

Kim swallowed hard, her eyes widening, "They–shrink–heads?"

"Not any more," Matthew felt around his head with his hands, "I don't think."

"Stop that," Cate punched him, "*not* funny."

"A very good thing," Kim said, with relief.

Matthew chuckled, "You girls have no sense of adventure."

"You're right," Kim assured him.

"Kim, there *is* more of a miracle here than you know," David said.

"How's that?"

"The *Jivaro* usually speak *Quechua*. Some speak a little Spanish, but very few speak English. Yours spoke English."

"Only through the providence and grace of God," Matthew's eye briefly glanced upward, "could what happened today happen."

"You mean that God orchestrated the events that caused this English speaking *Jivaro* and I to cross paths," Kim said.

David nodded, "Exactly."

Cate felt the emotion within her; *This is why I'm supposed to be here.* "How exciting!"

"God, is an awesome God," Matthew said.

Sarah had patiently and silently listened to the conversation, but when she heard Matthew say God is an awesome God, it triggered a memory. She began to sing. As she was finished, everyone applauded, Sarah smiled broadly.

Along with a waiter, Mama Rosa came from the kitchen bringing their food. She was always excited to offer them tastes of new dishes to the menu.

"I have brought you a selection of my new dishes. I would be pleased to know how you like them."

"You mean we are guinea pigs, Mama," Matthew smiled at Mama.

"*Si*," Mama smiled back.

David dug into one of the dishes, "I, for one, am most pleased to be Mama Rosa's guinea pig."

Everyone else joined him. Mama anxiously waited for their reaction.

After he had taken a bite, David proclaimed, "*Delicoso.*"

"*Muy bien,*" Cate said.

As he grabbed his glass of water, Matthew said, "*Picante.*"

"Matthew you're a wimp," David said.

Mama Rosa laughed and offered Matthew another dish to taste.

Kim took another bite of the first dish, "*Muy bien,* Mama."

Mama realized that Sarah had been eating steadily without a word. She patted her on the back and said, "*Muy bien, bambina?*"

"*Muy bien, Madre,*" Sarah replied.

Once she was sure each of the new dishes had been taste tested, she thanked them, wished them a good appetite, and returned to the kitchen.

They continued to eat and discuss the visit to the *Jivaro* village.

"When will you be leaving?" Cate asked.

"Maybe tomorrow," David added more food to his plate, "but probably the next day."

Not knowing whether she or Kim would stay, Cate tried to inquire tactfully, "What about Sarah?"

Sarah looked up from her food, and David and Kim looked at each other. "I'll let you know," David offered.

During the conversation, Cate watched Kim reach over and take David's hand.

When David saw Cate watching he looked away, but Kim seemed very comfortable as she held his hand and scooted closer to him. David appeared nervous, and Sarah was unhappy and her face revealed it.

While Kim was oblivious to what was going on with David and Sarah, Cate wasn't. She sensed that there might be trouble in paradise.

As they ate, Matthew slipped his hand over Cate's. This time it was Cate who was uncomfortable, and David was the one watching. Cate refused to look directly at David as Matthew scooted close. That's how the rest of the meal went: Cate looked at Kim, and David looked at Matthew, but not at each other.

Finally, everyone finished, the check was paid, and they began the walk home. Once again, Matthew held Cate's left hand while Sarah held her right, and David held Sarah's right hand while he held Kim's left. Half way home, Matthew, Cate and Sarah dropped behind, as David and Kim walked in front. Each couple made conversation, Sarah offered intermittent comments and Cate watched David and Kim as they walked. She noticed that Kim was holding David's hand more than he was holding hers. *What does it mean? Maybe nothing?*

As Kim and Cate arrived home, Kim asked if they could talk. They sat on the couch and Kim began, "Cate, I wanted to talk to you about–"

"About what?"

"Cate, I'm sorry, but sometimes I'm jealous of you and David and...Sarah."

"Jealous of me?"

"Yes, jealous of you."

The look on Kim's face revealed the extent of her jealousy, and Cate wondered if she *had* noticed something. "But, you don't have to be."

"I know. It's crazy. I know you have Matthew, but sometimes I..."

"Kim–"

"Cate, I know you and David have been friends for years. And, and, if you had wanted to be with him, you would be. Right?"

Before Cate could answer, Kim answered for her, "Of course, that's right, so you must not want him." Kim seemed comforted by answering her own question.

Cate breathed a sigh of relief that she was not going to have to answer, but it didn't last.

With a puzzled look, Kim looked her straight in the eye, "Why don't you want him? He's a great guy."

"Yes, he is, but Matthew's a great guy too." Cate hoped her answer would cause Kim to drop the interrogation, but it didn't.

"Cate, when you first arrived, I sensed there was something more than friendship between you and David. Was I wrong?"

Her tone revealed that she wanted Cate to tell her that she was. She needed reassurance so Cate decided to tell her about her divorce. "Kim, I'm going to tell you something because I think you need to know."

"Okay..."

"I'm divorced. Even if I was interested in David, it couldn't go anywhere."

Shocked and relieved, Kim asked, "I'm sure David knows, but does Matthew?"

"Yes, he does."

Kim narrowed her eyes, "Why didn't you tell me before?"

"It's not something I'm proud of. My husband left me for another woman."

"Oh, I'm sorry."

Cate shrugged, "Me too, but you see now why you shouldn't be worried about me and David."

"Yeah, but I still have a problem. I don't know what to do about Sarah."

"What do you mean?"

"While you were away, visiting your parents, I stayed with her while David was on a trip."

"And…"

"And," Kim sighed, "all she did was talk about you."

"Did you read with her and do the things she likes?"

"Sure, I did, but evidently I didn't do it like you do."

"I'm sorry. I—"

"Cate, I don't know what to do. That little girl loves you like she loved Jenny."

Cate heard Kim's frustration, "Kim, I'm sorry that my relationship with Sarah is causing you problems, but I'm not sorry that she and I have a close relationship."

"I know, I sound awful don't I, but I don't mean too. I love David and I want Sarah to love *me*."

Even though she knew Kim expected to marry David and become Sarah's mother, Cate was startled by actually hearing her say it. She worked hard to hide her true feelings.

"Cate, how did you get so close to Sarah after Jenny died?"

"I was just kind to her, and loved her."

"I can do that," Kim said.

Cate reached out and patted Kim's knee, "Sure, you can."

As those words filled the air, Cate was tangled up inside. *I can't believe I'm helping Kim marry David and become Sarah's mother.*

"Thanks, I feel better now," Kim said.

Cate masked her feelings, "You're welcome."

The phone rang and Kim answered. "Hello–Oh hi, David–Do I want to go with you to the village?–Matthew said that I could?–Dr. and Mrs. Patterson?–Of course, I want to go–When will we leave?–How long?–Sure, I'll let her know–Bye, darling."

Kim hung up the phone, her body radiating excitement, "I get to go to the village with David, and Dr. and Mrs. Patterson."

"That's wonderful," Cate said, "what about Matthew? Isn't he going?"

"He told David that because I led the *Jivaro* man to Christ, he thought that I deserved to go. He would cover my classes if I wanted to go."

"That's great," Cate was envious.

"Oh, one more thing, David wanted to know if you'd stay with Sarah."

"Of course, I'd be glad to."

At this point, for Cate, the trouble in paradise was that Kim was about to leave for several days on a mission trip with David, *While I stay home with the baby.* Even though she did not want to be, Cate was jealous.

Oh God, Cate prayed. *Please help me with this.*

Twenty

During the preparations for the trip, Cate and Kim saw very little of David. However, he did call Kim to make sure that she understood what she should take on the trip.

Once more, Cate had to deal with her feelings of jealousy and envy. She kept talking to God about it, and admitting to Him that she wished that she could be in Kim's place concerning David. She envied the fact that Kim could have a future with David while she could not, and she was jealous of the fact that Kim could say she loved David, while she could not. *Oh, Lord,* Cate prayed. *This is the same old battle. Please help me. Please dear God take my feelings for David away.*

God didn't take her feelings away, but He did provide the grace for her to deal with the envy and jealousy. She was able to watch Kim flit around the house singing and preparing for the trip, while she prepared to stay with Sarah.

The day came for the departure to the *Jivaro* village, and after prayer and appropriate goodbyes, David, and the others loaded their Land Rover and drove away. Matthew, Cate, Sarah, Miss Janet, and Mrs. Garcia waved until they were out of sight.

"I hope they find a lot of open hearts when they get to the village," Miss Janet said.

"Yeah, me too," Matthew agreed.

Knowing the power of prayer, Cate added, "Well, we can help by praying."

Matthew put his arm around her shoulder and hugged her, "You're exactly right."

Sarah slid her hand in Cate's and said, "I can pray too."

Miss Janet patted Sarah's head, "You sure can."

"*Si*, little one, you can pray," Mrs. Garcia added. "Would you like a snack, *mi bambina?*"

"*Si, Señora Garcia, gracias*" Sarah pulled her hand from Cate's and followed Mrs. Garcia into the house.

As she watched them enter the house, Miss Janet observed, "She's such a wonderful little girl."

"Yes, she is," Matthew and Cate agreed.

Miss Janet wiped at her eye, "Jenny would be so proud of her."

Cate turned to look back into the house, "Yes, she would."

Miss Janet asked, "Did you know Jenny well?"

"Yes, I did."

"Jenny was a great person," Matthew said.

Cate thought back to those earlier times, "Yes, she was. I liked her very much."

"I still miss her. I'm sure David does too," Miss Janet replied.

"Yes, he does, but unfortunately that's the past, and now, he's trying to look forward, to the future," Matthew said.

Miss Janet knew what he was implying, "Yes, he is. Maybe he and Kim will have a future together."

A moment of silence fell over the small group. Matthew was the first to speak, "Well, ladies, I hate to leave such good company, but I need to go to the school and take care of some correspondence. Unfortunately, it will not wait until tomorrow."

Miss Janet looked at Cate, "I need to get home too. I have to finish lesson plans for school tomorrow."

Cate knew that Miss Janet was beginning to teach from a new literature book, and commiserated with her. "I guess it *is* difficult to teach from a new literature book."

Miss Janet smiled at Matthew as she answered, "Well, it's not *too* bad. It's that boss of mine that's the problem."

Cate made an appropriate face at Matthew. "I know what you mean."

"Well, I *could* look for two new teachers," Matthew said.

Miss Janet winked at Cate, "Yes, we know, but you couldn't get two as good as us."

"I'm not so sure about that," Matthew teased.

"*I'm* sure, and even if you could replace me, I know you couldn't replace Cate. Matthew, I think it's time I told you something."

"And, what might that be?"

Miss Janet nodded toward Cate, "You were very wise when you hired her. She's a wonderful teacher and a fine young woman. Our school is lucky to have her,"

"I know it," Matthew responded, "I'm glad someone besides me recognizes it."

Red-faced with embarrassment, Cate offered a, "Thank you."

Miss Janet saw Cate's embarrassment, "Cate, I meant what I said. And, Kim and I are lucky to have you as a roommate."

"Thank you, Miss Janet. You're very kind.

"She is very kind," Matthew said, as he winked at Miss Janet. "But, she's also right."

Cate gave a mock curtsey, "Thank you, kind sir."

"You don't take compliments well. Do you?" Matthew asked.

"I guess you could say that."

"You need to work on that," Matthew winked, "I'm sure you're going to hear a lot more as long as I'm around."

"Sweet boy, isn't he?" Miss Janet said.

"Yes, he is," Cate answered, with a smile and a blush.

Matthew accepted the compliment, "I'm sorry, but this sweet boy really does need to go, correspondence will not take care of itself."

"Nor, will my lesson plans," Miss Janet agreed.

"Well, I am sorry to lose such good company, but I understand," Cate said.

"Miss Janet, could this sweet boy walk you home?"

"That would be lovely."

"Well, I guess it really is goodbye, then," Matthew hugged Cate and gave her a little peck on the check.

Miss Janet waved to Cate, "Goodbye dear. I'll see you at school tomorrow." Miss Janet took Matthew's arm and they began their walk down the street.

Cate went in the house to see what Mrs. Garcia and Sarah were doing. Sarah was still having her snack, and Mrs. Garcia was busy preparing dinner. Cate reminded Sarah of her nap time. "Well, Baby Girl, isn't it about time for your *siesta?*"

"*Si, Señorita,*" Sarah answered.

"Are you finished with your snack?"

"*Si.*"

"Well, let's go take a nap then."

"Are you going to take a nap too?" Sarah asked.

"I just might. Mrs. Garcia, do you need me to help you do anything?"

"No, Miss Cate. I am fine. Why don't you take a *siesta* too?"

Cate and Sarah went to the guest room, which was Cate's room when she was there. They lay down for a nap, and Sarah went to sleep while twirling Cate's hair. Sleep did not come as quickly for Cate. She lay there looking at Sarah, *Jenny would be proud of you. Maybe Jenny would even be proud of me, for the way I've taken care of Sarah.* She wondered if Jenny would approve of David and Kim, and concluded that she would. Kim looked a bit like Jenny, blonde like Jenny, but she had blue eyes while Jenny's were green.

Sarah was such a loveable, adorable little girl, and she looked so much like her father, but had ways and mannerisms like Jenny. Cate saw them often, as Sarah went about the business of being a five year old. She wondered if Jenny's ways and mannerisms would be lost as Sarah's memories of her mother grew fainter and fainter, and dropped into her subconscious.

Cate also found herself dealing again with feelings of impending loss. She loved Sarah; loved taking care of her. She loved Sarah needing her, and wanting her to be the one to take care of her, and the fact that David needed her for Sarah as well. But if things continued to go well with David and Kim, neither one would need her. Cate realized she needed to bow out, and give Kim a chance to take her place. That was the right thing to do, the mature thing to do, *but it's so hard.*

Cate hadn't realized she'd fallen asleep until Sarah woke her about two o'clock. They went to the kitchen for some juice and afterwards, watched a Veggie Tales video, and spent the remainder of the day in the backyard.

Spying the Hernandez children who lived next door, Sarah asked, "Can they come and play?"

"If their mother says yes," Cate said

"Will you ask?"

"Why don't you?

"Okay," Sarah hurried next door. She stopped to ask the children, after which she knocked on the door. Mrs. Hernandez came to the door and Sarah asked, "Can Suzi, and Diana come play with me?"

"Yes, they may," Mrs. Hernandez answered, as she waved to Cate.

Cate spent the rest of the afternoon watching the children play. Mrs. Garcia brought lemonade and snacks for the children.

As Mrs. Garcia poured her a glass of lemonade, Cate said, "Thank you for the refreshments."

"You are most welcome."

"I would have thought you would be ready to go home by now. I'm sure that you have a special project you want to complete while David is away."

"Yes, I do, but there was a special project here I wanted to complete first."

"Really, what project?"

"Dinner is ready whenever you want to eat."

"Thank you. That's very thoughtful."

"You are welcome, and there are extra meals in the freezer that can be re-heated."

"Mrs. Garcia, I appreciate that, but you didn't have too."

"I know *mi amiga*, but I wanted to. You can come home after school and relax."

"I appreciate your thoughtfulness."

"Thank you," Mrs. Garcia paused, as an expression of gravity took over her face. She lowered her voice, "And, there is another matter, I would like to speak with you about."

Cate clearly noted Mrs. Garcia's somber tone and mood, "Okay..."

"Maybe, it is none of my business, but I speak from my heart. You are a wonderful woman."

Cate smiled, "Thank you."

"Mr. David, he is a wonderful man of God."

"Yes, he is."

"Miss Kim and Mr. Matthew are fine people," Mrs. Garcia said.

Cate responded with puzzlement, "Yes, they are." *Where is she going with this?*

Mrs, Garcia looked to see that Sarah was out of earshot, "But, I see the way you look at Mr. David."

Cate blushed, "Mrs. Garcia."

"Miss Cate, I do not mean to upset you. I know that you care for each other."

"You're mistaken."

"I see what neither of you mean for anyone to see. I see that you love *him*, not Mr. Matthew, and he loves *you*, not Miss Kim."

"You're wrong," Cate protested.

Mrs. Garcia shook her head, "I do not think so *mi amiga*."

Cate melted, tears welling up in her eyes, "I do love him, Mrs. Garcia, but I don't think he loves me."

"I think you are wrong. I see it when he is with you, and when he speaks of you. You are wrong, and I know the little one, she loves you with all her heart."

"I don't believe that he does, but even if he does, we, we can't…" Cate clutched at her stomach, *Why can't I stop this?*

"But, *mi hija*, if you love him, and he loves you, he should be with you."

Cate took a deep breath, "He can't be with me."

"Why *chica bonita*?"

In tears, Cate explained, "Mrs. Garcia, I'm divorced, and if he married me, he couldn't be a missionary with the agency that sent him. He would lose his ministry here."

"I am sorry, Miss Cate." She reached into her dress and handed a handkerchief to Cate, "I did not mean to make you sad. I should not have spoken."

"It's okay. I know that you meant well," Cate wiped her eyes, "believe me, I wish that it could be as you say."

Mrs. Garcia comforted her, with pats of affection, trying not to draw the children's attention to what was happening. "Miss Cate, I will say no more. I will mention it to no one."

"Thank you and, I appreciate your good intentions," Cate sniffed.

"You are most welcome."

Cate quickly wiped her face when she saw Sarah came running toward them.

"Can we have some more lemonade?"

"Yes, *hija*, I will get more," Mrs. Garcia answered.

"*Muchas gracias* Mrs. Garcia," Sarah said.

"You are welcome, *mi niña*."

After she brought more lemonade, Mrs. Garcia said her goodbyes and went home.

For the rest of the evening, Cate's mind constantly replayed Mrs. Garcia's comments. It was evident to Cate that Kim must have noticed the same thing that Mrs. Garcia had. That was why she had confronted her about David. Cate wondered if Matthew suspected her feelings for David. *Maybe that's why he hasn't proposed to me?* Moreover, she wondered if Mrs. Garcia was right about David's feelings for her. Mrs. Garcia's observations caused her to have hopes-and regrets. Their situation was a 'no win' situation. She wished she could change it but, she knew there was no chance.

"I will never leave thee nor forsake you."

Hebrews 13:5b

And we know that God works all things together for good to them that love God, to them that are the called according to his purposes.

Romans 8:28.

Twenty One

The following day Cate awoke still thinking about her dilemma. She and Sarah gathered up what they needed for the day and went to school.

As she arrived, the first person she met was Matthew. She hoped that she did not appear as guilty as she felt. Mrs. Garcia's knowledge of her true feelings for David made her feel uneasy. She knew that if Matthew found out, he would be hurt, and she didn't want that. She did love him; *at least that's what I keep telling myself.* Anyway, he loved her, and she wanted to be married to a man who truly loved her. But, she could not convince herself to marry Matthew.

Cate welcomed the children to class and focused on her responsibilities, putting the thoughts that plagued her to a backburner. She was grateful for the break from her struggle.

The day was a normal school day. The children were excited about being back, and about seeing Cate. They were eager to learn, and Cate was glad. There was no time to consciously consider Mrs. Garcia's comments.

A few minutes before school was to end, Matthew poked his head in the door and asked to speak with her. As she walked slowly toward him, her sense of guilt took over.

"What are you and Sarah up to tonight?"
She tried hard to sound nonchalant, "Nothing special."
"Is it okay if I come over?"
"After a free meal, huh?"

"That's an added bonus, *if* you're inviting me to dinner, but I really want to spend time with my favorite girl."

Cate had no excuse to decline, "We're having leftovers."

"That sounds great."

"Okay, we'll eat about five."

When the bell rang, Matthew went to his office as Cate gathered up Sarah and started for home. Even though Sarah vied for her attention, her fear that Matthew might sense her inner turmoil captured her thoughts. Suddenly, a new fear took over, what if Matthew was coming over to propose? She prayed silently, but fervently for God's help.

When they arrived home, both changed clothes and relaxed for a few minutes, by watching a Veggie Tales video. Before the video ended, Cate went to the kitchen to re-heat some of the food Mrs. Garcia had prepared.

Matthew arrived at five on the dot. When he knocked, Sarah ran to open the door.

"Hello, Mr. Matthew. Dinner is ready."

"Very good, Miss Sarah, will you escort me to the table?" Matthew reached out his hand, for Sarah to walk him to the table. As they entered the kitchen, he saw Cate putting the final touches to the meal. "It looks great. I'm hungry."

"Dinner is served, Mr. Kennedy."

"Bragging about your cooking skills, huh," Matthew winked.

"Bragging about Mrs. Garcia's cooking skills." Cate corrected, as she asked Sarah to say grace.

Small talk about school and the trip to the *Jivaro* village made up dinner conversation, after which Cate did dishes, while Matthew helped Sarah practice writing her letters and numbers. Once finished with dishes and homework, they played Chinese checkers. Sarah won two games out of three.

Eight o'clock was Sarah's bedtime. As the clock struck eight, Sarah excused herself so she could put on her pajamas. When she came back, she said goodnight to Matthew and asked Cate to tuck her in.

"I'll be back shortly," Cate said.

As Cate tucked her in, Sarah grabbed Cate around the neck, "I love you Cate."

"I love you too, Baby Girl. Sweet dreams."

Cate made her way back to the living room, dreading being alone with Matthew.

When he saw her, he smiled, "Sarah's such a wonderful girl."

"Yes, she is."

Matthew's face took on a serious look and Cate said a silent prayer, *Oh, God no. Please no.* But, her prayer was not answered.

"Cate," Matthew said, as he took her hand. "Do you remember me telling you that once your mother was better that I wanted to talk to you about something?"

Afraid to look him in the eye, Cate stared at the floor, whispering, "Yes."

"Cate, I know that this should be done in a more romantic atmosphere, but I couldn't wait any longer."

Cate sighed and interrupted, "Oh, Matthew."

"Please, let me finish," he dropped to one knee.

Cate looked up and reluctantly, barely above a whisper, responded, "Okay."

"Cate, I love you more than I can say, and I want you to be my wife. Will you please marry me?"

She looked away, all the breath left her body, "Matthew…"

He was taken aback by her lack of an enthusiastic 'yes', "Cate, I know that you care for me."

"Yes, I do, I really do… But I–I can't marry you, not right now."

"Why?"

"Matthew, there is *so much* that you don't know about me."

"I know enough," he rose from his knee, and sat beside her.

"I don't think that's true. I don't think it's true at all."

He bent down trying to make eye contact, "If you think there's more I need to know, then tell me."

"I think we need more time to get to know each other."

"You mean *you* need more time." He sat erect, his tone betraying his hurt, "I don't."

"Yes, I guess, I mean-I need more time."

"But, you're not saying *no*. Are you? You're just saying… not now?"

Cate bit her lip and stared at the floor, "I'm saying not now."

"I can live with *not now*, because that means *maybe later*," he kissed her gently on the cheek.

"I'm sorry, Matthew."

"You don't have anything to be sorry about. I'll wait—until you *are* ready." He gently placed his hand under her chin, "Please look at me."

Cate slowly raised her head and looked at him.

Now he could see clearly the pain on her face. "Cate," he tenderly touched her face with his hand.

Cate placed her hand on his, "Thank you for being so understanding,"

"Sure," he looked at his watch. "I probably ought to be going. I need to get to school early tomorrow."

"Matthew, I'm sorry."

"I told you, it's all right."

"I'm not sure it really is," Cate took his hand and walked him to the door.

"Look, I love you, and I'd marry you tomorrow if I could, but if you need more time, you've got it. I want you to be sure. I want our marriage to last forever," he kissed her softly and said goodnight.

As she closed the door, Cate thanked God that Matthew was the type of man that he was. She prayed that God would help her stop loving David, and help her love Matthew.

She fell asleep that night praying and looking at the mountains in the distance. They never failed to remind her that God was an ever-present source of strength and help. Once again, she committed her life unreservedly to Him.

The next morning she awoke with a sense of peace. She might not know what her future held, but she knew *who* held it. That was enough for her.

The days following Matthew's proposal were busy. Not only did she have her regular teaching load, she had volunteered to supervise the kindergarten through second grade musical presentation for National Community Day on February 27. That took extra planning and meetings after school, and prevented her from spending time with Matthew.

David, Kim, Dr. and Mrs. Patterson came home the following Saturday. They had been gone for ten days and were excited about the results of their trip. Matthew, Cate, and Sarah listened with great interest as everyone recounted the events of the past ten days.

During the visit to the village, the group shared the gospel while the *Jivaro* man and others served as interpreters. By the end of that first day, more than 100 people had accepted Christ, and at week's end one thousand villagers had become Christians. David and Dr. Patterson promised to return in two weeks.

"It was a life changing experience," Kim said.

"For all of us," Dr. Patterson added.

"I've had the Lord bless my efforts in great ways before," David said, "but this is the first massive outpouring of His Spirit that I've been privileged to be a part of."

Touched by the group's excitement, Matthew said, "It must have been awesome."

Dr. Patterson nodded, "It was like our own Pentecost."

"It was wonderful," Mrs. Patterson said.

Matthew looked at David, "Did you say you were returning in about two weeks?"

"Yes, I did."

"Who's going this time?"

"If you're wondering if you'll have to cover my classes again, the answer is no," Kim answered.

"Probably, Dr. Patterson and I will go." David smiled at Matthew, "Do I hear your offer to join us?"

"You heard wishful thinking," Matthew answered.

"We'd love to have you," David said, as Dr. Patterson nodded in agreement.

"I wish I could, but with National Community Day coming up I have a lot to do."

"National Community Day!" Kim threw up her hands, "I totally forgot about that. I'm going to be so far behind at school."

"You *would* be, *if* you hadn't had a super substitute covering your classes," Matthew said.

"And, who was that super sub?"

"Me of course," Matthew answered, with a grin.

"You?"

"Me."

"Thanks boss,'" Kim hugged him, after receiving a nod of permission from Cate.

Mr. Patterson looked at his watch and stood, "I'm afraid we must be going."

"Are you sure you won't stay for lunch?" Cate asked.

"Thank you, but if we don't leave now, we won't get home until late afternoon," Dr. Patterson said.

"I'll walk you out," David offered. Sarah followed her daddy and the Pattersons out the door.

Kim turned to Matthew, "Anything interesting happen while we were gone?"

Immediately on hearing Kim's question, Cate and Matthew locked gazes. Matthew thought about his proposal to Cate, "Uh, nothing at all."

"Well, since you two are such good friends, *I* have an announcement." Kim's eyes sparkled with excitement, "While we were gone, David and I talked about marriage."

The words were like arrows through Cate's heart. There was an immediate visceral reaction, her heart began to beat rapidly, she felt flushed and faint. She tried to steady herself.

"That's great," Matthew said, as he looked toward Cate.

"I thought our discussion of marriage might give *you two* the same idea," Kim smiled at Cate and Matthew.

Matthew glanced at Cate, "We're doing just fine the way we are—for now."

Their discussion was interrupted as David and Sarah entered. Sarah ran to her room to play, and David joined the others in the living room.

"Well, I'm surprised at you Mr. Barnes. I can't believe that you're considering getting married without talking to me first," Matthew said.

"Huh?"

"I told them what we talked about," Kim said. "I told them we talked about getting married."

David's face became pale and he took an irritated breath, "Kim!"

"I know we said we'd keep it between us until we figured things out, but I didn't think you'd mind me telling Cate and Matthew," Kim said.

"We won't say anything," Matthew held up his hand, "Will we Cate?"

Still shocked by Kim's announcement, Cate shook her head in agreement.

"See, it's okay," Kim said.

Throughout the conversation, David never looked at Cate. She was glad no one looked too closely; she was afraid of what they might see.

David swallowed hard and changed the subject, "Did anything happen while we were gone?"

"I've already asked and they said no," Kim answered.

Matthew could see David seemed irritated with Kim so he intervened. "Pastor Luis will be glad that you're back. He's been anxious to hear about your trip."

"And I'm anxious to tell him, but it'll have to wait." David relaxed at this new discussion, "I'm driving into Quito tomorrow to talk to Dr. Patterson."

"Why, didn't you talk to him before he left?" Kim asked.

"He needed to get home today. I asked if I could drive in tomorrow." David's answer to Kim was curt.

It was quite apparent to Matthew that Kim and David weren't very happy with each other. He decided it was time for Cate and him to leave. "Cate, are you ready to go?"

"Yes, I'll get my things."

As Cate was getting her things from the bedroom, David came to the door. He avoided eye contact, "Can Sarah stay with you tomorrow while I'm in Quito?"

"Sure, she can."

"Thanks," David turned and walked back to the living room.

After they left, Kim tried to smooth things over with David, "Can I go with you to Quito tomorrow?"

"No, I'm sorry. I need to make this trip alone."

"Why?"

David answered, obviously irritated, "I just do."

"Why are you mad at me?"

"Kim, I'm not mad at you."

"Well, it sure sounds like it."

"I'm not mad. Could we please drop the subject?

"Are you angry about me telling Cate and Matthew?"

"Kim, please, can we just drop this whole thing."

"David, we need to talk this out."

"No, we don't. Please, just leave it alone."

"I don't want to."

David turned quickly and locked eyes with Kim, "Well, I do."

Kim took a step back and bit her lip to keep it from quivering.

"I'm sorry, but I'm tired." David reached out to touch her, "We'll talk when I get back tomorrow."

Kim backed further away, swallowed her tears, and stormed out the door. David didn't follow.

Twenty Two

Early the next morning, David dropped Sarah off at Cate's house and drove to Quito. He met Dr. Patterson at his church, and after the service, Dr. and Mrs. Patterson invited him to their home for lunch.

When lunch was finished David went with Dr. Patterson to the study. David paced the room, "Dr. Patterson, I don't even know how to begin."

"Begin anywhere you wish, my boy," Dr. Patterson's tone was fatherly.

"Dr. Patterson, I need your wisdom, and guidance. Even though the IMB frowns on dating on the mission field, Kim Davis and I have developed a, uh, close relationship."

"You two have known each other from the beginning of your mission work. Isn't that true?"

"Yes, sir, it is."

"If you're worried about violating IMB policy, Peguche does not lend itself to dating. Therefore, I don't believe you have to worry."

"The problem is Kim," David stopped pacing and took a seat in the chair facing Dr. Patterson. "She, she wants to get married, but I don't."

"Hmm," Dr. Patterson drummed the arm of his chair with his fingers. "Have you told her?"

"No, as a matter of fact, it seems I've let her think that I feel the same way."

"Why would you do that?"

David threw up his hands, "Because I'm a coward."

"My boy," Dr. Patterson chuckled, "you'll have to explain that."

"Kim is an attractive Christian woman, she's a good person, and I *do* care about her, but not enough to marry her. I've tried to tell her tactfully."

"Tact did not work?" Dr. Patterson studied David for a moment. "Sometimes we only see and hear what we want to. I take it Kim was not receptive to your hints?"

"No, sir."

"Maybe, you should try the direct approach."

"I'm not sure that'll work. She wants to get married-to me. Anyway, I can't bring myself to hurt her."

"I see. It's understandable, we don't want to bring pain and grief into other's lives. You're a good person, David, of course you don't want to hurt her."

"But, that's not all," David took a deep breath. "I need your advice, about Matthew and Cate."

"Matthew and Cate?" Dr. Patterson replied, with obvious perplexity.

"Dr. Patterson, I need to tell you something that no one else knows. I love Cate."

"Cate? And how does she feel about you?"

"I don't really know," David answered. "I wish I did, then again…"

"If you love Cate, why are you involved with Kim?"

David shook his head, "I'm with Kim because I can't be with Cate."

"Why?"

"Because she's divorced."

"Really?"

"Yes sir, but it wasn't her fault. Her husband abandoned her for another woman."

Dr. Patterson was silent. As one accustomed to counseling others he knew that silence often prompted the other to open up more.

David squirmed in his chair, "There's more. I was engaged to Cate, but she broke our engagement. She married this guy, Justin, and I married Jenny. When Jenny died and I went back home to Kansas, our paths crossed again. She helped Sarah deal with Jenny's death, and we became friends again. When she told me God was calling her to serve as a teacher at a mission school and Matthew told me that he needed a teacher, I put them in touch with each other, and I asked her to be Sarah's caretaker while I was away. Even before we got here I realized that I loved her now more than I ever did. But I asked God to take my feelings for her away, because I knew her divorce prevented us from having a future together."

"So, this love for Cate is *not* a passing fancy," Dr Patterson leaned forward, establishing a closer connection with David.

"No, it's not. I've tried to get over her." David sat back in his chair and stared out the window, "I even encouraged Matthew to pursue her."

"And, you're positive that you have no future together?"

"Dr. Patterson, you know the rules of the IMB."

"Indeed I do."

"I know for certain that God has called me to serve him as a missionary, and at this point as a church planter. If I married Cate, I'd lose the ministry that I have, and I can't do that. Regardless of how I feel about Cate, I have to be faithful to God and His calling."

"It's quite a dilemma. Isn't it?" Dr. Patterson took out his handkerchief and cleaned his glasses. "You're all good Christian people doing God's work, and you all care for one another."

"Yes, sir, it is. I never meant for things to turn out like this. I thought I could get over Cate with Kim, but it didn't work. And now Matthew intends to ask Cate to marry him and if she says yes," David ran his hands through his hair, "I don't know what I'll do."

"What if Cate says no? Where would that leave her-and you?"

"What do you mean?"

"Are you going to tell Kim that you can't marry her?" Dr. Patterson's voice took on a new firmness, "are you going to continue to have Cate take care of your child and love her from afar? Just where do you see this whole thing going?"

"I don't know. I guess I'll wait to see what Cate and Matthew do, and then, I'll- figure it out."

Dr. Patterson furrowed his eyebrows and crinkled his nose. "Are

you saying that you might marry Kim by default?"

"I'm saying, I don't know."

"David, you came to me for advice, so I'm going to give it to you, and it won't be anything you don't already know. God never meant for marriage to be a consolation prize. What you do about marrying Kim is your business, but you shouldn't determine what you do, by what Cate and Matthew do. If you love Cate like you say, you shouldn't marry Kim. It wouldn't be fair to Kim."

David knew that Dr. Patterson was advising him as a father would his son; he could sense his compassion. "You're right. I knew you'd know what to say. I've been letting my emotions control me, and I do know better."

"David, God has not only called you to missions. He's called you to be Christ-like, even in this, and you must discern how He wants you to do that with Kim, Matthew and Cate. You're not just deciding about *your* love life. You're deciding about your life and theirs. No matter how tough it gets, be faithful to God and His leading, and He will bless you."

"Yes, sir, thank you sir for reminding me."

"Let me say one last thing. I've heard you say that you have tried to deal with all of this in various ways. I've heard you say you got involved with Kim because Cate was involved with Matthew. I've heard talk about loving Cate and praying that God would take it away. I've heard you say that you fixed her up with Matthew because you knew you couldn't marry her. What I *haven't* heard you say is that you have surrendered the matter to God. You've been trying to fix things, or tell God how to fix things. Why don't you consider putting it into His hands and allowing Him to handle it however He sees fit."

They ended their conversation with a time of prayer. David said goodbye to Mrs. Patterson and began his drive back to Peguche.

He arrived at Peguche in time for the evening service, and sat with Matthew, Cate, Sarah, Kim, and Miss Janet.

After the service, he asked Cate if she would watch Sarah a little longer, so he and Kim could go for a walk.

As they were walking, he tried to summon the courage to say the words he had practiced during his drive from Quito. He'd prayed that God would give him the wisdom and strength to tactfully and honestly explain to Kim his position on getting married.

Kim spoke first, "I'm sorry about last night."

"Me too,"

"Did your visit with Dr. Patterson go well?"

"Very well."

By his tone, manner, and the preoccupied look on his face, Kim knew things still weren't right between them. She chose not to pursue it, deciding to let him tell her if he wanted to.

"How was the drive back?"

"It was fine," he summoned his courage. "Kim, I need to confess something to you."

Fearfully, Kim replied, "Okay,"

David paused, and sighed, as a tortured look overtook his face. He watched Kim brace herself for what was coming. He sighed heavily and paused before he spoke. "Kim, I owe you an apology."

"For what?"

"For allowing you to think that I wanted to get married, I don't."

"You don't?"

"I don't."

Kim wiped at her eyes, "Are you breaking up with me?"

"Not necessarily."

"Not necessarily?" She shrugged her shoulders and threw her hands in the air, "What exactly does that mean?"

"We can still spend time together," David said, "and go places together, but you need to understand that I don't want to marry you."

"Why? Is there something wrong with me? Something I can-"

"No. There's *nothing* wrong with you." David closed his eyes, searching for the courage and compassion to see this through. "I'm simply not interested in marriage."

Kim was hurt and unhappy with his explanation. The desire to be married consumed her, and David's words crushed her. She understood, but didn't like it: he wanted the question of marriage off the table. "You're saying you just want to be friends."

"That's right."

"David, I'm not sure I can do that."

"Kim, I'm sorry but that's all that I'm prepared to offer."

Silence followed. Neither one spoke as they walked toward her home. Everything had been said.

Upon arriving, she opened the front door, walked to her room and closed the door without saying goodnight. David went into the living room to retrieve Sarah.

Cate couldn't miss the tension, "Is everything all right?"

"It will be," David gathered up Sarah's things. "Thank you for watching Sarah."

"My pleasure, we had fun didn't we little girl?"

"We sure did," Sarah answered.

"I'm glad. Are you ready to go home?"

"Yeah, Daddy,"

"Tell Cate goodbye."

"Goodbye, Cate. See you tomorrow," Sarah took her daddy's hand.

"Sweet dreams, Baby Girl."

"Bye, Cate," David said, as he walked toward the door.

"Bye, see you later."

As David walked home that night, he felt great relief. He knew that Kim was upset with him, and he didn't know if she would ever want his friendship again. But, he knew that he had been obedient to God, and he knew that he'd done Kim a favor. She was too nice a woman to be a consolation prize.

Twenty Three

The next day Cate was about to go in to breakfast when Miss Janet warned her that Kim was in a foul mood. "I don't know what happened last night, but evidently there's been trouble in paradise. I'd tread lightly." Miss Janet nodded toward Kim's bedroom, "She's mad at the world."

"Yeah," Cate remembered the previous evening, "I noticed there was something wrong when she and David came back from their walk. I wonder what happened."

"I'm sure Kim will tell us if she wants us to know," Miss Janet went to her room to get ready for school.

When Cate entered the kitchen, she said 'good morning', and Kim grunted good morning in return. Cate ate breakfast and left Kim picking at her breakfast while staring into her plate.

Miss Janet returned and reminded them it was almost time to leave for school. Realizing how down she was, Miss Janet decided to try and help. "I know something's wrong. Is there anything that I can do?"

"I'd rather not talk about it," Kim stared morosely at her uneaten breakfast.

"Okay, but if you need a listening ear, I'm available."

"Thanks," Kim rose from the table and left.

Cate watched the scene unfold, "Kim is going to school today…. right?"

"Yes, she is," Miss Janet said, "She should be ready in a few minutes."

"Good."

"She's really preoccupied with something."

"I know." *I wonder if it involves David?* "I'm worried about her."

"Me too. When she came in for breakfast, her tone was so angry I decided to leave it alone. When I spoke to her a minute ago, her anger had turned to hurt and sadness. I asked what was wrong," Miss Janet's voice held its own sadness, "but she said that she didn't want to talk about it."

"Well, I guess, all we can do is be supportive and ready to listen if she wants to talk."

"That's right," Miss Janet agreed, as Kim walked out dressed and ready to leave for school.

Except for an occasional comment by Miss Janet or Cate, the walk to school was silent. Kim was obviously preoccupied and oblivious to everything.

By the end of the day, and throughout the week, nothing changed. Kim moped around, refusing to let either Cate or Miss Janet know what was wrong. They continued to respect her privacy, but decided that a change of scenery might do her good, and took her into Otavalo to the market.

Cate borrowed Matthew's car so they could get an early start. They wanted to arrive before the market became too crowded. They planned to window shop, enjoy the food, and take in the performances of the local musicians and dancers.

Everything was going according to schedule and Kim seemed to be enjoying herself, when they heard a voice call from the crowd,

"Cate…Cate…"

They turned to see a young man hurrying toward them.

"It *is* you!" he exclaimed, as he approached Cate and looked at her squarely.

"Tommy!" Cate yelled. *Tommy! Justin's younger brother-here-in Ecuador. Oh no!*

"Fancy meeting you here," Tommy grabbed Cate's shoulders.

"I could say the same thing," Cate said, as Miss Janet and Kim stood by watching.

Cate's pulse beat rapidly as she searched for what to say. *Is it time for me to reveal more of my past than Miss Janet or Kim know?* Tommy decided for her as he introduced himself, "Hello, I'm Thomas Timmons."

Cate realized she had not introduced her companions, "I'm sorry. Tommy Timmons may I introduce two of my colleagues, Kim Davis and Janet Cook."

"Nice to meet you ladies," he turned to three young men who had been following behind him. "Fellas, may I introduce you to Cate Timmons, Kim Davis, and Janet Cook, and ladies, may I introduce you to James Lovett, Austin Black and John Minery."

"Cate? Cate Timmons?" Austin Black repeated, as he made Cate's acquaintance.

"It's Cate *Jones*," Cate corrected, as she and the others exchanged hellos. Through a quick side-glance, she saw the puzzled look on Miss Janet's face.

"Hey Tommy," James asked, "how do *you* know such a beautiful lady," he nodded at Cate, "and why did you call her Timmons?"

Tommy shrugged, "She used to be my sister-in-law." Cate took another quick side-glance toward Miss Janet, who now had a look of total shock on her face.

"Used to be your sister-in-law?" John Minery echoed.

Tommy hugged Cate, "Yeah, my brain-dead brother left her for another woman. By the way, Cate, I really mean that. I think Justin was crazy to let you get away."

"Thank you—Tommy," Cate caught a glimpse of Miss Janet, who was taking it all in.

"You're welcome. So what, you're down here on vacation or something?"

"I'm actually teaching at a mission school nearby."

"Good for you. I always knew you were that kind of person."

"What are *you* doing here?" Cate asked.

"We took some time off from school. We thought we'd take advantage of the wonderful weather down here and do a little bicycling and backpacking."

"It *is* a beautiful country," Cate said.

"It sure is."

"When did you get down?" Kim asked.

Cate was thankful she joined the conversation. Both she and Miss Janet had been noticeably silent ever since Tommy had made his announcement that Cate was his former sister-in-law.

"We've been here a couple of days. We flew from New Orleans to Quito and are going to bike down the American Way to Cuenca, spend a few days sightseeing and catch a flight back home on March ninth," Tommy answered.

"You'll enjoy the scenery very much. Be sure and visit one of the historical haciendas before you leave," Miss Janet said, breaking her silence.

"Thanks for the suggestion. That's a great idea," Austin replied.

"Well, I guess we'd better let you ladies get back to your shopping," Tommy said.

"It's been great to see you Tommy. I wish you all the best," Cate hugged him bye.

"Yeah, you too," Tommy hugged her back.

"Fellas, it was nice to meet each of you. Take care of this boy, won't you?" Cate added.

"We always do anything a beautiful lady asks," John Minery joked.

Miss Janet and Kim joined in the goodbyes as each group went their separate way. Cate was anxious to know what Miss Janet was going to say. She didn't have to wait long to find out.

Miss Janet snapped her purse shut, "Let's call it a day."

"But, it's only early afternoon," Cate waved at the vendors.

"Why don't we have lunch-and a nice talk?" Kim suggested.

"I'd like to go home now," Miss Janet demanded, rather adamantly.

"Come on, Miss Janet, please. Let's have a late lunch at this open air café," Kim insisted, as she sat down at a table.

Reluctantly, Miss Janet sat down, and seeing that Miss Janet was quite agitated, Cate nervously sat down. The server came and took their orders. Though Miss Janet's body language was shouting, several moments passed without anyone saying anything. Finally, she broached the subject, repressed anger in her voice.

"So, Cate, why have you never told us that you were—divorced?"

Cate took a deep breath, *This had to happen sometime*. "It's not something that I'm proud of."

"I would certainly hope not," Miss Janet responded.

"I'm sorry that you're upset," Cate struggled to remain calm, "but that part of my past is something that's hard for me to talk about."

"Hard for you to talk about?" Or something you're trying to hide?"

"No! I *wasn't* trying to hide it," Cate sat tall in her chair, "but neither do I wish to openly talk about it."

"I would imagine *not*, since it would disqualify you to teach at the mission school."

"That's not why I didn't tell you, and it didn't disqualify me. *Matthew* knows. He knew when he hired me."

"Matthew knew," Miss Janet's eyes widened, "and he still hired you?"

"Yes, he did," Cate fought to maintain her composure.

Miss Janet rolled her eyes. "What in the world was he thinking?"

"Miss Janet, I don't understand why you are so upset."

"Why *are* you so upset?" Kim asked Miss Janet.

"I'm upset because," she paused-and looked at Cate, "*she* passed herself off as someone she isn't."

Cate's mouth flew open at the fierceness of Miss Janet's attack.

"*How* did I do that?"

"You passed yourself off as a dedicated, single young Christian woman," Miss Janet answered, with concentrated anger.

"Miss Janet, she *is* a dedicated, single young Christian woman," Kim attempted to mediate the situation. "The children love her, the villagers love her."

Miss Janet's eyes flashed with anger, "No, she's a young *divorced* woman, who passed herself off as a single woman."

Calmly, Cate said, "I didn't try to pass myself off as anything."

"A divorced woman is *not* a proper teacher, not according to mission rules."

"A few days ago, you told me that the school was lucky to have me."

"That—was *before* I knew you were divorced."

"Miss Janet, I can't change the fact that I'm divorced, but it's not the unpardonable sin. God forgives divorce, and God called me to teach in a mission school," Cate desperately tried to make Miss Janet understand.

Miss Janet rolled her eyes, "I don't believe God calls divorced people to missions to teach young and impressionable children."

"Miss Janet, we've lived with Cate for seven months. You know what kind of person she is," Kim tried to reason with her.

"I don't believe I *do* know her."

Cate shook her head, "How can you say that?"

"Because it's true, you're not the person that I thought you were," Miss Janet answered.

"Yes, I am. Miss Janet, I promise I am."

Miss Janet was unmoved. "I'm sorry, but you're not."

"What can I do to prove it to you?" Cate pleaded.

"I don't believe there is anything you could do-short of leaving the mission school."

Cate's mouth and eyes were both wide open, but she couldn't form any words.

Kim couldn't believe what she heard, "Surely, you don't mean that."

Miss Janet was filled with self-righteousness, "I do, and the sooner she leaves the better."

"But, Cate's a great teacher, and we need her."

"She's a *divorced* teacher. It's against the rules, against–the–rules."

The server brought the food; but no one ate. Miss Janet sat at one end of the table rigidly guarding her plate. Cate sat at the other end, her head down and tears falling in her food. Kim sat in the middle wondering how she could bring about reconciliation. Finally, she decided that at this point it wasn't possible. Kim asked the server for the check, paid the bill, and suggested that they return to Peguche.

The short drive home seemed to last for an eternity, and the silence was deafening. Kim drove, Miss Janet sat resolutely in the back seat, and Cate sat dejected in the front seat. Kim prayed for the situation all the way home.

When they arrived home, Miss Janet promptly got out of the car and stormed into the house while Kim and Cate took Matthew's car home. Kim asked, "Cate, are you all right?"

"No."

"I'm so sorry about Miss Janet's attitude."

"Me too, but I don't know what to do about it."

"Just give it time. I'm sure she'll see that she's over-reacted," Kim gave a half-smile. "She's a good Christian woman, compassionate, forgiving." *At least I thought so.*

"But, what if she doesn't? It hurt to hear all of those things she said, and to know her opinion of me."

"I know, but she'll come to her senses, just give her time."

"I hope you're right, but there's something else that really bothers me."

"What?"

"Did Matthew really hire me in violation of mission rules?"

"I don't know." Kim turned to look at Cate, "I don't know about any rules like that, but it wouldn't have affected *my* hiring you."

"I have to know," Cate said.

Matthew met them as they parked the car. He saw their anguished faces, "What's wrong?"

Cate walked up to him, "Matthew, did you hire me in violation of the mission rules?"

He held up his hands, "Whoa! Where did that come from?"

"Miss Janet said the rule is that a divorced person can't teach at the mission school. Is-that-right?"

"That… It was my father's policy, but I don't think it's written down anywhere."

"So, Miss Janet was right," Cate sighed.

"No, she's not. *I'm* the head of the school and the mission agency. I decide policy, not my father."

Cate seemed to collapse into herself, "But, technically, it's still your father's organization and therefore, written or not, his rules apply."

Matthew grabbed her shoulders, "No, Cate that's not correct."

Cate shook her head, "Yeah, it is, and I'm sure if he knew, your father would be terribly upset with you."

"*I* make the decisions here, not my father."

"But, I don't think he'd approve of your hiring me," Cate's teary eyes found Matthew's, "and I don't want to cause trouble between you two."

Matthew held her at arm's length, to get a good look at her, "You're thinking about resigning. Aren't you?"

Cate tearfully nodded, "Yes".

Looking to Kim for help, Matthew pleaded, "Tell her Kim. I'm running things, so *I* call the shots."

"He's right," Kim nodded. "He's been running the school for the last three years. Surely, he has the authority to decide policy."

Matthew pleaded, "Don't resign. I promise; my hiring you was okay."

Cate avoided his eyes, and remained silent.

"Please, Cate. Listen to him. Just give the situation time," Kim said.

Matthew gently touched Cate's chin, turning her face to him, "She's right, Cate. Just give the situation time. I'll talk to Miss Janet. Everything will be okay."

Although Cate agreed, the next day things were the same. Miss Janet refused to go to church with Kim and Cate. She brooded all day. On Monday she stormed into Matthew's office and confronted him about Cate. "Matthew Kennedy, I'm disappointed in you."

Matthew sat back in his chair and folded his hands, "About…"

"Don't play dumb with me. I'm sure that Cate told you about Saturday."

"Yes, she did, and I must say, I'm a little disappointed in you too."

Bristling with anger, Miss Janet responded, "Don't try to turn this thing around. You know you had no business hiring her."

Matthew rose and offered a chair to Miss Janet. "Look, I'm the head of this school and the mission agency. I have the authority to hire whomever I think is right for this school." Matthew spoke with calm determination.

Miss Janet reluctantly sat, her eyes flashing with anger, "Your father would've never considered her."

"You don't *know* that—and neither do I." Matthew remained polite, but firm.

"Yes, I do. Your father's rule was no divorced teachers in the mission school."

With anger of his own shining through, Matthew continued, "Miss Janet, my father is no longer in charge. I am."

Miss Janet's voice rose, "The rule always has been no divorced teachers. It's biblical, and traditional."

Matthew arrested his anger and tried to de-escalate the situation, "I don't understand your attitude at all. You know what kind of person Cate is. How can you act this way?"

"I'm trying to protect this school and its reputation. I *know* how it's supposed to operate, even if you don't!"

"I cannot see how Cate Jones is going to hurt this school's reputation. She is one of the godliness women I know."

Miss Janet shook her finger at Matthew, "That woman has you hoodwinked. If she is such a godly woman, why did her husband leave?"

"Maybe, because *he* was such an ungodly man."

"Do you even know the particulars of why she got divorced?"

"Do you?"

"No, I do not, and I don't want to," Miss Janet sat rigid in her chair, her arms tightly crossed.

"That's the problem."

"No, the problem is *that woman*."

His anger took hold again, "No, she's *not* the problem, Miss Janet. You are."

Matching his intensity, Miss Janet responded, "The problem is you violated mission rules when you hired someone unfit to teach here."

Matthew carefully considered his next words, "If you are not happy with my decisions as headmaster, maybe you ought to think about leaving the school."

"I can not believe you're making this about me. She's the one! I came in here with good intentions. Now you're trying to fire me, instead of her."

"I'm not trying to fire you. I'm trying to get your attention, to get you to calm down and see my side of things—and Cate's side."

Miss Janet's voice was hard as flint, "I won't abandon my convictions to accommodate *your* policy."

"I'm not asking you to. I'm asking you to be compassionate and forgiving. Cate's divorce was not her fault. Her husband lied to her about being a Christian, began seeing another woman, and told her one night that he had filed for divorce."

"Did she tell you this?"

"No," Matthew took a breath, "David did."

Miss Janet's eyes narrowed, "That's right. David would have had to be a part in this too."

"What do you mean?"

"I mean that he knew her before. He would have," she corrected

herself, "*should have* known about her unfitness to teach. His mission agency wouldn't have allowed her to teach," Miss Janet answered.

"You're right, his mission agency wouldn't have, but I did. From the very beginning, I knew the truth about her marital status, and the circumstances behind it. David vouched for her. Everyone had only good things to say about her. I felt that we were very lucky to get her, and I am now more convinced of that than ever."

Miss Janet was unmoved by Matthew's explanations, "I think that you, David, and that woman pulled a fast one, and I don't think you ought to be able to get by with it. Dr. Kennedy established the rules of the mission for a purpose. How can we teach godly Christian values if we don't uphold those very rules?"

Matthew tried a different tack, "Will you please pray about the situation?"

"I'll pray, but I warn you. I won't change my mind."

"I hope that's not so. After you've spent some time praying about it, come back and see me again, and we'll proceed from there," Matthew said.

As she rose to leave, Miss Janet warned, "Matthew, you might as well be prepared to proceed in another direction."

Twenty Four

Nothing improved with the passing of two weeks. Miss Janet's icy coldness caused Cate to stay at school as late as possible, or spend more time with Matthew. She went home only to sleep. Kim and Matthew encouraged her to give God time to work things out.

Cate prayed non-stop that God would help her make sense out of everything. "Oh God, will I have to pay for my wrong decision forever? God, will this always pursue me and cause problems for those I love and for me? God, please help me. I don't know what to do."

Miss Janet's praying did not change her mind. In fact, it reinforced her opinion of the whole situation. She decided to notify Matthew's father and Dr. Patterson of the situation, but kept this fact to herself until her plans came to fruition.

When Miss Janet called Dr. Patterson, she asked if he could drive to Peguche. She did not give any specifics, only saying she needed to discuss a matter with him face to face. When he agreed to meet her the next day she asked him to make sure that David be present at their meeting.

On receiving Dr. Patterson's call, David suspected Miss Janet's nefarious purpose for the meeting. Matthew had informed him about what happened in Otavalo and Miss Janet's subsequent visit to his office, and how Matthew hoped that prayer would defuse the situation. Dr. Patterson's call made him believe that had not happened.

David returned Matthew's favor, and informed him of the meeting the next day. Matthew and David both thought it best not to say anything about it to Cate until the following morning.

Since Miss Janet had insisted that David be involved in the meeting Dr. Patterson suggested that it be held at David's house. The meeting was set for the afternoon. Dr. Patterson arrived first, and Miss Janet five minutes later. When David opened the door for Miss Janet, he knew immediately that he had been right about the purpose of this meeting. "Good morning, Miss Janet."

Very curtly, she answered, "*That* remains to be seen."

"Dr. Patterson is in the living room."

"Thank you," she stomped into the room.

Dr Patterson rose to greet her. "Good morning, Miss Cook."

Despite her frosty attitude, David played the perfect host, "Won't you have a seat, Miss Janet?"

"Thank you."

"Well, I believe we are all here now. Shall we get started?" Dr. Patterson suggested, in his usual pleasant voice.

"You may wish to wait," Miss Janet corrected. "There'll be two more shortly."

"Two more?" Dr. Patterson looked to David, who merely shrugged.

"Yes, I decided this morning to include Matthew Kennedy and Cate Jones."

David shook his head and let out a sigh. He hoped to avoid Cate having to go through what was about to happen.

Dr. Patterson noted David's distress, "Miss Cook, what is this meeting about?"

"I'd rather wait until everyone is here before we proceed."

As she finished her statement, Matthew and Cate arrived, and David went to invite them in.

He saw the nervous apprehension on Cate's face. "It'll be okay," he whispered, as he led them into the living room.

"Matthew, Miss Jones, how are you today?" Dr. Patterson rose and greeted them.

When everyone was seated, Dr. Patterson nodded to Miss Janet to begin.

"Dr. Patterson, this is difficult for me. I have always had the deepest respect for David, and the utmost confidence in him as a man of God. Therefore, I deeply regret to inform you that I believe he is guilty of a misjudgment that will tarnish his reputation-and that of your mission agency."

Cate immediately looked at Matthew for encouragement and briefly glanced toward David, who was watching Miss Janet. Cate saw the shocked expression on David's face as Miss Janet leveled her charge.

Dr. Patterson allowed her to finish before he asked, "Exactly what is your accusation against David?"

"He willfully conspired with Matthew to violate the rules of our mission agency."

"How did he do that?"

"He encouraged Matthew to hire this *divorced* woman as a teacher for our mission school," Miss Janet nodded her head toward David, Matthew and Cate.

"Miss Cook, am I understanding you correctly? Your accusation is that David encouraged Matthew to hire Miss Jones to teach at the mission school," Dr. Patterson tried to clarify.

"That is correct. He encouraged Matthew to violate the mission rules in order to get *her* a job."

"Miss Cook, even if what you say is true, I don't know why I'm here," Dr. Patterson said.

"It's true. Just ask them. They'll tell you," she pointed toward them with her hand.

"But, madam, I'm trying to tell you—"

"Just ask them!" Miss Janet insisted.

Dr. Patterson saw her agitation and reluctantly gave in. "David, did you encourage Matthew to hire Cate?"

"I recommended her for the job, if that's what she means."

"See," Miss Janet's eyes flashed with vindication.

Dr. Patterson continued his questioning, "How did you know there was an opening?"

"Matthew wrote me about it."

"And, why did you recommend Miss Jones?"

David answered, "Because God called her to teach in a mission school, and if Matthew agreed, why not this one?"

"Did you know that the Kennedy Agency had rules against hiring divorced people?" Dr. Patterson asked.

"I didn't know if they did or not."

Matthew sought to remove David from the hot seat. "David told me upfront that Cate was a divorcee, and asked me if that would be a problem; and I said no."

"So, you made the decision to hire Miss Jones, knowing that she had been divorced."

"I did," Matthew said empathetically.

Dr. Patterson was silent for a moment as he studied the group before him. "Miss Janet, I'm afraid I don't see any grounds for your complaint."

Miss Janet sat tall in her chair, her jaw firm, "Would *your* agency have hired her?"

Reluctantly, but truthfully, Dr. Patterson answered, "No, I'm afraid not."

"So, my complaint is that your missionary should not have recommended our agency hire her."

Miss Janet's words pierced Cate's heart. She knew it was true; the IMB had strict rules against appointing people like her, and most mission agencies followed this policy, regardless of whose fault the divorce was, or whether there were biblical grounds. This prevented David and her from having a future together. Now it threatened to destroy her ability to teach in the mission school. Cate's anxious thoughts were interrupted as Dr. Patterson continued.

"Miss Janet, all that you say about the IMB is true, but your agency is not the IMB. Matthew is the head of your agency and as head, he has the right to decide whom to hire. I don't see how this has anything to do with David, or our agency."

Miss Janet fidgeted in her chair and clenched her fists, "So, you're not going to do anything about this?"

"No, Miss Cook, I am not," Dr. Patterson said.

"Well, I know someone who will."

Matthew feared he knew what she meant, "And, who might that be?"

"Your father," Miss Janet answered.

"Miss Janet, there is no reason to bring my father into this."

"I beg to differ with you. Anyway, he's already involved. I called him this morning."

Matthew's head dropped, "Janet, I wish you hadn't done that."

"I'm sure you do. I had hoped that Dr. Patterson would help resolve this, but the more I thought about it yesterday, I realized that a resolution would require your father's intervention, so I called him. When I explained the dilemma here, he was very upset. You'll be hearing from him shortly. I know *he* will straighten the whole thing out."

Unable to be silent any longer, Cate confronted Miss Janet, "How could you dislike me so much that you would create such havoc and hurt so many people?"

"I didn't do that, *you* did."

"Is divorce the unpardonable sin to you?"

"No, a *disqualifying* sin," Miss Janet corrected, with smug self-righteousness.

Matthew came to Cate's rescue, "It *is* a sin God forgives. Any way, Cate didn't cheat and leave, her husband did."

Miss Janet narrowed her eyes at Matthew, "So, *you* say."

"Miss Janet, Cate was blameless in the divorce," David backed Matthew up.

"I'm sure that you two would say anything to help her," Miss Janet's lips curled into a smug smile.

"Her father, Dr. Johnathon Jones, told me the details of her divorce. She's blameless," David said.

Hearing his words, Cate's eyes widened and her mouth flew open.

"I don't think anyone is blameless in a divorce."

Pointing to Matthew and himself, David asked, "Are you accusing us of dishonesty?"

"No, I'm accusing you," Miss Janet looked at both David and Matthew, "of being in love with her."

Dr. Patterson tried to defuse the situation, "Now, Miss Cook, I'm sure all of this can be handled in an amicable manner."

"I'm quite sure it can't," she replied vehemently. "I think you're *all* in collusion."

"We're not in collusion. We're just trying to understand your attitude," Dr. Patterson said.

"The fact that you don't is why I called Dr. Kennedy," Miss Janet rose to leave.

Matthew tried one more time, "Miss Janet, I have to ask you one more time to please reconsider what you are doing."

"Not on your life," Miss Janet answered, as she stormed out the door.

Cate stifled a sob, "I am so sorry that all of you have been dragged into this."

"You have nothing to be sorry for my dear," Dr. Patterson assured her.

"She's not ordinarily like this. I-I don't understand her attitude at all," Cate said.

"Sometimes we Christians are terribly self-righteous, unforgiving people. If I understand correctly my dear, you've done nothing wrong," Dr. Patterson handed Cate a handkerchief.

Cate looked at Matthew, "What if she's right about your father?"

"I told you, I am head of the agency. I have the authority to hire whoever I think I should."

"But, will your father feel the same way?" Cate's voice held understandable concern.

Matthew took a deep breath and glanced at Dr. Patterson, "I don't know, but I'm ready to defend my decision."

"Dr. Patterson, you're not directly involved in this fiasco. Therefore, may I ask your advice?" Cate inquired.

"Of course, my dear,"

"It appears to me that Miss Janet wants me gone. If-you were me-what would you do?"

"May I call you Cate?"

"Yes, sir."

"Cate, why did you come to Ecuador to teach?"

"Because I believed God wanted me to."

"So, you were obeying God when you came here."

"Yes, sir that's right."

"Has all of this caused you to feel differently about God's leading?"

"I–I don't know sir."

"I'm sure that you've been praying about this situation?"

"Oh, yes sir, constantly."

"What have you sensed God leading you to do?"

"I don't know." Cate looked at Matthew and David, "I haven't receive any clear guidance."

"So, if God hasn't made clear what you should do," Dr. Patterson put a fatherly hand on her shoulder, "keep praying until He does."

"But, this situation, it's so hard to endure."

"I know. God knows too, and you can trust His grace to be sufficient to sustain you."

"Yes, sir, thank you," Cate said.

"Dr. Patterson," Matthew interrupted, "Under the circumstances, I think it would be wise for Cate to find another place to live. Don't you?"

"That might help calm the situation some. I'm sure it will help ease the stress a little."

"The problem is the agency has no other housing." Matthew looked at Dr. Patterson, "Does your agency have any here that we could use temporarily?"

"Not at the moment," Dr. Patterson answered.

"I'll stay where I am," Cate said. "I'll give Miss Janet her space like I've been doing."

"Maybe, I can help," David said. "I might know somewhere Cate can stay for a while.

"Where?"

"At the Garcia's."

Matthew considered David's suggestion, "You really think so?"

"Yes, if it's agreeable to Cate, how about you and I go ask them?"

"Of course, Mr. and Mrs. Garcia's house would be fine," Cate said.

Dr. Patterson suggested that he stay with Cate while the two young men talked to the Garcias.

"Cate, did I understand correctly?" Dr. Patterson asked, "Your father's name is Johnathon Jones."

"Yes, sir. It is."

"Did he attend Southwestern Baptist Theological Seminary?"

"Yes, he did," Cate wondered how he knew.

"I believe I know your father. I had a very good friend by the name of Johnathon Jones while I was in seminary. He married a girl name Carolyn Jane Smalley."

Cate smiled, "That's right. Smalley was my mother's maiden name."

"John, Carolyn, my wife and I lived in the same apartment building."

"You remind me of my father," Cate said.

"I'm honored." Dr. Patterson patted her hand, "After seminary, he took a pastorate in the South and I took one in the Midwest. We kept in touch for a while, but we lost touch after I began to prepare for the mission field. I moved to go to language school and your father moved to another pastorate."

"That was probably the church in Charleston. We moved from there to Kansas City. My father has been pastor of the Bethsaida Baptist Church ever since."

"Cate, I'm sorry for all that you are going through. If I, or my wife, can be of any assistance to you, please let us know."

"Thank you, sir. I appreciate that very much."

"It's the very least we can do for our old friends' daughter," Dr. Patterson said, as Matthew and David came through the door.

"It's all set," Matthew said.

"Mr. and Mrs. Garcia will be very glad to have you," David added.

"Good," Cate felt immediate relief.

"The agency will pay a monthly rental for you to live there," Matthew said.

"Oh, Matthew, I'm so sorry about this."

"I've told you over and over that you have nothing to be sorry for. I'll call Kim and ask her to gather up enough of your clothes for tonight, and we'll get the rest while Miss Janet is at church tomorrow," Matthew said.

Cate frowned, "I don't like bringing Kim into the middle of this."

"Nonsense, she'll be glad to help. She told me so."

"Well, I'll leave this with you young people, and make my way back to Quito," Dr. Patterson said.

David walked him to the door. "I'm sorry Miss Janet dragged you down here."

"It's part of the job, my boy," Dr. Patterson replied.

"Thank you for all that you've done," Cate said, as she and Matthew joined them at the door.

"Yes, sir, thank you," David shook hands with Dr. Patterson.

"You all are most welcomed," Dr. Patterson replied. "Cate, be sure and tell your parents that my wife and I said hello, and that they are in our prayers."

"I'll walk you to your car. Be back in a few minutes," Matthew told David and Cate.

Cate and David were alone. They had not been for a long time, and they were uncomfortable with it.

"Cate, I'm very sorry this is happening."

"Thanks, I don't know what I'm going to do. I've prayed continually since this began. It's like the heavens are brass. I wonder if God's trying to tell me something."

"Like what?"

"Like maybe I made a mistake in coming here? Maybe I misunderstood God's leadership."

"Cate, I don't think that's true. I've never known anyone who was so convinced about God's leadership," David's voice held conviction, and he moved closer to her.

"You're right," she nodded, "I don't really think I misunderstood, but I *am* confused about why this is happening. Tell me why," Cate turned and grabbed David's hand, "when I am obediently following God's leading, suddenly, everything falls apart."

David heard the anxiety, perplexity, and discouragement in her voice.

"I can't answer all of your questions, but I do know that God *is* in control, and He has a purpose in everything He allows."

"The only purpose I can see in this is Miss Janet's."

"I'm sure there's more here than you know."

"I'm not!"

"Cate," David said, with deep tenderness.

His tone caught her off guard, and she immediately looked up. They looked deeply into each other's eyes. Neither said a word; time stood still.

Hearing Matthew and Kim's voices as the door opened, they both looked away.

"Well, I hope I got all of the things you needed," Kim said, as she sat down on the couch. "We'll get the rest of your clothes and stuff tomorrow."

"I've filled Kim in," Matthew informed them.

"I knew when Miss Janet came home this afternoon that something had happened," Kim said, "but I was afraid to ask."

"Kim, I am sorry that you're caught in the middle of this," Cate apologized.

"It's not your fault. I'm on your side, but if I say it openly, I'll be looking for a new place to live too."

"Maybe Miss Janet should be looking for a new place to live and a new job," Matthew said.

"No, Matthew," Cate insisted, "I won't have her lose her job because of me."

"If she loses her job, it will be because of her attitude," Matthew responded.

"Cate, we'd better get you to the Garcias' so you can get settle in," David suggested.

When they arrived at the Garcias', Cate and David got out, and Matthew took Kim back to her house. Mr. and Mrs. Garcia and Sarah met them at the door.

"Ola, Miss Cate," Mrs. Garcia greeted them, "You are very welcome here. We have a nice room waiting for you."

"Cate, will you be living here now?" Sarah asked.

"Yes. Baby Girl I will."

Sarah scrunched up her nose, "You're not going to be living with Kim and Miss Janet?"

"No, Baby Girl I'm not."

"You'll have lots of fun at Mrs. Garcia's house. I always do," Sarah assured her.

"We are most glad to have you," Mr. Garcia greeted Cate too.

"Thank you both. I hope this won't be an imposition."

"No, you are most welcome. With all of our children grown, we have plenty of room. You will add sunshine and joy to our home," Mrs. Garcia assured her, while Mr. Garcia nodded his agreement.

"Where should I put this?" David held up Cate's suitcase.

"Come, I will show you," Mrs. Garcia said.

Mrs. Garcia led the way. It was not a big room, or a fancy room, but it was a bright cheery room. One of its best features was that its windows faced the same mountains that had become the symbol of the Lord's strength and protection for Cate.

"I hope this will be fine, Miss Cate."

"This is beautiful. Thank you both for allowing me to stay here."

Sarah pulled at David's hand, "Daddy, can I stay with Cate tonight?"

"Honey, I don't think so. Cate needs her rest."

Cate held out her hand to Sarah, "I really don't mind, if Mrs. Garcia doesn't."

"No, it is no problem," Mrs. Garcia said.

"Come on, Daddy," Sarah begged.

"Yeah, come on Daddy," Cate laughed.

"Are you sure?" David asked.

"Sure, I'm sure. She can help me get use to my new room."

"Well, I guess, it's all right then."

"Yea!" Sarah yelled.

"Well, I guess I'll see you all in the morning. I'll bring Sarah's church clothes and we'll take care of that—other matter," David winked.

"Thanks that would be great."

As Sarah was busily playing on the bed, David walked over and asked, "Don't I get a goodbye kiss?"

"Sure," Sarah grabbed him around the neck, hugged and kissed him goodbye.

"Bye, Lady Bug I'll see you tomorrow."

"Daddy, give Cate a goodbye kiss too," Sarah said innocently.

Surprised by the comment, Cate and David locked eyes, but aware that Mrs. Garcia was in the room, they quickly looked in different directions.

"Sarah, your daddy has to go home. He has many things to do," Mrs. Garcia said.

"That's true," Cate agreed.

David sheepishly said goodbye to Mrs. Garcia and dismissed himself.

After dinner, Cate helped Mrs. Garcia with the dishes while Sarah helped Mr. Garcia feed his collection of animals. Mrs. Garcia took the opportunity to offer Cate her condolences. "Miss Cate, I am very sorry about your troubles. I do not believe that Miss Janet is behaving as God would like."

Cate leaned against the sink, running a dish towel through her hands, "Mrs. Garcia, I am sure that Miss Janet thinks she is doing what God would have her to do. She believes I'm unfit to teach at the mission school."

"*Mi querida*, I do not believe that you are unfit. *God* has made you fit. I know that you are a godly woman." Mrs. Garcia spoke with conviction.

"God has forgiven me of my sin, including any that had to do with my divorce. But, that doesn't matter to some people. They see divorce as anathema," Cate explained.

"Ana-anna-anth-"

Cate smiled, "Anathema, it means a terrible sin, an unforgivable sin."

Mrs. Garcia shook her head, "I am so sorry *chica bonita*."

Cate smiled at the "beautiful girl" reference, "I'm sorry too."

"But, God forgives all sin," Mrs. Garcia reminded her.

"That's true, but some people don't," Cate said, with great sadness.

Mrs. Garcia glanced upward, "Everyone should be like God."

"That would indeed be wonderful," Cate replied, "but I fear that won't occur this side of heaven."

"I am glad you are here with me," Mrs. Garcia hugged Cate, "I will take care of you as if you were my own daughter."

"Thank you," Cate hugged back.

Once they had finished the dishes, Cate and Mrs. Garcia relaxed in the back yard, and watched Mr. Garcia, as he allowed Sarah to play with the animals. As the sun went down, they enjoyed a spectacular sunset and later, a beautiful star-studded, moonlit night.

When Sarah fell asleep sitting in her lap, Cate carried her into the house, and tucked her in. Cate turned out the light, but she didn't go to bed; instead she stared at the mountains in the distance. She found herself meditating on Psalm 46 and praying that God would be her *present help* in this time of trouble. "Please Father work in this situation however you see fit. Help me know if I made a mistake in understanding Your guidance when I came here. Please help me know what to do. I'll do anything you want." She prayed fervently with tears for two hours before falling asleep.

Twenty Five

She awoke the next morning with a verse of Scripture on her mind. Psalm 57:2: "I will cry to God Most High, Who performs on my behalf and rewards me, Who brings to pass His purposes for me and surely completes them." It was confirmation to her soul that God had answered her prayers and was indeed working out His will for her life. For the first time she felt a sense of peace, and found herself silently praising the Lord for His love, grace and goodness.

She had been reading her Bible and praying for about thirty minutes before Sarah woke up. Cate watched as she began to stir, *I couldn't love her anymore if she were my very own.* She prayed that whatever God had in store for her that it might somehow include Sarah. She wanted very much to continue to be a part of Sarah's life.

As Sarah opened her eyes, Cate welcomed her to the day. "Good morning sleepy head."

"Good morning."

"I guess we better rise and shine so we can get ready for church," Cate sat down on the bed beside her.

"Yeah, I like church."

"I know, and I'm very glad that you do."

"Ever since He came to live in my heart, I like to hear about Jesus and to sing songs about Him," Sarah said.

"I'm glad you asked Him to come to live in your heart."

"He'll live in my heart all my life, and someday I'll go to heaven to live," Sarah said, with child-like simplicity.

"You're exactly right."

"You know what else."

"What else?"

"I'll see Mommy again someday."

Cate paused, "You sure will, Baby Girl," and hugged her.

Sarah looked up, "Cate, I miss Mommy."

"I know."

"Do you think she misses me?"

Sarah's question tugged at Cate's heart, "Of course."

"Do you think Mommy's sad when she misses me?" Sarah continued, with a child's inquisitiveness.

"No one's sad in heaven; so if she misses you, Jesus reminds her that she'll see you again one day and that makes her happy."

"I'm glad Jesus is taking care of mommy, and that you help take care of me."

"I'm glad too," Cate looked toward the window and blinked her eyes.

Mrs. Garcia's knock on the door ended their conversation. "Good morning Miss Cate, breakfast is almost ready. You and Sarah must get up now if you are to eat breakfast before church."

"We're up. We'll be in shortly."

Cate and Sarah dressed quickly and went to breakfast. Before they finished eating, David arrived and shared breakfast with them. With David's arrival, there was an added dimension to the conversation. Mr. Garcia and David talked about Mr. Garcia's animals, his work at the school and his participation at church while Mrs. Garcia, Cate and Sarah ate and listened. Mrs. Garcia and Cate smiled as they observed the two men's mutual respect and admiration for each other.

When the service was over, people milled around and visited. Cate tried to avoid Miss Janet's glare. It had begun as a glare of disapproval, and morphed into a glare of condemnation, but more recently, it had mutated into one of bitter resentment.

The pastor was still greeting people. As Cate, David and Sarah approached, he reached out his hand and greeted them warmly. Each one including Sarah told him how much they enjoyed the sermon. He thanked them sincerely and wished them a blessed day.

During the drive home Cate was silent. She was absorbed in her predicament. She couldn't help but hold herself responsible for what was happening. After all, her sin of rebellion had opened the door for the unwise marriage which resulted in the divorce that seemed to be the source of all of her present problems. *Therefore, I'm at least partially responsible for Miss Janet's attitude.* She also found herself wishing that she could talk to her dad.

Once again, Mr. Garcia insisted that David join them for lunch. The fact that Cate was preoccupied during the meal did not escape Mrs. Garcia's attention, nor did the fact that David watched Cate throughout the meal.

After lunch, Mrs. Gracia suggested that David and Cate enjoy the beautiful day by taking a walk. Much to her surprise Cate agreed without a protest.

They left Sarah and Mrs. Garcia washing dishes and Mr. Garcia in the backyard with his animals. Cate and David walked down the street toward the path that went down to the stream that had its source in the mountains. At first, they walked silently, Cate still absorbed with her thoughts, and David not quite sure what to say.

After a few minutes of walking, he decided to speak. "Cate, I know this situation is hurtful to you. I want you to know that I'll do whatever I can to help you. I wish that there was a way that I could make things better."

"Well, there is one thing."

"Name it."

Cate stopped walking and turned to face David, "Could I possibly use your phone to call my dad?"

"Sure, would you like to do it now?"

"Yes, if you don't mind."

"Not at all," they picked up their pace and headed toward his house.

When they arrived, Cate went to the phone and made her call. Wanting to give her privacy, David went to the backyard.

"Hello," Cate heard her dad answer the phone.

"Daddy," she said, a depressed tone in her voice.

"Catie what's wrong?"

"Oh, Daddy, almost everything,"

"What can I do to help?"

"I need to tell you about what's happened. I need your advice."

"Okay," her dad replied.

Cate gave a detailed account of what had happened, Miss Janet's attitude, the meeting with Dr. Patterson, Miss Janet's call to Matthew's father and Cate moving in with the Garcias. She told him about the verse in Psalm 57 that the Lord had awakened her with and how she felt it was a confirmation that He would work out His will in her life. "Daddy, she won't listen. It's like she's got it in for me and there's nothing I can do to change that."

"I'm sorry Catie," her father's voice was tinged with deep love and empathy.

"Daddy, what do I do? This woman wants to drive me out of Ecuador."

"Cate, what I am going to say may seem like preacher talk, but honey, it's daddy talk. What you need to do is trust God. From what you're telling me, you've done all you know how to do. You've prayed, searched God's word, talked to Miss Janet, and sought her forgiveness for your perceived sin. Honey, you've done everything you should do. Now you must trust God to honor your obedience and faith."

"Daddy, this is the most difficult situation that I've had to deal with since Justin. This woman, who was my friend, now hates me and says I'm unfit to serve God."

"Honey, if she hates you, she's wrong and *she's* the one who needs forgiveness."

"I know. I have forgiven her, and I've been praying she'd realize that her attitude is wrong."

"Catie, you *are* fit to serve God. God's forgiveness and grace is not just for most sins. It covers all sins. I know what kind of relationship you have with the Lord, and I know He has, can, and will use you."

"Daddy, I don't know what Matthew's dad is going to do about Miss Janet's accusations." Desperation tinged her voice, "I may have to leave Ecuador."

"If you do have to leave, you can still trust God. Even though this woman may be successful in her machinations, God is still in control. Trust Him no matter what.

Remember too, if you have to leave, your mother and I will be waiting for you."

"How's mom?"

"She's doing very well. She has two more treatments, and recently the treatments haven't made her so sick. We're very hopeful that there will be no signs of cancer when it comes time for the CT-scan."

"Can I say hello to her?"

"Sure, honey," he called for his wife to come to the phone.

"Hello, Cate."

"Hi Mom, how are you?"

"I'm okay honey. How are you?"

"Not so good Mom. Dad will fill you in."

"Cate, what can I do?"

"Pray for me. I need lots of prayer. Please pray for David and Matthew too."

"Honey, you sound so upset."

"It's okay, Mom. Well-not really, but I'll be okay as long as I know that you and Dad are praying for me."

"Mom, since I'm on David's phone, I better say goodbye. I love you."

"I love you too," her mom said.

"Mom, can I speak to dad one more time?"

"Sure, honey."

"Yes, Catie,"

"Daddy, can we pray together right now over the phone? Mom too?"

"My thoughts exactly," he took his wife's hand and began praying for his daughter.

During the prayer, Cate's mother realized how difficult a time Cate was having in Ecuador. Once Dr. Jones had concluded his prayer, Mrs. Jones took the phone once more, "Cate I love you. I'll be praying for you."

"Thanks mom. I love you too," Cate swallowed hard, wiping away tears.

They exchanged one more goodbye, and hung up the phone. Cate was sobbing. Talking to her parents had helped, but it caused her to miss them. She cried for a little longer as she continued to pray.

Because the windows were open to take advantage of the February breezes, David had overheard Cate's conversation. It broke his heart

to hear her recount everything to her father and it pained him to hear her talking about the hurt she was experiencing because of the situation. But, the thing that really wrenched his heart was hearing her say that she might have to leave Ecuador. He had known that was a possibility, but he hadn't allowed himself to think about it because he didn't want her to leave. He found himself hoping and praying that Miss Janet would leave so Cate wouldn't have to, but he knew that Miss Janet's leaving would not completely solve the problem. Cate's fate was in Dr. Kennedy's hands. Helplessly, he sat outside, listened to her sob, wished that things were different, and prayed that God would comfort her.

Ten minutes later, she stopped crying, and went to David. "I'm sorry I took so long."

"That's fine. I wanted you to take as long as you needed."

"I appreciate you allowing me to use your phone to call my parents. It really helped."

"I'm glad, are you ready to return to the Garcias now?"

"Uh-huh."

As they were about to leave, they heard a knock at the front door. It was Matthew and Kim.

"We thought we might find you here," Matthew said, as David opened the door.

"Cate, wanted to call her parents."

"I thought she might," Matthew said.

"We missed you both at church this morning," Kim told David.

"We were there," David responded. "We just sat in the back and stayed out of Miss Janet's line of sight. I figured Cate had taken enough glares and verbal shots from her."

"I don't blame you for that," Kim said. "After the meeting yesterday and especially when Cate didn't come back to the house last night, she ranted and raved about what had happened and the special treatment that Cate seemed to be getting. When we got home from church today and she discovered that Cate's things were missing, she crowed with triumph, thinking that maybe she had gotten rid of her."

David shook his head, "I would never have believed that Miss Janet could be like this."

"Neither would I," Matthew agreed.

"It's as if Miss Janet hates her now. She has no kind word for her."

Kim turned to Cate, "I'm glad you found another place to stay. Frankly, I wish I could move too."

"I'm sorry. I didn't know it was that bad for you," Matthew said.

"It's not like it was for Cate. She's okay with me. I just can't stand her attitude toward Cate." Kim sighed, "I don't like being around anyone with an attitude like that."

"Have you tried talking to her?" David asked, grasping at straws.

"Sure, but I got absolutely nowhere. I'm telling you her attitude is etched in stone. I can assure you; she is *not* going to change her mind."

"That doesn't bode well for Cate," David said.

"No it doesn't," Kim agreed.

"Matt, have you talked to your father?" David hoped he could offer Cate a glimmer of hope.

"No, I haven't. I tried to call him several times yesterday, but got no answer. To tell you the truth, I'm rather surprised that he hasn't called me."

"Yeah, I'm surprised too. I heard Miss Janet on the phone when she called him. She put things in the most terrible light possible," Kim said.

As they walked out, Matthew could see how down Cate was and tried to cheer her up.

"Hey, beautiful, how you doing?" Matthew walked over and kissed her on the cheek.

"Okay," Cate tried to sound convincing.

"Hang in there Cate. This too shall pass," Kim advised her.

"I sure hope so."

"Cate, no matter how this thing works out, remember God's in control, and we are in your corner," David said.

Cate gave a halfhearted smile, "I'll remember, but all three of you are on Miss Janet's *bad* list because of me. Maybe it would be best if the three of you aren't seen with me until this thing has been settled."

"Not gonna happen," David said.

"Exactly," Matthew put his arm around her shoulder.

"Sorry, Cate, you're stuck with us. We aren't going anywhere," Kim stated, with firm resolution.

David and Matthew took Cate back to the Garcias, picked up Sarah and offered the Garcias a ride to church.

Home alone, Cate was free to pray aloud and unburden her heart to the Lord. She played her father's words over in her mind, and begged God to help her learn whatever it was that she was suppose to learn from the situation. She asked fervently that He would help her to trust Him to work out His will and help her to be completely submissive, even if it meant leaving Ecuador.

Twenty Six

Today was National Community Day, a national holiday of sorts, so she needed to be there early. It wasn't a normal school day; it was a day of celebration and festivities, during which the students at the mission school would perform a musical program. After it was over, everyone would go home and celebrate with their families and neighbors.

When she arrived, she discovered it would definitely *not* be a day of celebration and festivities, *not for me*. Matthew's parents had arrived the night before and his father wanted to settle the matter concerning Cate in an expeditious manner. He had decided to take advantage of National Community Day. This would give him the opportunity to meet with Matthew, Miss Janet and Cate without pulling them away from their normal duties.

When Matthew informed him that Cate was in charge of the music program of the kindergarten through third grade, Dr. Kennedy asked him to put another teacher in charge so that they could go ahead with their meeting. Matthew met Cate shortly after she arrived to inform her of what was about to take place. "Cate my parents arrived last night."

"Oh," Cate never imagined the Kennedys would arrive this quickly. "Have you spoken with your father about the situation?"

"I tried, but he wanted to wait until everyone was present.
Cate rolled her eyes, "I'm sure that he's heard *Miss Janet's* side."

"Probably so, but I managed to share bits and pieces of yours and mine. Uh," Matthew paused, a concerned look on his face, "there's something else I need to warn you about."

"What?"

"My mother and Miss Janet have been good friends for years. Mother will almost certainly take Miss Janet's side." Matthew saw what he said deeply discouraged her.

"So, you're telling me to expect the worse."

"No, Cate, I'm trying to prepare you if the worse happens."

"Isn't that the same thing?"

"No, it isn't. My father is a fair, compassionate, godly man. I'm certain that he'll listen to all sides and make a thoughtful, biblical decision."

"Thanks, that's all I really want." Cate breathed a heavy sigh, as tears welled up in her eyes.

Matthew took her hands in his, "Cate, it'll be all right."

"I hope so, Matthew."

He put his arms around her, and pulled her close, "Whatever happens we'll make it all right."

"Do you have any idea when your father wants to have the meeting?"

"In about thirty minutes."

"Thirty minutes! What about the music program?"

"He wants you to get someone to take your place."

"Catlin's my assistant, I'll need to inform her and go over a few details."

"Sure, I'll walk with you."

Cate was glad for company; she felt like one of the early Christians about to appear before Nero or Diocletian. They found Catlin and briefed her on what needed to be done. Now it was time to face the "trial" in Matthew's office. She was nervous; she couldn't help it, and prayed silently that the Lord would give her wisdom, strength, courage, and a sense of His peace and presence, as she faced her accuser. Matthew offered her his arm as she walked boldly into Matthew's office where his father, his mother and Miss Janet waited.

Dr. Kennedy sat at Matthew's desk, with Mrs. Kennedy and Miss Janet on his left. He asked Cate to have a seat in front of the desk. Matthew escorted her and took the seat next to her.

As she sat down, she felt a sense of courage, strength and peace that she had prayed for, and best of all a distinct awareness of His presence. She breathed a sigh of relief, as Dr. Kennedy began.

"Miss Jones, may I introduce myself. I am Marcus Kennedy, Matthew's father and founder of this mission agency and school," he nodded to his left, "and this is my wife, Martha."

"It's nice to meet you both," Cate said politely.

As Cate spoke, Mrs. Kennedy rolled her eyes in Miss Janet's direction.

Dr. Kennedy maintained a formal mood, "Thank you Miss Jones," He glanced toward his wife and Miss Janet, who were obviously irritated with him, and continued, "Well, Miss Jones, it seems we have a problem."

"Yes, sir," Cate answered, surprised by how unaffected she was by his statement.

"From what Miss Janet tells me you are a divorced woman. Is that true?"

"Yes, sir, it is."

He glanced at Matthew, "Did my son know that you were divorced when he hired you?"

"Yes, sir, he did," Cate looked first at Matthew and then back at Dr. Kennedy.

Once again, he surveyed his son's face and asked, "Did you tell him you were divorced?"

"Yes, sir."

"What part did David Barnes play in your being hired?"

"Matthew told David that he needed a teacher and David told him about me."

"What did he tell Matthew?"

"He told Matthew that I felt that God wanted me to teach in a mission school, but that I was divorced. He asked Matthew if that would prevent the possibility of hiring me. Matthew said no."

"So both Matthew and David knew, from the very beginning, that you were divorced."

"Yes, they did."

Dr. Kennedy looked directly at Miss Janet while he continued to question Cate, "Did you in any way try to hide your marital status?"

"No, sir," Cate said, "I did not."

He turned his eyes to his son, "Matthew, did you know my long standing rule not to hire divorced people?"

Matthew met his father's eye contact, "Yes, I did."

"Then why did you hire Miss Jones?"

"Because I checked her out thoroughly, and everyone gave her their highest recommendation as a teacher. David knew what kind of Christian she was, *and* the particulars of her divorce. It wasn't her fault. Her husband left her for another woman. She had biblical grounds for divorce. He did not; *he* divorced *her*. Knowing all of this, I hired her and she has been an excellent teacher."

Dr Kennedy listened intently to his son. It was apparent the two had great love and respect for each other.

"I see," Dr. Kennedy turned his attention back to Cate. "Miss Jones, I know you feel like you're on trial here and that I'm the judge and jury. I'm sorry for that, but I need to have a clear understanding, so I need to ask you some more questions."

"That's fine, sir."

"Okay then, if you had not come to Ecuador, could you have gotten a teaching job in the United States?"

"Yes, sir."

"Had you had a teaching job prior to coming here?"

"Yes, I did."

"Where did you teach?"

"Glendale Elementary School, Kansas City, Kansas."

"How long did you teach there?"

"Three years."

"Why did you leave that job to come here?"

"Actually, I left that job to go to teach in a mission school in Mexico."

Dr. Kennedy paused, considering her answer, "You taught in Mexico?"

"No, sir, that job fell through because of funding issues."

"That occurred just before you came here?"

"No, sir, it occurred a year before I came here."

"I see," Dr. Kennedy asked, "What were you doing right before you came here?"

"Attending seminary and working part-time at a pre-school."

"And, you found out about this job through David Barnes, who found out from Matthew."

"Yes, sir."

"And, you took this job because…you felt God was leading you here?"

"I did, yes, sir."

"And, you never tried to hide the fact that you were divorced."

"No, sir. I didn't. It's not something that I'm proud of, but I never tried to hide it. I felt that the people who needed to know, knew."

Dr. Kennedy removed his glasses and folded his hands as if in thoughtful prayer, "Thank you, Miss Jones, for being so forthcoming. You have given me much to consider in making my decision."

Impatient with his approach, and venting her frustration, Miss Janet asked, "Do you mean that you are going to consider keeping her as a teacher while you're deliberating on a final decision?"

"Janet, I want to be very fair to Miss Jones. Therefore, I want to consider the matter carefully," Dr. Kennedy answered.

Miss Janet's eyes blazed, "I do not see what there is to consider. Your policy has always been not to hire divorced people."

"That *was* the policy."

"Do you mean to say that you are considering going against your own policy?" Miss Janet bristled with unvarnished anger.

"I *am* considering it."

"Marcus!" Mrs. Kennedy gasped in disbelief.

"Why in the world would you change the policy to accommodate *this woman*?" Miss Janet shouted.

Dr. Kennedy looked directly at both his detractors, "I'm not considering changing it to accommodate this woman, but to be in line with the scriptural allowances for divorce."

"I *cannot* believe this. Of all people, I thought that *you* would do the right thing." Miss Janet shouted again.

"Me too!" Mrs. Kennedy expressed obvious displeasure.

Realizing the situation was escalating, Matthew stood, "Dad, before this thing goes any further, I need to tell you and mom something."

"Okay, son,"

Matthew looked directly at his mother and Miss Janet, "I've asked Cate to marry me."

His father's expression did not change, but his mother's eyes widened and her mouth flew open. Miss Janet gasped.

Cate looked at Mrs. Kennedy and Miss Janet, "Don't worry, I said no."

"That's not what you said," Matthew corrected. "You said maybe."

"I'm sorry Matthew, but *now,* I am saying no," Cate directed her words at his mother and Miss Janet.

Miss Janet quickly tried to turn the tables. "*There*, you see what kind of woman she is. She led your son to believe that she'd marry him, but now she won't."

Mrs. Kennedy shook her head in agreement.

"The way you two looked at her when you heard about his proposal, I would have said no too," Dr. Kennedy replied.

"Marcus!" Mrs. Kennedy said angrily.

"Martha, your friendship with Janet has compromised your ability to see this thing clearly. I believe you to be much more compassionate and forgiving than you seem to be at this moment."

Miss Janet interceded for her friend, "Marcus, it's *you* who can't see clearly. This woman is making a fool out of you and your son."

Cate and Matthew were shocked at Miss Janet's boldness and Dr. Kennedy was nearing the end of his patience.

"Janet, you seem to have an ardent, unreasonable dislike for Miss Jones. You wanted an immediate decision so I'll give you one, but you're not going to like it. My decision is that Miss Jones can continue as a teacher at the mission school, and from what I have seen and heard, my son would be a fool to take no for an answer to his proposal."

"Well, you can be sure of one thing, if she stays, I'll go," Miss Janet threatened, loudly and adamantly.

"*That*," Dr. Kennedy said, "is entirely up to you, however, from what I have witnessed here today that might be a good thing."

Miss Janet was dumbstruck.

"Dr. Kennedy, she doesn't have to leave." Cate spoke calmly, with steadiness of purpose, "I will."

"But, Miss Jones, you don't have to leave."

"Yes sir, I believe I do. Miss Janet has given her life to this school, and I don't want her to leave because of me." Turning to look directly at Miss Janet, Cate continued. "Miss Janet I'd like to thank you for all of the past kindnesses that you have shown. I'm sorry that things turned out like they did between us and I hope someday you'll change your mind."

Miss Janet moved nervously in her chair, turned her head away, but remained silent.

Cate turned to Dr. Kennedy and summoned up the courage to finish. "If it won't be too much of an imposition for Matthew to get someone to cover my classes for the rest of the school year, my resignation will be on his desk this afternoon."

"Cate please don't," Matthew's voice held sadness.

"Matthew, I have to."

"Miss Jones, I'm sorry that you have chosen to leave us. I would have liked to get to know you better. However, if you are sure leaving is what you want, Matthew will make arrangements to take care of your classes," Dr. Kennedy said.

"Yes, sir, it is what I want. Thank you. Now, if you'll excuse me, I'll go clean out my desk."

"Of course my dear," Dr. Kennedy stood as Cate resolutely rose from her chair and left the office. He looked pointedly at his wife and Janet, "Now, do you see what kind of woman she is? It seems to me that you both could learn a lot from her."

Matthew hurried after Cate, catching up with her as she entered her classroom. "Cate please don't quit."

"I have to."

"No, you don't. Didn't you hear my father?"

"Didn't you hear Miss Janet, and didn't you see your mother's face?"

He took her in his arms, "Cate, you can't leave."

"Matthew, I can't stay. I just can't," she answered with sadness and regret.

"Please," he begged, "marry me and stay."

"Matthew, I can't marry you," Cate tried to let him down as tenderly and compassionately as possible.

"Cate, if you marry me, we don't have to stay here."

"Who'll run the mission agency and school if you leave?"

"I don't know, but I do know that I want to be with you."

She knew there was no way to avoid hurting him, so she spoke plainly. "We can't do that to your parents, and I can't do it to you."

"Do what to me?"

"I can't marry you when I don't love you with my whole heart."

Matthew's voice was quieter, "I–I was hoping you did love me, like that."

"I know, and I wish I did. I'm sorry, but I don't."

"There's no hope, no changing your mind?"

"There's always hope," Cate answered.

"I don't think so, not for us. I suspect that there's something you're not telling me. Right?"

"I don't think you'd like to hear the answer to that," Cate hugged him and softly whispered, "I'm sorry."

Matthew forced a slight smile and changed the subject, "I think you were about to clean out your desk when I stopped you."

"And write my letter of resignation."

"Would you like some reluctant help?"

"Sure," Cate took his arm and walked toward the desk. Realizing that she would need a box or two, Matthew went to find them, while Cate sat down to write her letter of resignation. It was as if she were operating in two worlds-one visible and the other invisible. She looked at the children's pictures on the wall and saw them for the first time. Her eyes focused on an ant as it scurried over the leaves of a potted plant. From the point that Matthew informed her of his father's presence, she had been in unceasing prayer. During Dr. Kennedy's interrogation, she felt a sense of total peace. She was intensely aware of God's presence and power, and she knew no matter what happened that God was in control, and would work out His will. When she told Dr. Kennedy that she would resign and leave, she was sure she was following the "still small voice" of God's leadership. She was just as sure that He was leading her to leave Ecuador as she had been sure of His leadership to come there.

She completed her letter just as Matthew returned. He handed her the boxes and she handed him her letter of resignation. He sighed and put it in his pocket. They both worked at packing her things, the entire operation taking only an hour. When it was finished, Matthew walked her out and offered to drive her to the Garcias. Cate asked for a few last favors.

Sure," Matthew said, "I'll do anything you need me to.

"May I use a phone to call Dr. Patterson?"

"Of course," Matthew answered, as he led her to the phone in his office, which had been long since vacated by his father, mother and Miss Janet. He stepped out of the office to give her some privacy. When she finished her call, she asked, "When we get to the Garcias' house, will you wait while I pack my things, and if they are not there will you help me find them, as well as Kim, David and Sarah so that I can say goodbye?"

"Sure, I will."

"There's one more thing."

"Yes…"

"Will you drive me to Quito?"

"To the Pattersons'?"

"Yes."

"I'll be glad to."

When they arrived at the Garcias' house, Mr. and Mrs. Garcia were home. Cate packed her things and prepared to say a very tearful goodbye. They were waiting for her in the living room. Matthew took her things to the car so that she and the Garcias could say their goodbyes in private.

"Thank you both for your friendship and generosity."

"You are most welcome Miss Cate," Mr. Garcia said.

In tears, Mrs. Garcia said, "*Mi amiga*, do not go, *por favor*."

"Mrs. Garcia, I have to go."

"But, why?"

"I just have too."

"Carla, can't you see how difficult this is for Miss Cate? It is okay *mi esposa*. Say goodbye to your friend. She must be on her way to Quito," Mr. Garcia put his arm around his wife, trying to comfort her.

"*Adiós, amiga. Que Dios este contigo.*"

"Mrs. Garcia, I would appreciate it very much if you would please take special care of Sarah. I don't think she is going to understand my leaving."

"*Por supuesto mi querida.*"

"Thank you Mrs. García." Cate wiped away her tears and hugged both of them. "I will never forget either of you."

"Nor, we you," Mrs. Garcia replied.

"Well, I guess it's time to go." Cate walked to the front door where Matthew was waiting. The Garcias followed them to the car, and

Cate and Mrs. Garcia hugged one last time. As they drove away, the Garcias shouted, "*Que Dios vaya contigo*," and waved until the car was out of sight. Cate breathed great, deep sighs, knowing the other goodbyes would be more difficult.

They stopped by the house that she had shared with Miss Janet and Kim to see if Kim was at home. Matthew went in and returned with Kim. As she walked toward the car, Cate realized Kim was crying. Cate got out of the car and embraced her. They cried together, as they exchanged goodbyes. Kim lodged one last protest. "I don't know exactly what happened today, but I do know Miss Janet said you were leaving. I can't believe Dr. Kennedy took her side."

"He didn't," Matthew said.

"Then, I don't understand why you're going," Kim stepped back while holding Cate by the shoulders.

"I just have to go, but I need you to promise to do something for me."

"Help take care of Sarah?" Kim asked, tears in her eyes again.

"Yes, please. Will you take my place and stay with her when David's away?"

"I will if David agrees, but I'll never be able to take your place. She loves you too much for that."

Cate wiped her eyes, "I don't know how I'm going to be able to say goodbye to her."

"Then, why say goodbye? Stay Cate; please stay."

"I can't Kim," Cate hugged her again, said goodbye one last time and got in the car.

Matthew had already returned to the driver's side. As Cate got in, he asked, "Ready to go?"

With tears streaming, Cate nodded and they drove away, leaving Kim wiping tears and waving goodbye.

Cate dreaded the next stop most of all. She prayed earnestly that God would give her unwavering resolve to do what she had to. Knowing how difficult the next goodbyes would be, Matthew glanced at her a time or two as they drove to David's house. He dreaded it for her.

When they arrived, Matthew told her that he'd stay in the car and wait for her. She took a deep breath, grabbed the door handle and started to get out when Matthew reached over , "I'll be praying for you."

"Thanks," she sighed. As she stopped in front of the door and reached to knock, David opened the door.

With deep sadness he asked, "Please come in."

Before she could say anything, David spoke again, "I was expecting you. I know why you're here."

"You do, how?" She could see that he was upset.

"Kim told me that you were leaving," he avoided full eye contact.

"Yes, I am," Cate answered, as she lowered her head and choked back the tears.

There was silence. Both worked hard to maintain control of their emotions. Finally, she found the ability to speak again. "I wanted to tell you and Sarah goodbye."

"Sarah's napping. I can wake her up," David said, "but, before I do, I'd like to ask you to stay."

He was making it difficult for her to be obedient to the Lord's leadership in leaving, but she answered, "David I can't."

"Cate, I don't know what we are going to do without you."

Cate tried to take control of the subject so he would not ask her again to stay, "I asked Kim and Mrs. Garcia to help you take care of Sarah."

"I'm not talking about that. I'm talking about *you*. We'll miss you."

Hearing those words Cate struggled again with her resolve to obey God and leave Ecuador.

"I'll miss you too," she said, and then added, "both of you."

"Yeah..."

Fearing she wouldn't see him for a long time, she decided to try to apologize again for the past. She summoned the courage, took a breath and began. "David there's something I'd like to say to you. There are lots of things in my life that I wish that I could change. One is the way that I treated you seven years ago. I'll always be sorry for that. I–I wish I could change it."

He nodded, "I know, I wish I could change some things too."

"But, we can't. Can we?" She wasn't sure why she had asked that. *Maybe, I'm still searching for a glimmer of hope that one day we'll be together.*

"No, we can't," David answered.

"But, it would be nice if we could." She couldn't hold back the tears any longer.

"It would be-very nice," David said, as she began to cry.

He shuffled his feet nervously unsure of what to do as Cate lowered her head and wiped tears.

"I've got to tell Sarah I'm leaving, but I don't know how to say goodbye to her, and I don't know how to make her understand about my leaving."

"I know," David swallowed hard and cleared his throat.

Cate stood, shaking her head, "I just don't know."

"Why don't you let me tell her? Maybe, it will be easier coming from me?"

Cate was grateful for his offer, but knew that it was something that she had to do. "I need to tell her, but I don't know how to make her understand."

"I don't think she's going to understand no matter which one of us tells her, but it'll be easier for you if I tell her."

"I can't leave without at least seeing her," Cate raised her head, with tears in her eyes.

Hurting for Cate, himself and Sarah, David answered, "Okay…she's in her room."

Cate walked slowly to Sarah's room; she found the child sleeping peacefully. She walked softly to the bed, bent over, and kissed her gently on the forehead. As she did, her long brown hair brushed Sarah's cheek, and roused her from her sleep. Catching Cate's hair in her hand, she opened her eyes. Seeing Cate leaning over her, she caught her around the neck and pulled her closer for a hug.

"Hey, Baby Girl," Cate said, trying to hide her sadness.

"Hello, Cate. I missed you at the music program this morning. Where were you?"

"I–uh–I had something important to take care of."

"But, you didn't hear me sing." Sarah said, disappointment in her voice.

"I'm sorry, Baby Girl. If my meeting hadn't been very, very important, I wouldn't have missed your singing."

"Would you like to hear me sing my song now?"

"Sure," Cate said.

Sarah began to sing, and Cate's eyes filled with tears.

Seeing Cate with tears in her eyes, Sarah stopped singing, "What's wrong?"

Cate tried to answer, but the words wouldn't come. David had followed her into Sarah's room and seeing Cate's distress, he said, "Sarah, honey, Cate's going home."

"Home? To the Garcia's' house?" Sarah asked, with furrowed brow, and a confused expression.

Cate was trying hard not to cry, but tears trickled down her face and she couldn't answer.

"No honey," David said, "she's going home to Kansas."

"Is your mother sicker?" Sarah tried to decipher what was going on.

Cate shook her head 'no' and forced the words, "No, Baby Girl, I'm going home to stay."

"You're not coming back?"

"I don't know honey, but probably not," Cate answered, with lots of tears and a big sigh.

"But, I don't want you to go," Sarah protested through tears.

"I know," Cate hugged her.

Sarah sobbed, "Who's going to take care of me?"

"Kim and Mrs. Garcia will help daddy take care of you," Cate answered, trying to comfort her.

"But, I want you," Sarah protested again tearfully.

"I know, but I've got to go home," Cate hugged her tighter. "Don't cry. I'll see you when you and daddy come home to Kansas again."

Taking Cate's cue, David joined in, "Sarah, honey, Cate's right, we'll see her again."

"But, not for a long, long time," Sarah protested, with her arms still tightly around Cate's neck.

Maybe not," David said, trying to comfort her.

Cate knew she had to try to bring an end to the grief they were all feeling and begin the drive to Quito. She took a deep breath and said, "Well, I've got to get going. Matthew's driving me to Quito, and I don't want it to be too late when he drives back home tonight."

"Where will you be staying in Quito?" David looked directly into her eyes for the first time.

"I'm going to stay with the Pattersons until I fly home," she answered, as she surveyed his eyes.

"When are you flying home?"

Cate saw the marked sadness in his eyes.

"As soon as I can make arrangements, I guess," Cate answered, as she rose with Sarah still in her arm. As they walked to the door, David put his arm around Cate's shoulder and walked with them. When they reached the front door, Cate hugged Sarah tightly and whispered good-bye.

"I love you, and I'll miss you," Sarah said, with tears streaming down her face.

"I love you too. I'll miss you too."

Cate hugged her tightly one more time and handed her to David. As he took her, his eyes met Cate's eyes. For a moment, they shared another silent, sad gaze. Cate's tears were flowing again. David's face took on a tortured look, and he lowered his eyes. Sarah was crying deep sobs.

Reluctantly, Cate turned and began to walk away. She took four steps, whirled around and walked briskly back to where David and Sarah were standing. With an arm around Sarah, she hugged David tightly. She quickly turned, hurried to the car, and got in. As Matthew drove away she watched David and Sarah in the side mirror until they faded from sight.

Twenty Seven

The drive to Quito took two hours, but Cate didn't notice. She was thinking about the goodbyes, and thankful that God gave her the strength to obey Him. Matthew was content to allow her to sit quietly and process what had happened. He was glad that she had asked him to drive her to Quito. That would allow him to spend more time with her before she left for Kansas.

They arrived in Quito at seven o'clock. When they pulled up in front of Dr. Patterson's apartment building, Cate breathed a very long sigh, looked at Matthew, and got out of the car. Dr. Patterson invited her in and offered to help Matthew with the bags while Mrs. Patterson showed her to her room.

Matthew took the opportunity to share his feelings about Cate's leaving. "Dr. Patterson, she doesn't have to leave, and I can't understand why she's going."

"I'm sure she has her reasons," Dr. Patterson said, as they entered the elevator.

"But, I don't get it."

"I'm sorry my boy," Dr. Patterson replied, "but these things have a way of working out for the best—eventually."

"I've prepared dinner for all of us," Mrs. Patterson said, as they returned.

"Thank you, that was very kind of you," Matthew replied.

Knowing that Cate would not want to talk about why she was leaving everyone made small talk.

After the meal, Matthew decided it was time to head back to Peguche. Cate walked him down. Once at the car, she hugged him, thanked him for driving her, and told him a last goodbye. He reluctantly got in his car and drove away.

When Cate returned to the apartment, Dr. Patterson was waiting for her.

"Cate, are you sure leaving is what you want?"

"No, sir, but I do believe I need to go."

"But, Matthew said that you could stay, if you wanted."

"Dr. Patterson, I'm leaving because I think that's what God wants me to do," Cate said.

"You can't argue with that," Mrs. Patterson said to her husband.

"Indeed I can't," Dr. Patterson said.

"My dear, we'll be very happy for you stay with us as long as you wish," Mrs. Patterson added.

"Thank you, but I think I should leave as soon as I can make arrangements."

"Afraid you'll lose your resolve, my dear?" Mrs. Patterson asked.

"Yes," Cate brushed a lock of hair from her face, her eyes were red and tired. "Dr. Patterson may I talk to you about something?"

"Of course, my dear,"

"I'll give you two some privacy," Mrs. Patterson excused herself.

"You don't have to," Cate responded. "Please stay?"

"If you're sure," Mrs. Patterson said.

"I'm sure. I'm convinced that God wants me to leave Ecuador, but I don't know why. I know He led me to Ecuador, and I can't figure out why He's leading me away."

Dr. Patterson sat back in his chair, his hands touching his lips, as he considered what he had heard, "You say that you are convinced that He led you here and that He's leading you away."

"Yes, sir, as far as I know I am absolutely surrendered to God, and today when I met with Dr. Kennedy, I knew God was leading me to leave, and though I don't know why He wants that, I am trying to be obedient."

"My dear, I applaud your obedience," Mrs. Patterson said.

"Cate, trusting and obeying God, when you do not understand is a very courageous thing. Many Christians couldn't or wouldn't do that," Dr. Patterson said.

Cate choked out a small laugh, "I don't know how courageous it is, but I do know that I want to be totally surrendered and obedient to God. There was a time in my life when I wasn't. I married the wrong man because I was afraid to say, 'God I'll do whatever you want me to do.' I messed up my life and others' too. But, I'm not afraid of surrender anymore." She paused, changed her position in her chair, and continued. "Dr. Patterson, there's something else that I need your advice about."

"I'll do my best," he said, in a fatherly tone.

"This ordeal with Miss Janet has made me think a lot about what she said. I know that God has forgiven me for the rebellion that led to my marriage to Justin, but that doesn't change the fact that I'm divorced. I didn't want the divorce, but that doesn't change anything. I know many people feel the way Miss Janet does. They're convinced that divorce disqualifies a person for lots of things. My dad told me that God in his forgiveness has made me fit to serve Him, but there are Christians who don't believe that. I–I don't know how…"

"My dear, if we repent and confess them, God forgives all our sins, but He doesn't remove all of the consequences. His forgiveness is eternal, but we often have to deal with the temporal consequences of our sin. Unfortunately, your divorce is one of those temporal consequences."

"Yes, sir," Cate said, with a tone of dejection.

"However, there are other things that you need to consider," he added. He had Cate's full attention.

"Like what, sir?"

"Cate, God's forgiveness gives renewed fellowship, fullness of His presence, the opportunity to be back in the center of His will, and the opportunity for service, joy, meaning, and purpose. I've seen that purpose-in you."

"I'm glad."

"There's something else. This concerns your marriage. If I understand correctly you thought your husband was a Christian when you married him, but he wasn't. Is that correct?"

"Yes, that's right,"

"And, he left you for another woman?"

Cate sighed and her shoulders sagged, "Yes, sir."

"I'd like to remind you of two things. The Bible gives us guidance in both areas. First, you married a man who was not a Christian. In first

Corinthians 7: 14 Paul tells us that one who is married to an unbeliever should seek to be the kind of godly example that He can use to win them to Himself. You sought to do that. Correct?"

"Yes, sir. I tried, but...I failed."

"Cate, we *never* fail when we seek to follow God's word. He can take our feeble efforts empowered by His Spirit, and work a miracle in hearts and lives that respond to Him. Your husband refused to respond, and he left you. In first Corinthians 7: 15, Paul tells us that if the unbelieving spouse leaves, the believer is not morally bound to the marriage vows. Secondly, in the gospels, Jesus tells us that adultery is biblical grounds for divorce."

"I don't understand."

"Cate, you're divorced, that's true, but it's also true that there were biblical grounds for your divorce. Therefore, according to God's word-you're free to remarry."

"So, you're telling me that even though I'm divorced, that biblically I'm not disqualified from being remarried."

"Exactly my dear, and, there's more. I want you to understand that regardless of what people like Janet say, God can use you. God has a habit of using those whom others think are unusable."

Shifting uncomfortably in her seat, Cate looked at the Pattersons and confessed, "Dr. Patterson, I appreciate what you've said, but there's something no one here knows, and I'd like, no, I need to tell you both.'

"Of course, my dear,"

"When I married Justin, I was rebelling against becoming a preacher's wife, David Barnes' wife in fact. By the time, I realized my mistake, I was already married. After Jenny died, when David came to Kansas, I realized that I was still in love with him, but I was divorced and he was an IMB missionary, so there was no hope for us. So you see, even though God's word says I can remarry," she choked back a sob, "I can't marry the man I love."

"Oh, my dear, I'm so sorry," Mrs. Patterson said.

"Does he love you?" Dr. Patterson asked.

"I don't know, but I came awfully close today to telling him how I felt. I stopped because I knew God was telling me to leave Ecuador and I have no idea what God is going to do with me."

"Cate, I'm afraid I can't tell you what God is going to do, or if you and David will ever work out, but I realize you think that you and David might be able to be together, *if* he wasn't an IMB missionary."

"Dr. Patterson, I don't know if that's true or not. I don't even know if he loves me-or wants me."

"I'm afraid I can't solve your dilemma as far as David's feelings go, but I can tell you that David's calling to be a missionary doesn't mean that he has to be an *IMB missionary*."

"He loves his ministry and all the people," Cate's eyes held a far away look, "I can't see him *not* being an IMB missionary. If I ever remarry," she sighed, "I don't think it'll be him."

"I'm sorry my dear. I hope I've helped-a little," Dr. Patterson said.

"You've helped more than you know," Cate responded, as she saw how late it was. "I'm sorry. I didn't realize the time; I hope I haven't kept you up too long."

"You haven't at all," Dr. Patterson said.

"Friends always take precedence over bedtime," Mrs. Patterson said.

"We are honored that you confided in us and asked our counsel," Dr. Patterson added.

"You're both very kind. If it's all right, I'd like to turn in."

"Of course, my dear, you must be very tired," Mrs. Patterson said.

"Yes, I am,"

"And, Cate please make our home yours for whatever time that you're here," Mrs. Patterson said.

"Thank you very much. Goodnight to you both," Cate rose and went to her bedroom, She spent time in prayer and meditation as she considered what might lay ahead for her, and fell asleep while doing so.

The following day found Cate with the fixed resolve of being completely obedient to God and leaving her future in His hands. She spent time in Bible study and prayer, dressed, went in for breakfast, and called the airport to arrange her flight home.

Discovering that a flight was leaving at six o'clock that night, she knew that she would have to hurry to get everything in place so she could leave.

It was three o'clock in the afternoon by the time she finished everything. Dr. Patterson insisted that he and Mrs. Patterson drive her to the airport. When they arrived, Dr. Patterson helped her with her luggage.

She checked in, thanked the Pattersons again for their hospitality and told them goodbye. Cate spent her last few minutes in Ecuador thanking God for the opportunity of serving Him there, and asking Him to prepare her and strengthen her for whatever was ahead. She asked that He take special care of David and Sarah, and confessed that leaving them was probably the most difficult part of leaving Ecuador.

She didn't arrive in Kansas City until two o'clock in the morning. After she had passed through customs, she found her parents waiting patiently for her. She tearfully grabbed them and hugged them tightly.

"How are you doing Catie?" her dad asked.

"I'm okay."

"Are you sure?" her mom asked.

"I'm sure. Let's get my luggage and I'll explain on the way home," Cate answered with a calmness that surprised her parents. "Dad, Mom I want to try to explain why I came home."

Her parents listened with rapt attention.

"First, you need to know that coming home was my choice, or rather God's. Dr. Kennedy gave me the opportunity to stay, but I felt God leading me to resign and come home. Yet, I don't know why; I'm totally bewildered."

"Cate, you're sure about this?"

"Yes, mom I am."

"Well, Catie. If you are sure of His leading, He will bless your obedience," her dad said.

"But, Dad, *I* don't understand."

"Understanding is not essential, obedience is. If you'll leave it in God's hands and continue to obey, He'll reveal the next step."

"Okay, Dad, but this walking by faith and not by sight thing is hard."

"I know Catie, but it's the only way to please God."

Her mother, who had been listening thoughtfully, decided to add her testimony. "Cate, I know living by faith is difficult, and sometimes God calls us to go through hard things so our faith in Him can be perfected. I can tell you by experience that walking with Him can bring great joy as we realize how faithful and trustworthy He is."

Cate spent the following weeks trying to be open to God and to discern his leading. During this time, God's presence was very real, and His fellowship was sweet as she quietly meditated upon His Word and prayed. She sensed that He was saying, "Trust Me. Depend on Me," and she was determined to do that.

As the weeks passed, her parents were a constant source of encouragement. They prayed with her, counseled her, and loved her. They were, as they had always been, examples of practical Christianity.

Two and a half months had passed when her mother called her to the phone. When she answered the phone, she heard Matthew's voice on the other end.

"Hello Cate, how are you?"

"I'm doing well."

"Really? I'm glad. I've got news that may help you do even better."

Cate held her breath, "What news?"

"Miss Janet has decided to retire. Her last day at the mission school is Friday."

"Why did she do that?"

"I'm not sure, but perhaps it's a guilty conscience over how she treated you."

"Matthew, I'm not sure how you expect me to react to that, but I wish Miss Janet no ill will."

"I didn't think you did, but I did hope, as does everyone else, that the news would cause you to consider returning here to teach."

There was silence on Cate's end. Afraid of what the silence meant, Matthew tried again.

"Cate, won't you please consider returning to Ecuador?"

"Matthew, I don't know. I'll pray about it."

Matthew tried another approach. "Cate, my dad asked me to tell you that he really wishes you would come back."

"I'll pray about it, but I can't promise anything."

Matthew chuckled, "I'll just have to leave it in the Lord's hands."

"By the way, how is everyone?"

"Everyone misses you."

"I miss everyone too," she heard Kim in the background.

"Matthew, let me talk to her."

Kim came on the line, "Cate please come back. It's not the same without you."

"Kim, it's nice to hear your voice."

"Yours too, and I *am* serious about what I said. You'd make a little girl and a big boy very happy if you'd come back."

"I know, I miss Sarah and Matthew too."

"I don't mean Matthew. I mean David." Kim's implication could not be missed.

"David..."

"Yes, David. He loves you, Cate."

Cate held her breath, "Why do you say that?"

"Because it's true, I made him admit it."

"What?" Cate couldn't believe what she was hearing.

"Since you've been gone, he's been moping around as if he's lost his best friend. Suspecting you were the source of his sadness, I shared my suspicions with Matthew, and he agreed with me. When we confronted David he tried to change the subject. I decided to ask him point blank if he loved you. When I did, he admitted it."

"Kim, I'm sorry. I know you're in love with him. I-I never meant-"

"Yeah, about that… I thought I loved him, but I suspected all along that he didn't love me. Now, I realize that I never really was in love with him. Rather, I was in love with the thought of being in love. David and I were over before you left."

"Really…"

"Yep, we broke up before the whole thing with Miss Janet began. I'm sorry I never told you about it, but at the time, I was really mad at him and jealous of you."

"I'm sorry."

"It's okay now. I've found someone that I might have a chance with."

"That's great. Who?"

"That would be me," Matthew said, as he and Kim shared the phone.

"Matthew," Cate's voice reflected her surprise, "that's great."

"We might have found each other sooner had we not been detoured by you and David," Matthew joked.

"Sorry," Cate wondered if he really was joking.

"That's enough about us. Let's get back to David and you," Kim interrupted.

"Cate, *are* you in love with David?"

"Like you have to ask," Matthew said.

"Ssssh!" Kim scolded. "Cate *are* you?"

Hesitating a moment, Cate answered, "Yes, I am."

"So come back, and *do something* about it," Kim said.

"I can't. The fact that we love each other doesn't change the fact that we can't be together."

"It's the divorce thing again. Isn't it?" Matthew asked.

"Yep."

"But, you two should be together," Kim said.

"We can't be. He's an IMB missionary. If he marries me, he loses his ministry, and I know him well enough to know that he'd never do that. And I wouldn't want him to."

"No, Cate you're wrong." Matthew's voice had the same warm, counseling tone of his father. "He wouldn't lose his ministry. He'd lose his financial backing, not his ministry."

"To him that's the same thing. He's convinced, as I am, that God led him to serve as a church planter in Ecuador. He can't do that without financial backing; no money, no mission. He needs the IMB."

"No, he needs financial backing. What if another agency was willing to back him?"

"Yeah, another agency could back him," Kim said, picking up Matthew's cue.

Cate's eyes widened, "You're talking about your agency. Aren't you Matthew?"

"Sure, I am. My agency could back him and that would solve the dilemma so he could marry you."

"I'm not sure that he'll go for it." A multitude of thoughts swirled through Cate's head, "I don't know that what you're proposing is God's will for him, or me."

"Neither do I, but I'm going to make the offer to David, and we'll all pray and leave it in God's hands."

Ecstatic about the possibilities, Kim said, "That's a great idea Matthew. We'll pray and leave it in God's hands. Right, Cate?"

Once again, Cate was silent. She was being asked a pivotal question that could change her life, *What do I say?*

"Come on Cate. Are we all agreed?" Matthew asked.

After breathing a very heavy sigh, Cate finally answered, "Agreed."

As she hung up, Cate could hardly wrap her head around what had happened. Could it be that David loved her after all? After all this time, was God working out a way for them to be together? Did it all happen in Ecuador to pave the way for this? She might be on the verge of having what she never thought she could. Only prayer and time would tell. She savored the possibilities for a few minutes before she shared the conversation with her parents. Her parents looked at each other in amazement and smiled.

"Cate, that's wonderful," her mother said.

"Maybe, Mom. I don't know yet. I'm not sure what God is doing."

"Just continue to be open and submissive to His leading," her dad said. "And, he'll make it all clear in time."

"I know, Dad."

They joined hands in prayer, praying that God would provide unmistakable guidance. Cate felt grateful and humbled by the experience and was confident that God would answer their prayers.

During the weeks that followed, she spent more time in prayer, meditation and fasting in order to discern God's will. God's answer to her request for guidance was continually the same. He brought three verses of Scripture to her mind. One He had given her in Ecuador, Psalm 57:2 and two new ones, Psalm 37:7 and Psalm 91:1-2. Reading them in the Amplified Bible, Cate fed on what they said, "I will cry to God Most High, Who performs on my behalf and rewards me—Who brings to pass [His purposes] for me and surely completes them! Be still rest in the Lord; wait for Him, patiently stay yourself upon Him; fret not yourself because of him who prospers in his way, because of the man who brings wicked devices to pass. He who dwells in the secret place of the Most High shall remain stable and fixed under the shadow of the Almighty [Whose power no foe can withstand]. I will say of the Lord, He is my Refuge and my Fortress, my God: on Him I will lean and rely, and in Him I [confidently] trust."

She shared with her parents what God was saying to her heart. They continually prayed for her and with her, and encouraged her to submit herself and the situation with David completely in His hands, and to trust what He was saying to her heart. She humbly and patiently heeded their advice.

More weeks passed and God's guidance remained the same. He constantly asked her to trust Him and she submissively clung to the verses in the Psalms.

Three months had passed since Matthew's call, and she'd heard nothing from him, Kim or David. She believed David had been praying and seeking God's leadership as well, yet since so much time had passed, she concluded that God had not led David to accept Matthew's offer.

"God please help me. If you have said no to David and me, I want to submit to Your will. I don't understand why you brought me home, or what you're doing right now, but I know that You love me and You're wise and good in all that You do. I admit that my heart is broken, but I know You can mend broken hearts. Please help me. I want Your will to be done and not mine."

Things happened quickly after that prayer. One bright sunny morning Dr. Jones answered a knock at the front door, smiled, quietly greeted the visitors and said loudly, "Cate it's for you."

Rounding the corner from the den, Cate suddenly stopped as she realized that David and Sarah were standing before her. Her mouth flew open, her face lit up with surprise and happiness, as tears of joy filled her eyes.

"Hi Cate," David said, with a smile.

"Hi!"

"Ask her Daddy. Ask her," Sarah ran from her daddy's side toward Cate, who immediately scooped her up into her arms.

"Ask me what?"

David took a deep breath and moved toward Cate and Sarah. For the first time in seven years, his eyes revealed exactly what was in his heart as he looked deeply into Cate's eyes. She saw it plainly and melted at its presence. He took Sarah from her arms and put her down, took Cate by the hand, and said the words that she never thought he would.

"Cate... Will you marry me and be Sarah's mother?"

"Yes, yes I will." She fell into his arms, sharing the kiss she'd always dreamed of.

"Hooray," Sarah clapped her hands with joy.

As David hugged her and Sarah clung to her leg, Cate lifted her teary eyes heavenward. *Thank you Lord, for my husband and child, and for my calling.*

About the Author

Deborah A. Hodge was born in Camden, Tennessee and attended college and graduate school at Union University, Jackson, Tennessee, earning a Bachelor of Science and Masters of Arts in Education. She completed thirty-three hours at Luther Rice Seminary in Lithonia, Georgia.

Presently, Deborah is a teacher at Bolivar Central High School. She teaches United States history and Theater Arts. She is the chairperson of the Social Studies Department at Bolivar Central and an adjunct instructor in history for the University of Tennessee at Martin.

Breinigsville, PA USA
31 October 2009
226780BV00002B/2/P